ADDITIONAL PRAISE FOR

WHITE DANCING ELEPHANTS

"The seventeen stories in this debut collection take place around the world, exploring queer and interracial love, extramarital affairs, and grief over the disappearances of loved ones. The book provocatively probes the aftermath—the aftermath of death, of grim diagnoses, of abandonment, of monumental errors in judgment. Passages jump back and forth in time to dissect how the consequences of a fraught event shape and unravel the lives of innocent casualties....An exuberant collection."

—*Kirkus Reviews* (starred review)

"This enthralling, vivid debut collection...provides powerful glimpses into experiences of grief, violence, and betrayal."

—*Southern Living*

"Bhuvaneswar's daring mix of ancient, contemporary, and dystopic stories carries us to the heart of rarely exposed longing, loss, and the politics of violence and endurance in remarkable, elegant, heart-stopping prose."

—Jimin Han, author of *A Small Revolution*

"Reading Bhuvaneswar is like receiving Lasik via literature—the world you return to is a little clearer and sharper for the time you've spent in her pages. She is a formidable talent, formally accomplished and intellectually alive."

—Anthony Marra, author of *The Constellation of Vital Phenomena*

"These stories show impressive dexterity and range. The prose can be rich and intricate one moment, then shifts registers into sharp

humor; Bhuvaneswar's ability to take on larger topics and to locate and intensify their complexity within individuals is amazingly fine."
—Peter Rock, author of *My Abandonment*

"Filled with dark music, nuance, and intelligence, *White Dancing Elephants* takes readers on a thrilling journey. This unforgettable collection will hold its readers captive to the very last page."
—Diana Abu-Jaber, author of *Life Without a Recipe*

"Bhuvaneswar is a master of literary stealth. Authentic, fearless, and wholly original, *White Dancing Elephants* is a knockout collection."
—Jillian Medoff, author of *This Could Hurt*

"A timely stunner, a wild collection that touches on everything from motherhood, race, and privilege to Rachael Ray and Jay Z....This is one of those rare books that refuses to look away."
—Kelly Luce, *Electric Literature*

"Books open up people, books open up the world, books open up history to us—but it's very rare that a book does all three. Bhuvaneswar's debut is a remarkably written, insightful book, wise and wide as the world."
—Amber Sparks, author of *The Unfinished World*

"Bhuvaneswar has the gift of precision, the ability to fit whole novels into her stories. This is fiction as unafraid of the intimate—pulsing and tender—as it is of the big questions of life and death, love and betrayal, belonging and dislocation."
—Allegra Hyde, author of *Of This New World*

"So rich and full of rage and beauty...incredibly well written and so brave."
—Courtney Maum, author of *I Am Having So Much Fun Here Without You*

"Bhuvaneswar's stories reveal a rare sensitivity to the strange and complicated acrobatics of the human heart. Astonishing, urgent portraits of people trying to see the world for what it is and what it might be."

—Emily Geminder, author of *Dead Girls and Other Stories*

"Bhuvaneswar writes with a clear eye, precise hand, and a compassionate heart. This is a collection of stories that reward the reader's mind and spirit."

—Dohra Ahmad, author of *Rotten English*

"*White Dancing Elephants* dazzles from the start. Readers are treated to deep characters, mesmerizing language, and a story that propels forward across a city and the landscape of a mind effortlessly. This is a new, gifted voice in contemporary literature, and we are so lucky to have it!"

—Victoria Chang, author of *Barbie Chang*

"Bhuvaneswar's deft and poignant stories bring the whole damned world into clearer focus. A pure pleasure to read, *White Dancing Elephants* is a remarkable book that will stay with me for a long time."

—Skip Horack, author of *The Other Joseph*

"Bhuvaneswar's stories are as insightful as they are ineffable and as devastating as they are delightful. As I read these important and hilarious tales about the lives of queer people of color, I kept asking myself, you can do this in writing?"

—Emma Eisenberg, author of *The Third Rainbow Girl*

"Radical and searing, the stories of *White Dancing Elephants* demand and warrant an attentive, listening audience."

—*Foreword Reviews*

WHITE DANCING ELEPHANTS

WHITE DANCING ELEPHANTS

—STORIES—

CHAYA BHUVANESWAR

DZANC
BOOKS

DZANC BOOKS

5220 Dexter Ann Arbor Rd.
Ann Arbor, MI 48103
www.dzancbooks.org

Library of Congress Cataloging-in-Publication Data

Names: Bhuvaneswar, Chaya, 1971- author.
Title: White dancing elephants : stories / Chaya Bhuvaneswar.
Description: Ann Arbor, MI : Dzanc Books, 2018.
Identifiers: LCCN 2018005798 | ISBN 9781945814617
Classification: LCC PS3602.H54 A6 2018 | DDC 813/.6--dc23
LC record available at https://lccn.loc.gov/2018005798

First US edition: October 2018
Interior design by Leslie Vedder

Stories in this collection appeared, sometimes in different form, in the following publications: "White Dancing Elephants" in *Asian American Literary Review*; "The Story of the Woman Who Fell in Love with Death" in *Bangalore Review*; "Talinda" in *Narrative Magazine*; "A Shaker Chair" in *Story South*; "Jagatishwaran" in *Nimrod*; "The Bang Bang" in *Michigan Quarterly Review*; "Neela: Bhopal, 1984" in *Narrative Northeast*; "Newberry" in *The Write Launch*; "Asha in Allston" in *r.k.v.r.y. quarterly*; "The Life You Save Isn't Your Own " in *aaduna*; "The Orphan Handler" in *Ellipsis*; "In Allegheny" in *Santa Fe Writers Project*; "The Goddess of Beauty Goes Bowling" in *Chattahoochee Review*; and "Adristakama" in *Del Sol Review*.

Printed in the United States of America

10   9   8   7   6   5   4   3   2   1

CONTENTS

who would connive
in civilized outrage
yet understand the exact
and tribal, intimate revenge.

—Seamus Heaney, "Punishment"

WHITE DANCING ELEPHANTS

I WALK OUT TO THE LOBBY, wanting to prolong my dream of you, thinking that I'll gain some control by staying awake. Impossible—I'm too aware that people are staring at me. The lobby is tiny, compact but cool as glass. I walk with my hands loose, hair disheveled, my pajamas covered by a trench coat. Someone glides out from behind a front desk and presses an umbrella on me because it's pouring. The rain is tropical. It's June in central London, financial district, the back of Deutsche Bank, the first building I walk past, with its gargoyles and angelic flourishes so unlike its German-constructed, super-efficient front façade. I'm half a block away from the hotel when, shivering, I open the umbrella. The rain makes it possible to wipe my face and have people think that I was caught in a downpour. I hate metaphors of rain, fecundity, gushing water from a hidden space. There wasn't anything macabre in your passing—no rush of blood, no horrifying trickle down my legs. Just two clear stains, understated, as quiet and undemanding as your whole life had been; only enough blood for me to know.

When I was younger, in my early twenties, and couldn't imagine having a child, I would stare at myself as I jogged past office buildings, appreciating the slim reflection and promising myself to stay that way. Now I don't look. The curve of my belly is meaningless—indulgence, fat, no longer where I'm carrying you. But all the signs are still there, superfluous: the fuller breasts—not tender anymore the young skin, the shiny hair that were all gifts from you.

"You all right then, luv?" A cabbie leans out his window when I stop for the light and he sees my tearful face. I nod, then make an unintended turn and keep on walking.

Without realizing it, I've reached a subterranean sort of Euromall. Octagon Arcade, it's called, though looking at the glossy bus-shelter type of walls gives me too much of a headache to bother counting to see if they're eight. Things are never named reliably, I understand. Boots is not a shop where shoes are sold; Monsoon has nothing to do with India. W.H. Smith isn't a person but a generic chain of newsstands selling cheap sandwiches and tabloid rags and things called "health foods," like tiger balm, which isn't made from tigers at all. (If we were only in the forest together, we wouldn't sleep. We would stay up. You would nestle against my breast, picking it up and stroking it and arranging it under your ear like a pillow, and eventually you would say, "Mama," though not right away. Before you could speak you would make sounds, and because the sounds would tell me you were listening, I would kiss your head and tell you stories, stories within stories, stories of elephants in the forest, stories of tigers.)

I go down the steps into the mall, heading into the pharmacy. I need pads. The first day, the way I mopped up blood was cautious, hopeful, as if by showing that it could be quickly absorbed, I was collecting proof that you were still alive. After that I stopped measuring. Only one moment caught me unawares, like getting soaked by rain—the moment that, smiling, thinking of something else from long ago, I actually saw you on the pad. Your flesh was hard, less darkly bloody than the rest of it, more than just a part of me. Your hardness froze my smile. You had existed, formed; I could see light outlines, the shape of limbs. You were hard enough to have formed bone, if you had lived more than an inch.

The English pharmacy is impossibly friendly and bright.

"You all right then, miss?" inquires a security guard. I look away from him, my attention fixed on the bellies of women gathering into a line. The line of them divides between the self-pay registers and the one or two cashiers who stand, bored, only as polite as required. The women's bellies divide into flat, obese, and then the one in front of me, a petite woman with long dark hair, pregnant, I recognize, maybe even in the final trimester. She looks perfect. I turn away from her and find the one who is obese. Perhaps she's never been pregnant, I think, and she's just fat—until the woman's three children follow in her wake, sullen and palely beautiful the way dark-haired English children are, their lips a thin and natural red, their eyes pale blue. She's probably my age, I realize suddenly, early forties, but she has not spent her life on mistakes. My eyes can't leave her or her three growing daughters. The same security guard who talked to me just before comes up and gently accosts me.

"You all right then? You know what you're looking for? D'you need a basket or something?" and I nod my head, "Yes," letting him put a shopping basket in my hand, even though, my darling, I have accepted nothing.

You could be alive. The hard thing could be from inside of me. A piece of a fibroid, a tumor from inside my uterus that my body was smart enough to get rid of to make room for you. The ultrasound could have been blocked by bowel, air, artifact, ignorance, an act of God, because you weren't meant to be seen. (How much more clearly I would see it all, if I could only rest under a tree with you kicking me awake in my belly.)

In the hotel, I change my pad again but try to get some rest, really try, the way I would if I knew beyond a doubt that you're alive, so that I would take care of us. I churn the sheets around my heated limbs, taking off clothes and putting them on again, remembering how my younger sister told me she couldn't sleep before her son was born.

"Where can I go where there's green space?" I find myself asking via telephone, pressing "0" in the dark and conquering my jetlag with high-heeled boots. Still holding the phone, I put them on, as if I might go out dancing, the way my sister and I did when we were young. Now my younger sister has a son and a daughter and, before she knew that I'd lost you, my lucky sister confided in me that she is trying for another one. (I'd never give you to her, my darling. I'd never even let her wish for you.)

Then a grey cab with the caption "Radio Cell"—modern and sleek, nothing like the battered yellow cabs in Manhattan or even the quaint-looking, black, old-fashioned London cabs—pulls up in front of the hotel and lets me slip inside, and with the side windows open and the dust of the city rushing in, I finally fall asleep. Years from now, my sweet love, I imagine you will be a man, and you will crane your neck to look at things your driver tells you to ignore. The thought of you seeing all of it opens my eyes. The Gold Shop with the sign, "We can melt down anything"; the gleaming Tesco with the two homeless men, too tired to stand up while they wait for it to be noon on a Sunday so they can buy cheap wine; a beautiful brown prostitute at the edge of the pavement, almost in traffic, talking to a man leaning out of a van. Her skin's identical to mine. She has one hand on her hip and the other on the handle of a baby's pram, its front wheel alarmingly close to a red double-decker bus. My taxi stops near enough for me to see her painted but young face when she steps back; I see her shaking her head at the driver of the black van; she will have other babies, I am sure of it, and they will live even though she smokes, exhaling blankly while she pokes the milk bottle into her baby's face. Crushed beer cans come flying out of the van window, aimed at her, but she sidesteps and laughs, looking around, not moving the bottle from where her covered-up baby must be sucking for dear life. She's seen all of this before. When you come here, you will not stop the car to talk to her. But you will watch her pushing the baby, like I do.

"Primrose Hill?" the driver asks suddenly, reminding me of what I told him. Before I know it, I'm standing outside in a wet meadow abutting a suburb. I walk deeper into this corner of green, smelling the cars parked outside the park's small fence, seeing a rectangular sign with directions right at the entrance. The sign is blurred from the rain; I ignore it. (But if you were here, I would have hoisted you up to look at it; I would have taught you how to locate yourself on a map.)

You would have played right here. Not would have—*will*. You will play here, through my sheer will, and years from now it's possible that you will have a child who loves this park. I can hear a three-year-old's laughter at finding a big enough stick to shake at an adult. Grandson. That child will run to the fence that separates the grass from the curb, where cars are squeezed into makeshift parking spaces, and stick his face through it, hoping a pretty girl will talk to him. Then he will turn his little face to look in the direction of a sound—the tinny melody coming from a truck selling ice cream. He will beg for some, but turn his face away from the ice cream when you give in. You will lift your smart boy in the air, throw him up, catch him. Each second he laughs will be exquisite joy, if you would only stay with him, my love.

The blood has stopped; my underpants feel dry. No one has been inside my womb and actually seen you, checked your eyelids, passed a hand under your mouth, to catch you breathing. Everyone has sympathy, but no one really knows. (In the forest, no one can stop us from dreaming. The rustling of leaves could be elephants unfolding and folding back their ears; the ground shifting could be armies of tigers lying down to sleep. The sound of a motor could be the enormous animals' rumbling snores. The soft breeze you feel on your face could be a beauty's breath or even her hesitation before she kisses you; she could be one of the invisible girls who live in heaven, dancing while celestial musicians endlessly perform. One of those girls could be your bride.)

I walk faster, ignoring how my high heels tear at the lawn. The path I follow cuts across the park, and on either side, there are great swaths of uncut grass interrupted by patches of clover, by dandelion stems with puffs blown off. At the end of this littered, broken path, with its deflated and discarded rubber balls, its trash, its posters for farmers' markets and festivals and radical meetings, are two walkways, one next to an expensive-looking running track. A left turn leads to London Zoo.

Years ago, before I conceived of you, I went inside. In the first cages, monkeys bait the onlookers, sitting in branches high beyond their view and swinging their tails, then suddenly flinging their bodies hard against the glass for one instant, before retreating into the leaves. There are two jungle gyms, each sized for each sized for children of different ages, and low-slung exhibits where small hands can press buttons and run their fingers against tactile squares, one with a lizard's skin, another with a fox's fur.

I can't make it into the zoo. My feet slow in the mud outside the main entrance, where crowds will line up in a few hours to buy tickets. The zoo is closed. All I get is a glimpse of an office—"The London Zoological Society"—that looks like it's been there for hundreds of imperial years, since back when it might have been a hoot to go see Hottentots and Pygmies, tribesmen of India, captured gypsies who were locked up, exhibited, meticulously caged and labeled. (The doctor had said: "If you pass tissue, bring it in for us to analyze," but I will not, my darling love, I would never give up any part of you.) I stand, uncertain of the time but clear that it must be before eight, waiting for a compassionate employee to arrive and slowly realizing no one is coming.

Finally, a taxi whizzes by, empty, pausing inquisitively, and I signal, get in and mumble my destination, then sleep until Oxford. Long before I thought of having you, that's where I lived. I hated the town, and I hated myself for parts I loved—the sanctity of the libraries, their vastness and capacity. The hushed and exquisite museum, laden with things I thought They shouldn't have, like the Diamond Sutra scrolls, sixteen feet long, stolen from a Buddhist Cave;

the "They" from Lenin's angry description of tourist monuments to Trotsky when the two men visited Europe. But the coldness of those buildings didn't change the loveliness of tea, funny TV commercials, *doner* kebab carts with egg and meat packeted in foil, food smelling divine and tasting perfect after a night out. I didn't drink liquor even before this pregnancy; I abstained for months in case you suddenly came into being. When I studied at Oxford, I found moments of quiet, when I jogged in the Deer Park around Magdalen and saw the lovely ones behind the fence, or when, by myself, I had tea and buttered scones on lonely afternoons, or when I sat near the window of some ancient common room and recited words from memory that you might hear from multitudes, if you come back to me—"Namo tassa bhagavato" and "Namo tassa bhagavato arahato samma sambuddhassa." Imagining white elephants and dreaming of your birth. Sometimes boys would edge close, curious, asking me to repeat the prayers, giggling nervously at the strange words. But I took no offense—I liked it when the English boys couldn't tell what the words meant. It gave me an excuse to stay away from them.

This morning I travel to Oxford from the London Zoo. The spot where the cabbie lets me off will turn out to be a familiar corner near a bridge. The bridge leaves Magdalen and Green and graduate houses and a street that, if you follow it, leads to the Bodleian Library across from the King's Arms. But when I walk over it, instead of turning back toward the colleges, the bridge leads to a different place, to Cowley Road and strong-smelling Indian fish-curry takeaways and a plebeian, exotic Oxford that I had secretly found comfort in, full of dreadlocked white hippies with mangy dogs, coupons at Sainsbury's, and plastic-covered public library books. Sometimes, I would disappear into the normalcy of cardigans and quiet disparate streets with shops displaying porn magazines and fifty-pence boxes of Oxfam and cheap licorice, and there I would eat, slicing the bittersweet pink and yellow layers of the candy with my teeth, flipping with curiosity through *Hot Indian Babes* until some white woman, blowsy, unwashed with bad skin, would interrupt my reading, asking, "Cheap, aren't they?" daring me to defend the beauties taunting her from the pages. (My sister posed once for her husband and he painted her, as he would paint you in her arms if she had you—if you ever came back to this world, my love, and found me gone.)

Over the years, I have lost time being afraid. Hours lost as I hid in my bed, or stood on a chair staring at my face in the mirror over my small sink, anguished over what some boy or some very English tutor said, the state of my hair, the exact size of my body. The fact that I was not yet married and didn't want to marry anyone I knew. I couldn't walk or read or write or even hide in the basement of the foreign language institute, to feel less foreign.

I thought I felt rage when someone shouted a slur at me from three feet away, while sitting on the tube from Paddington Station, or when someone called me a "cheap tart" when we were waiting in a line for a dance club and I was wearing silver shoes and a black dress that had a pulse, or when a law passed in the US that I didn't agree with, or when, years after Oxford, I married your father and loved him, and despite that love, he could not save your life.

Before my last morning with you, my love, I didn't know rage. I didn't know how empty rage is, like a bag of bones.

Now I am walking across the Isis River, looking down, hearing the sound of my heels on the bridge. Once when I was here at Oxford, fifteen years ago, I stood wearing a towel, looking through the curtain at the garden below my room, making note of its beauty as if I were far away, because I would leave it soon; because it would never be mine. Not even noticing that I was beautiful. The radio was on, and I heard the reporter talking about a girl. She had been found in the river just before the May Day festivities. The girl could have been me.

This morning at 0400 hours the body of a young, uniden.
Asian woman was found floating in the Isis River in Oxfor.. . ...
details are available from the police. The woman appeared to have been
dead for a few days.

In all the years I've lived, I haven't realized that my body is dying.
But you perceived this right away. You heard the thud of elephants,
the dancing procession, the march not of a wedding but a funeral.
You were so quiet, but you knew when the end came; you were silent
as our blood leaked from my body.

Every May Day, here on the riverbank where I'm stumbling now,
there is a festival with Ferris wheels and carnival contraptions, displays
and tricks that can cause accidents. And there are animals—swans,
horses, maybe even dancing elephants. I lie down on the grassy bank
and dream of you. I dream of elephants, thumping a distant melody,
disrupting the forest. (If you were here now, my darling, how we'd
dance, my love. And if you were old enough and strong enough to
move your feet deliberately, you'd sing. You'd speak to me.)

I lie down now and feel the weight of it on me, a white dancing
elephant that I can see with my eyes closed, airy and Disney in one
dream, bellowing despair and showing tusks in another. In the last
dream, a gash of red stains the white hide, and I am forced to watch
an elephant dying. It makes me want to sink into the earth, ashamed
and finally mindful of my own blood. The sound of people walking
on the bridge becomes a din. I close my eyes, drained, dreaming of
six white tusks entering my flesh. I slide off my shoes. Now I could
roll underwater. Now I could write the words describing how and
why I ended my life.

The woman found in the Isis River in June of this year was for-
ty but was found to be pregnant. She was on her way, authorities
learned, to give birth at her father's home outside of London, as is
the custom for Asians, but by the time she reached the river she had
lost the pregnancy. Or it is possible, though less likely, that the child
was born along the way and disappeared below the ripples of water,

along the bank, under the trees, before being rescued and taken home by someone else watching.

I get up, put on my shoes again. If I were to disappear, you would be taken home by someone, I believe it. My body, this body, could be discarded. But you could live. It isn't that your soul came to me in a body that wasn't durable. It's that my body was failing, too late, too careless, too empty; but after my death, you could live. In my absence, my sister would love you like a prince.

I walk away from the river, toward the road and the traffic, knowing one day, my own sweet love, you'll come here and walk along this riverbank, and cross over this bridge, and sit calmly under a tree here—and not know me. But you will be awake when I'm asleep. Yes, you will be.

THE STORY OF THE WOMAN
WHO FELL IN LOVE WITH DEATH

In an armchair at the center of a Starbucks, nearly hidden by its arms, a young boy reads, perplexed but concentrating hard:

Once upon a time, there lived a man of little importance. But his fine young daughter did belong to him: her lovely face, the soft and the angular parts of her body, her hips, her strong legs, her glorious laugh—everything that made her worth the highest price.

Naturally, the father had to search for some suitable person to bid for her. Every day the daughter offered a million prayers, begging for the blessing of a lover who wouldn't pay money, and every night she lit a million candles, facing the lights away from where her father was always watching her. She'd occupy herself for the whole night with this one task, so that her father would be asleep by the time the sun came up, too tired to come into her room.

The god of death was fed up with the piteous pleas of that tenacious girl, who asked for a salvation he would not be able to grant. Finally, either to avoid hearing the subterranean, growled prayers of her father (which the girl also heard), or out of some divine mercy, the god of death performed a miracle. But neither the girl nor her father were aware of it at first.

The god of death sent her a lover. The lover who would become the husband of the girl had to walk fifty miles.

With time, the lover found their house, but he limped like an old man. The finest clothes awaited him, but the blisters on his feet prevented him from standing up. But once he healed, the girl could see how strong and independent he would be, how the god of death had sent her the right one after all, if she could be patient with him.

After anxious days of waiting, the girl broke down and begged the man to marry her.

He barely walked. He lacked the strength to lie on top of her. But the clever girl found a palanquin meant for brides and promised that, after the wedding, he could rest on its cushions. And since she had no horse, she promised that she would carry the palanquin's long handles on her shoulders.

The first night, instead of making love, the man slept a dreamless sleep. The girl stayed awake. When the sun rose on the marriage bed, there he was with his feet in bandages, the girl with her gown tightly fastened.

The girl then stole a bigger palanquin that would allow more room for making love and sought out men who could take up her burden, so she could lie with the man. There was another sunrise, another dreamless sleep, and the restless girl searching out another palanquin, to be carried by a litter of strong fearless men whose legs could easily outrun her father's, and another when her father seemed about to track her down, and another, and so on.

Soon enough, the girl was left penniless with just the man, who could walk, albeit slowly, and without a sense of where to go. But soon, the stranger promised her, when he was healed, soon they would make mad, fierce love. As the hours crept on, the girl's father pressing on their trail with his good horse, the girl and her husband, who had still to become her lover, lay down on the fifth night of their marriage, on the road next to their last broken palanquin, whose carriers had gone. The road was still. The girl and her lover rested, drifting to sleep then waking and kissing passionately, and every time she kissed him, she gave him strength.

Just when he had almost recovered, a horse with a masked, heavy rider slashed the ground with steel-shod feet, striking the man in the head before streaking down the road.

Instantly the god of death appeared.

As the horse and his rider stopped, seemingly preparing to turn back, the god of death cushioned the dying man's head in his hands, silently urging him to close his eyes. To stop her from lamenting the man, the god showed the frightened girl his own solemn face.

But he is so beautiful, she thought with joy.

The girl knew, from the stories she had read, and from the story that might be told about her, that she was to bargain with the god of death. Plead for her husband's life. Show that her devotion extended beyond tears. Inspire the god of death, by her courage, to spare them both.

But she could not look away from the god's bleak, handsome face. The sound of the horse with its rider—deafening against the night's silence, pressed closer and closer, growling desire, impatience.

The girl unfastened her dress, offering her bare skin.

"Hurry," she whispered, winning him.

In the Starbucks in Greenwich Village near West Fourth, the boy shut his book and sighed in contentment. He wasn't old enough yet to drink coffee, let alone see the illustration in the book of the girl's bare chest, though he lingered over it, not realizing that a barista with floppy soft hair was looking over his shoulder, admiring her breasts too.

"My man," the coffee meister purred. "My little man. What you got there, huh?"

The boy, small for his age but nearly twelve, nodded with solemnity. Yes, there was something fruit-like and dark and perfect about the girl's breasts in the book—without wanting to touch them, exactly, the boy felt content looking at them. He wasn't a boy who had ever seen *Playboy*. His father wouldn't allow it. And his sister—once long ago he *did* have a sister, though no one in the house, not father, not aunt, not the mother who had died when the boy was three, none of them ever mentioned her, the sister-girl, with breasts like these. He'd seen them in the other photograph, the one in his father's sock drawer, the place where a picture of the boy's lost sister was hidden, buried under softest cloth, dust motes like petals on her cheeks, her skin a lustrous color and unlined, his father's fingerprints confined to the very edges of the photograph, as if that might keep his sister from being consumed.

No one at school asked the boy anymore, "Where's your sister? Did the cops ever find her?" No one seemed to worry about her. Only the boy, who'd once missed her whenever she ran away from home, the boy who had promised when he was four or five (though he didn't remember saying the words) that he would somehow rescue her.

Now in the Starbucks, the boy licked the foam off the plastic lid of his paper cup and put it down, reflecting, wondering.

"What if she hadn't gone?" he thought. He couldn't get that question out of his head. Of who he would have become, if she had stayed. Of what would have happened to them.

In college it became worse, the wondering, once it was coupled with an edgy curiosity. Not only just: *Where did she go?* But also: *How do I bear it, that she left for good?*

By then, some of the questions were answered, of what the boy's father had done. The family knew, but no one else imagined. By then the boy could make sense of some things—loud arguments, crying and shouting, slapping, pushing, pulling, then silence, the girl emerging afterward, quiet, appearing overcome.

In the years since the boy discovered his favorite storybook, there had not been any news. Silence again, but this time not following any loud noise; only silence following on silence, building in intensity, proving the truth of what happened—she was gone, no one could dispute it. "Must have had her reasons," the neighbors said.

At first when the boy had become a young man—post-sex, post-fumbling around, post-fantasies, counting himself lucky for the one summer he had hitchhiked before college, not telling anyone, breaking away from the quiet house with his glowering father and talkative, overbearing aunt—the boy felt he was lucky to have been younger than the girl, younger and small for his age, no threat. No one could ever think him the reason for the girl leaving.

"You should have taken me with you," he'd say softly, touching the book that he still had in his dorm room, turning to the place where he had tucked the stolen picture, the one his father had stolen before him.

In the city, the boy had felt anonymous. Walking through the Village or sitting in a public square where construction workers watched pigeons just as closely as women; sneaking coffees at Rafa-ella Café or eating a slice of pizza slowly, to savor it, at Two Boots; or waiting, just waiting, not really doing anything.

But out in the country, where the college was, the boy felt ex-posed, even when others were not drinking or looking for a tall boy to go home with. Their gazes settled on him, not knowing how much his face resembled his beautiful sister's. He felt put upon. Girls ex-pected him to prove to them what boys were like: shallow, callous, laughing animals that could smell irresistible. Other boys wanted to see if he realized he was handsome, if he knew how to use it against them. And teachers mistook his quietness and matter-of-fact dili-gence for respect, when in fact the boy just didn't know what to say to anyone, in the small, underground classrooms he could have mistaken for tombs.

No subject moved him to express himself. Art history, geology, architecture, engineering, poetry: he liked classes about things, objects he could draw inside of books, whose intricacies absorbed and dis-tracted. Protected him from being left with a blank page.

Without fanfare, he finished his studies. The father called. The aunt came to visit, only once or twice, enough to make his neigh-bors look at him with sympathy. A querulous woman whispering too loudly about all the foreigners, the slutty girls, the subpar cafeteria.

The aunt's presence hadn't always been noxious. After his sister disappeared, the boy remembered his aunt making hot chocolate and frosted cakes, day after day, as if by feeding herself and the boy, and sometimes the father, she could fill the absence, as if she were preparing extra food, stocking a wake.

The aunt had been married once. The boy could remember an uncle. This uncle, his father's brother, had taken his sister aside and said in a voice probably meant for others to overhear: "You deserve better. You can get out."

Then the uncle had driven a long way, for miles, returning in a bleak snowstorm. He had passed through country and city, driving on high roads, on the most remote mountains. The father had gone to help the uncle with a jump but had come back alone, refusing to say when the uncle would follow. When the aunt heard that the uncle's car was lost, she hadn't wept. "Foolish beast," she'd said. "He would never listen to me. He'd never behave." Hoping to bring back their uncle, the boy's sister had gone out in the same snowstorm without wearing proper shoes and walked and walked alone.

The sister came back to the house with blistered feet and her face chapped from crying, not telling the boy that the police believed the uncle had been killed. His aunt was the one who shared that truth.

After the uncle disappeared, the father relaxed some but watched more carefully, controlling both the sister and brother, warning them that if he ever caught them doing wrong, he'd cut off their hands, no questions asked. Even once the threat was no longer a promise the boy believed in, he fled the house as often as he could. The Village Starbucks became less an ordinary shop, instead a kind of dirty, well-loved living room, where the boy knew each upholstery intimately, knew where the crumbs had spilled and by which newspaper-reading man, knew the barista's name was Stan, short for Stanley, that he liked reading dirty books behind the counter before sweeping his floppy hair aside with a broad hand and granting the customers, especially the pretty girls, an even broader smile.

If only his sister had run off with a Stanley, the boy thought, watching the baristas play and laugh, dance to the same prepackaged music as if it were new, watch the clock even while customers waited. If only there had been some boy—strong enough to rescue her. Some boy to carry the palanquin, the kind that protected young women. A friendly boy she could have used to get away, and then get away from, if he bored her.

A boy like me, the brother thought. A kind of older brother to them both.

Once the boy finished college, paid his dues, worked for a time in a Starbucks. It wasn't the one in the Village, where he first read that book.

Then, when he saved enough , he saw the world. He saw a brilliant red palanquin bearing a rich man's wife in the middle of a rushed street in China, then a white elephant in India gravely carrying a wealthy groom. Bejeweled princesses; palaces that might be considered relics, their walls made of mirrors, where the boy could see his reflections.

It was never deliberate, how he would look for his sister, backpacking and hitchhiking and sleeping in rough places for cheap. It was just that he'd never believed she was dead. She could have been a thousand places—on a movie poster, pouting at him, or peering from the window of a café, or mindlessly shopping, wearing furs, or teaching a classroom of children, looking out the window at the precise moment he passed.

The boy imagined life for her, a life she might reveal to him, her children and his children playing together, his wife coming to love her as a sister.

The images eventually made him get married, and in the marriage, he was happy but waiting. Waiting for his sister.

There was life in between the years of searching and imagining— a job for him, first at another Starbucks, then medical school, because it fully distracted him.

Then a fine day at the hospital where he worked as a doctor and where, through no accident, the body of his sister was brought in, though he wasn't sure at first.

She looked the same. He knew not to tell his father—and that was a great gift, not telling, not even whimpering out loud in front of anyone—because in the end he only had his memory to reckon with. How did he know for certain it was she? It was a young woman his sister's age, face still familiar and beautiful but body wrecked— a car accident, her husband's or boyfriend's or lover's car struck by another motorist. The man, too weak from some illness to turn the wheel in time, deconditioned, had died at once. But she had been six months pregnant, and there was the pale gold band on her ring finger, and wedding pictures in her wallet too, of gorgeous red palanquins from an Oriental honeymoon, a *Doli* for a bride, the kind meant for queens and deities, the inside obscured by curtains, and pictures of a smiling family, probably her husband's relatives. But not a single one of him, the boy and the brother she had left, or the father, the mother, the family she started with. Only the family she had been trying to make.

The boy, the brother, couldn't bear to conclude that his sister had been defeated. So, he would say to his own wife, instead of saying his sister was dead: "I couldn't be sure that was my sister. I never had proof. She had a slightly different name—unless she changed it, I suppose. And how could I remember her body? I was so young. So, I don't really know. I really don't."

But the story stayed, a story that he knew—though his sister had left him behind when she escaped. Though she'd left him alone, to remember. Though her body had endured—what? He couldn't know. Only that she'd left so that her body would be hers to give away.

TALINDA

1.

So, here I am sitting in the doctor's waiting room, hoping no one talks to me or intuits why I'm fat, when the door that says on the outside DO NOT ENTER swings open and Talinda storms out, not long for this world.

The young, blond nurse stands there, bracing the open door with one hand, holding a clipboard with the other. "We should have the results back any day," she calls, though it's obvious my best friend isn't listening. "Later this week. Do check," her voice wafts out, like she's a woman working in a shop. Not an announcer of life versus death.

Not long for this world. "Don't say things like that," I would've pleaded with Talinda, if she had said the words out loud. One of her usual angry and dapper turns of phrase.

"You'll fight this thing," I said when she first told me she had stomach cancer, and for once she nodded, not ridiculing the cliche. That was a year ago, before I became this wretched person. A woman sleeping with her best friend's husband, a woman waiting to take over a life.

"Aren't *you* full of surprises, Miss Narika Kandelwala," Talinda would have said. "You're not as boring as I thought." If she had known.

But Talinda doesn't know what her husband and I were—are—capable of. Cancer is what she's come to know. How its cells lived as shameless parasites of the body, the dark and mocking children who'd never leave home. Talinda could caution you about genes that whispered false instructions. Genes speaking louder and louder over rivers of gushing new blood vessels, these rivers mindless and cruel as they crossed in confusing directions of their own, greedily serving the cells of destruction.

This is Talinda Kim, and what she's been given: age thirty-seven, Korean American, born to a waitress in Flushing. Board-certified internist and geriatrician, married, no children, signet cell gastric carcinoma, stage four, prognosis six months.

Six months. If I weren't betraying Talinda, I'd use what I know for her benefit. My arm around her shoulder, I'd describe Audre Lorde's cancer journals, her dignity, her hope. Then Talinda would be forced, as usual, to turn on me with her mix of affection and contempt, the potent and honest combination that I've always counted on. She might say, "Narika, you don't win any points for reading some poor woman's private diary, whose problems you can't even understand to begin with. Amazing how you're trying to read books for a living. At some point you have to stop going to school and get a job. At some point, you have to accept it. The real world isn't made of poetry."

I'd urge her on in making fun of me. I'd do anything to distract her. Talk about Dadaist art or North Korean politics or Bette Davis movies, her favorites. *Now, Voyager,* with a childless Bette Davis trying to make do by being a cool aunt. *Of Human Bondage,* Bette as the pregnant, vulgar, coercive, determined Mildred. *All About Eve.* What it is like to have your life, bit by bit, stolen by a woman you trusted.

But all I do instead is slink down in the passenger seat of Talinda's black Benz, hoping she doesn't really notice me.

A real friend would take Talinda out to a movie, after her day at the oncology clinic. Some Bette Davis old romance, but who was that actress, after all? Some skinny, overbearing, self-important white woman who bears more than a passing resemblance, I realize suddenly, to Talinda's husband George's mother. She'd never remarried after George's father left her for one of his students, a beautiful Asian woman, the two of them traveling to go teach at a university in Singapore.

All Talinda has is a mother-in-law who, like Talinda's own mother, hasn't been told anything about the cancer. A mother-in-law who's expressed the wish, loudly at times, that George had never married Talinda. Who wished Talinda had never existed.

If I loved Talinda, really loved her, I'd tell her that her husband seduced me, and vice versa. That the three of us should get far away from each other. That she deserves a better life, friend, and lover. If I were good, I'd exit, pursued by a bear.

For once, I'd be the one with adult knowledge Talinda didn't have, and I could tell her what was what.

My affair with her husband began six months ago, well after she'd been diagnosed, after she'd tried to keep working as if nothing were happening but was fatigued and couldn't stop losing weight.

I gave in after George called me in the middle of the night, crying for me to come help cook something she could eat. After George and I started meeting up in grocery stores, hospital cafeterias, places where we could help Talinda together, while she was going through surgery and modified chemo.

Tired by marriage—or maybe by his marriage to Talinda specifically, with its burdens, the heaviest of which was extreme privacy—George pulled me in. The lingering touch on my arm, my back, my hand. The grateful smiles that never felt straightforward. Then his expression when I told him how I'd tried and failed a few times to have a child with donor sperm.

"I know what it's like to hope and be disappointed," he'd said. "To wait, and want, and not have children. To be the only people waiting in the world. Believe me, I know what it's like."

George and Talinda tried a lot too. It wasn't clear now if her in vi-tro might have speeded the cancer. She would've kept trying. George was the one who couldn't try again, unable to bear how relentless she was. They'd just gotten to the point of discussing adoption when her new symptoms started. Then Talinda had to tell George that she'd never make him a father.

Had she reached for him the way I reached for her, when I found out she was dying?

When she got sick, Talinda forbade her husband from getting his family involved. No mother, and no sisters, and George's father was long gone. So George made more and more frequent calls to me in the middle of the night, while locked in the bathroom or sitting in his car.

Many calls, talking alone, and then finally, we *were* alone. He lavished long, splendid kisses on me, after he'd undressed me at my place, more recently kissing my round belly.

Talinda isn't one for gaining weight, not even back in her col-lege pre-med classes when she didn't leave her room for days. Even after hormone treatments, trying to get pregnant, she was all angles and petite, high-fashion sinews. George is tall, over six three, blue-eyed, ever so gentle with his slightly stooped posture. She was the one who'd poked fun at his rumpled-professor demeanor, complained be-hind his back about how low his salary remained even after he'd been tenured. She didn't see him for how brilliant he was. She'd never re-ally made him feel special, I told myself, even though I'd never touch the truth of them and I knew that.

Years ago, the only time that George ever came close to leav-ing Talinda—early on when they were living together but not yet engaged, during the harshest days of Talinda's medical residen-cy when she would stay at the hospital for four days at a time without calling once—she'd finally bucked the routine and come home before the end of her shift, trading with someone, running all the way. It was unthinkable to her not to work the hardest, not to dominate, not to be the best. Unthinkable to take the time to answer George's calls.

Even though George had said that if she didn't cut down her hours, they'd break up.

The night they almost broke up, when she got home, she cried when she didn't find George, calling me to come over so she wouldn't "act like a dimwit" when he did show up. Disheveled, she sat at my feet waiting for him, saying that if I breathed a word about how desperate she'd become, she'd murder me. When he let himself in later that night, I saw how Talinda pretended not to care, but how she then came up behind him as he sat eating alone. How she touched him so gently, without asking anything.

Today, waiting for Talinda to be done at the clinic, by avoiding certain patterns of thought, by walking fast whenever I passed by mirrors, by keeping in my mind an image of Talinda not loving George, never really loving him, I made it all right that I would be the one having George's baby. Just for a few seconds, I told myself that once I started really showing, I would tell her this was a baby conceived from donor sperm. Accept it when she teased me about using the sperm of a white man.

But it's possible Talinda will be gone before the birth and never know my baby is half white. We'd have our joy once she was gone. Once our goddess Talinda had risen fully out of reach.

High in a white palace, the king's daughter, the golden girl—

That image from a book the two of us read in high school. From an old story of infidelity and careless, childless adults.

By thinking of Talinda as always being high above me, I could sometimes think of her as being untouched by what I had been doing with George. Like she had too much pride to be hurt by it. Like she had better things to do.

But here I was, a little more than four months pregnant with a boy. With George's son.

2.

Many hours after Talinda's doctor's appointment, long after she's started one of her eight-hour shifts at the hospital, George calls me at eleven p.m., exactly when he said he would.

I've done my good deed for the day, I tell myself. Sitting with her for hours, at the doctor's. It doesn't make me good for a second, but it was something she needed.

Now I'm tucked away and snug inside the little studio that goes for just two grand a month on Cornelia Street, not far from where we both teach. George found the apartment a month ago and paid to rent it in my name, since I'm still only an assistant professor, and I might not have a job next September. My tenure clock is running down. The signs are good, and George's advocacy has made it easier. But nothing is certain.

I teach big courses in South Asian studies that use movies and music. I attract future photojournalists, Peace Corps volunteers, missionaries' children. They're good young people who wouldn't condone what I have done.

George shuts a door behind him so he can be completely alone, even though Talinda isn't there with him. He always tries to call from a bathroom, as if calling from the bedroom would make what we're doing worse.

Then he makes a silly liquid kissing noise into the receiver, joking, "That's for the baby, not for you."

"We just have to sit and wait," he adds. Then more softly, "Goddamn, I can't stand watching all this. This is her third straight ER shift. She just won't rest. I don't know what to do with her."

"Why not tell her now," I say, suddenly wanting to be mean, as if that is what I, what both of us, deserve. As if George and I were awful people, stuck with each other. "Tell her you're shacking up with your pretty, plump brown piece. Tell her we did it just enough times to knock me up. Then did it extra, just for kicks. That'll give her more strength to fight. We would be helping her if we made her hate us. Trust me, I know her."

"What's wrong with you?" he asks in a whisper. "If you weren't pregnant, God—"

"Well, but I *am*," I say, suddenly crying even though I don't want him to come over. "I *am* pregnant, and I'm feeling impatient."

"About what?" he asks. "You've got five months. You have to learn to be patient."

"George, we're too greedy and not cunning enough," I whisper. "And she'll find out."

"No matter what anyone does, she hasn't got more than another six or seven months," he says, sounding like a different man, the kind who might have run a hedge fund with arrogance, instead of living as a Communist academic. I'd never suspected, before George, how much some men could yearn for a child, and how poorly that desire could match up with the women they married. How a man's yearning for a child could make his marriage vows less binding, more porous, help him forgive himself.

On some level Talinda knows about this. She's always joked about George's running off with some coed. Some sociology major from the Midwest seemingly swept up in George's work against police brutality. Some younger scholar who has really been a wife-in-waiting, praying to marry George and settle down, thinking it easier to shag him than compete for funding.

"We have to wait," George repeats. Defensive, grim. "We don't have rights to anything. We only have the right to wait and see. Just waiting isn't hurting her."

I want to say, *Everything we've done is hurting her.* But that would take hostage our whole night, make George come here this minute, only to pace, drink, and agonize for hours before we fuck, instead of just taking off my clothes without much talk, as I prefer.

After this morning Talinda might come over to see me tonight. Just to complain about that nurse who wouldn't speed up her biopsy result. "Blondie couldn't get into med school," she'll say, "and now she hates women doctors."

George throws me another kissy-kiss, and I do the same over the phone, wishing that months ago we'd had the decency to stop at phone sex.

Once we hang up, I take the time to look in the mirror. In my otherwise tidy bathroom, where I have been talking to George on the new iPhone 6 he bought me, there's a little blood in the sink from where I broke a glass. It looks worse than it is. I'm not that sort of person, never was. Crazy. Cutter. Unstable bitch. In general, I don't tend toward destruction.

I'm a decent—no, more than decent, *good*—academic with papers, even a book in press. I took loving care of my mother when she was dying of diabetes complications, one foot amputated and the other holding contagion, vision gone and fingers constantly tingling. When we were little I was the one who invited Talinda home, serving my mother's mediocre Indian food to her in big portions.

Whenever she came over, she smiled vaguely when asked if she'd have more, only to whisper, "We need to go to Taco Bell," the minute my mother left the room.

I was the only one who ever made sure Talinda didn't have to eat dinner alone.

I would have shared my father with Talinda too, if mine had stayed. And for years, though I barely knew Talinda's younger-man husband, I was the one who told her to treat George kindly, to make sure he knew how intensely she loved him. A year ago, Talinda told me about the cancer and admitted to me, "You know, Narika, you are the first person I've told. Even George doesn't know yet."

A year ago, all three of us were different people. A year ago, I could have answered the question, *Why do people want to have children so much?* Now I don't know. The instinct, the hunger to have a child—it's no different from what drives the cancer growing inside Talinda. It's involuntary and primal. Primordial. I'm an academic; I should be able to tell stories about foreign words that mean "ancient" and "first." Instead the two words make me think of screaming, or of blood. But Talinda has been quiet so far, as composed as she was when she first understood that she might die.

3.

The scene one night a year ago, around Easter: the night I found out my best friend was out of time, a woman I'd known and somehow loved since I was ten and she was a bossy but affectionate, precocious twelve. Setting: a Korean restaurant she'd picked out for dinner in Flushing. Characters: Narika, a well-respected Asianist, an up-and-coming junior faculty member in the social sciences, the humanities. Not much of a slacker, despite what Talinda implies. In certain circles admired. Also: Talinda, a well-manicured Flushing beauty, a local girl made very good, in line for the next junior chair of the geriatrics department of a prestigious university. A dedicated physician. Bill: Talinda's first boyfriend, a train wreck, a playboy, luckily not present in person, but talked about, even lusted after, long after college. George: Talinda's new love, at that point married to her for seven years.

And me—the new me—nowhere in evidence. I was Narika the academic, not Narika the "friend." Not me, the one who cut herself today on a piece of broken glass, not wholly by accident, in a flash of self-loathing and dread, the woman afraid to go swimming even though it might be good for the baby; the former respectable citizen. Now regressed to seeing the same old black-and-white movies I saw in high school, imagining Talinda gone so I can go and live in her big house in Long Island. Sleep in her big bed with her husband, when pregnancy will make good sleep harder to get. When sleep alone will comfort me.

I remember me and Talinda like from a movie. Scene, action, dialogue.

One year ago: "You're late," Talinda said. Narika slid into a fake leather booth. It's where Talinda's parents first met. Neither had lived in America more than a few years. The laughing acupuncturist insisted that the too-serious, pretty girl who brought his food sit down with him. That was when the very idea of Talinda first began, frivolous as that was, serious as Talinda Kim is today. Hard to imagine Talinda's sensible mother ever being pliant, giggly, tractable, but Talinda's doctor father, telling strangers the story, always insisted she was. In a booth like the one where Talinda and Narika sat, the confident man, years before he would leave Talinda forever, must have pulled Talinda's mother by the hand, maybe even caressed her roughened fingers. Charmed her enough to make her stay.

In the restaurant, several feet behind Talinda and Narika, near the sushi bar where two men of indeterminate age in white aprons and chef hats busy themselves cutting vegetables, one of the waitresses sat, chubby and tense, perched on a bar stool. She wore a red uniform with sausage-casing cleavage that looked highly uncomfortable. An alert, compact golden retriever sat at the woman's feet, trim and obedient, panting when it saw Narika looking its way but not attempting to get up. Narika was used to Korean food, but for a second she worried for the dog, saw grim images of paws floating in soup, the waitress's thin fingers flicking a torn, shaggy ear. She shrugged it off; they came here often during childhood, when Talinda's mother had to go back to work after Talinda's father divorced her, disappearing overseas, leaving them without money.

Often Narika thinks that the facts of her parents' divorce have defined Talinda: abruptness, condescension, pride. Even bare-faced lying. A cynical indifference and yet a kind of quiet and unshakable loyalty, the same kind that made Talinda's mother send money to her in-laws in Korea for years after the father absconded. Before leaving, he'd taken money from his parents as well. Talinda's mother, eventually Talinda herself, sent them thousands.

Talinda is much easier to love than to like. But then again, Narika thought, she herself is not that easy to even tolerate.

"You've lost weight," Narika said when minutes passed and Talinda did not speak or even make eye contact. The woman knows how to give a cold shoulder—actually, an icy one, as punishment for Narika's being nearly half an hour late to their dinner.

Talinda looked up from her menu.

"No, I mean it," Narika said. "A lot of weight—like, what, at least thirty pounds? Don't tell me you did this on purpose. It isn't chic. You look almost skeletal." Narika aspired to be mean, as she often did when in Talinda's company. She's always told herself that this is only in anticipation of Talinda's bona fide meanness, which she has been so interested in and enraptured by since the fourth grade.

It *is* bracing, watching Talinda eviscerate some stranger with verve. The last time they'd come to this cheap Korean restaurant, a few months before, Talinda sported a new, thin, but unmistakable magenta streak in her hair, like some Japanese teenager rebelling against her high school principal. Despite Talinda's Chanel suit and pearls, Narika always half-expected to see her slinging a Hello Kitty knapsack across her chair. That time, Talinda had picked up a brochure in Korean, with one phrase in English only: *Water bar.*

"*Mizu shobai* is the Japanese name for it," Talinda said. Narika remembered the contemptuous curl of her lovely lips. "It's from an expression about good luck and bad. A matter of chance, as shifting as water. So, might as well live it up now with hot baths, massages, and lots of you know what."

"Wait, why do they call them water bars?" Narika asked.

"Don't ask boring questions. Do I look like a tour guide?" Talinda snapped, just as a waiter came over to replenish their water glasses. He was the owner of the restaurant. Narika recognized him from the large photo near the front entrance.

He also had the appearance of being some daughter's father. This is how Narika's own father could have been—serene, present, working, instead of disappearing, unemployed, and indifferent. It had been Narika's mother, and not Narika herself, who waited anxiously for his letters and cards, not even insisting on a check. Narika's mother who spent her modest salary on beauty treatments, facial creams, hair oils, expensive clothes, so that the house had to be sold to pay all the debts once her mother was dead. Narika's mother who, upon hearing that Talinda had lost her father too, wondered aloud why Talinda's mother hadn't tried harder to persuade the man to stay.

"What are you nice girls doing, talking about water bars?" the genial man said, pausing with the half-full pitcher of water on his tray. "Those aren't innocent places."

For his intrusion, Talinda rewarded the man with a cold smile. "I'll have the dinner plate," she said, giving him her menu while looking straight at Narika. Instead of taking the hint, the good-looking Korean man caught Narika's eye, leaned closer than he had to, and said: "You know the secret of the water bars? They're favorite places of water demons, the *kappas*. That's why you should never go to a host club or, God forbid, work in a hostess club, near any body of water. The *kappa* will wait for you under the water, and then he'll ravish you. Seduce you into giving him pleasure, maybe even give you a baby."

"You know the only way to avoid him?" the man had asked Narika, bedroom-eyed. Narika shook her head, ever the wide-eyed ingénue.

Talinda, weary, answered him like she was sick of his type. "Yes, yes, you have to be polite. Bow to the *kappa* as deeply as you can." Talinda bowed her head to illustrate her meaning.

The man smiled, but Talinda was determined that he not be complacent, not be charmed. "The goal is to kill the bugger with your politeness. You bow to him only to make him bow to you. As soon as soon as the water falls out of the cup on top of his head, he cannot move. He's stuck there, and you move on, and then you're free of him. I mean, totally free of that demon. Like you don't ever have to talk to him again. Like he'll know enough not to come near you. Ever." Raising her eyebrow slightly, she glanced at the man as he stood there transfixed with his tray of water. He never approached their table again, not that night or any other night.

Talinda's instinctive sharpness had been there since she was twelve. One day in homeroom, Talinda, a seventh-grade monitor, announced that the fifth-grade Narika's generic puppy-themed lunchbox was no good, and if she was lucky she would get a better one on sale. Somehow, the very act of being criticized had comforted Narika. She'd felt that they were both marked as outsiders. Not just because Talinda was the new girl in school and, for a time, the only Korean, or because Narika remained the darkest brown girl in the class for all six years of elementary, but because they were both fatherless. Because they'd found a way to do without.

Twenty-five years later, Talinda has become a successful doctor specializing in the care of older people and writes influential papers about feeding tubes. Narika is an academic expert in Indian history—assistant professor, tenure track, no longer an adjunct. She's on the eve of the publication of her first book on Hindu women in politics and the ambiguous meanings of the mother goddess for Communists in India, a successful expansion of her dissertation. "I never know what you're talking about when you try to explain what it is you do for a living," Talinda often says. Or else she drops one of her sayings—elusive, a pearl: "Narika, don't try so hard to live inside a story that's not yours."

That evening, dinner a year ago, Korean restaurant, Talinda was, as usual, practical. "What are you doing these days, anyhow?" Talinda asked, probably just to change the subject from her dramatic weight loss. "Still chasing after dead bad white guys, or what?"

Often Talinda sounds exactly like Narika's dead mother, comforting for her familiarity, for her constancy. Narika's mother was stubborn. She'd held onto the house where she'd raised Narika until the end, though she'd been riddled with bad debt.

She'd never stopped preparing herself for her husband's return after he'd left them for another woman and another child. Narika was sixteen then; her father's mistress, barely twenty. Only Talinda, out of all her friends, knew why he'd gone. Only Talinda knew how intensely Narika came to despise her own mother's house, how peaceful it had been to finally be rid of it.

"I mean, I know you're a teacher, a professor, I do understand that," Talinda went on, emphasizing "that" and spitting a little when she talked, which Narika made a mental note of but didn't comment on. "But the subjects you study? Something about colonialism, which I understand is over now in India and elsewhere in the world, and like, has been over for the last hundred years or so? So what does studying that do for anyone, what purpose does that have? And are you at least teaching your students other skills? So they can do research on topics that matter?"

"Like curing cancer," Narika said, unaware and trying to make Talinda smile. "Like being, oh I don't know—a doctor?"

Talinda laughed. "Well, what's wrong with that?" By then the waitress on duty, who recognized the subtlest changes in expression and mood of a table, had brought them water and sake. The liquor stung Narika's throat and eyes. She never drinks except with Talinda—like so many other things, it is a ritual separate from her life, from her identity as a nose-ring-wearing Indian-origin academic. A dark brown woman who does yoga on the beach.

Talinda was impassive as she drank. She never seems to manifest the Oriental flush that is a peculiarity of cytochrome enzymes' genetic heterogeneity, she always liked to say. But she never drinks to excess either, not like the Asian man who'd once sat next to Narika on a bus ride from Washington, D.C. to New York with two six-packs on his lap, and who brought his sweaty arms and thighs too close to Narika as she sat next to him, trying to outline her lecture notes. There might be something Talinda had to tell her, Narika got the sense, but couldn't be sure of, couldn't force it out. It would probably emerge as they were settling the check. "Bill and I broke up" was how they'd finished a similar dinner eight years before, before Talinda met George, back when she assumed her college boyfriend Bill would be the one.

That time, she and Talinda still in their twenties, Narika only had two hours left before catching a flight to O'Hare for a conference. She'd tried in vain to get Talinda to "talk more about her feelings" (a phrase her friend uttered with a snarl) by taking her to a lovely candlelit dessert place in the Village, with a French name and little tables and perfect espressos served in demitasse with chocolate croissants. The coffee and the pastries had been fine, Talinda remarked afterward, but "please spare me all that psychological whatnot. Bill left me and that's that. What am I going to do about it? What would I change by talking? Not a thing. Maybe it would've been different if his mother liked me. She was no fan of 'slant-eyes,' as she put it, but that's fine. I'll live."

Perhaps the not-talking had worked, for only two years after Bill left, Talinda had met George at an art gallery, a show Narika dragged her to. George the academic, well read, definitely humanities—the kind of man Narika herself hoped she might marry someday. But back then, Narika was dating a woman, not the first. Something she and Talinda didn't talk about. Either because it would spotlight, uncomfortably, how beautiful Talinda still was to Narika, even after so many years—or else because it would raise the question, equally uncomfortable, of what Talinda had intended when they were fifteen and seventeen, respectively, and Talinda, sleeping over at Narika's house, crawled into her bed to; watch and laugh at a slightly campy Roman Polanski movie where two beautiful women made love, and afterward they tried it themselves.

Slightly nervous now, at Talinda's continued silence, Narika ordered her usual Buddha's delight—a vegetarian version of *bibimbap* with tofu instead of beef, a fried egg on top of tender noodles, sprouts, and lots of vegetables smothered in Korean hot sauce. Talinda's mother was the one who'd made it for her the first time, along with Korean spareribs that Narika refused, first provoking mild insult then pity as the older, still lovely woman sat with Talinda and they contentedly tore into the meat, picking at the bones afterward, unselfconscious, pinching large pieces of pickled cabbage with gleaming black chopsticks and popping them into their mouths between bites of gristle and beef, even burping occasionally without casting a glance at Narika, their guest, who at age eleven had sat in shocked but amused silence.

Talinda ordered a small miso soup and another side dish with tofu.

"I haven't decided yet; I'll tell you in a while," Talinda said to the waitress, speaking in English to prevent conversation, something she routinely does with other Koreans. The waitress bowed and retreated as a busboy refilled their tumblers of green tea.

"You *are* starving yourself," Narika said in triumph. "But now it's going to stop. I'm not leaving here until you've had at least one order of either Korean spareribs or the *bulgogi*. Take your pick."

Talinda shrugged. "So, tell me about this book of yours."

"Well, it's coming out finally, not that there'll be any money in it. But there is a book tour if I take the initiative, and I think it'll be taught at the undergraduate level."

"That's good."

"And it ended up being shorter than the original five hundred pages, even with the photographs I took on my trip back to India—"

"What do you mean, 'back'? Girl, you are not from India. You are from Flushing, Queens."

"*I* know that. But the publishers want to pitch me as Indian." Their food came quickly, came quickly, as always. The waitress gave another little bow, perhaps wondering if they'd be there all night, bickering and picking at their food, and what kind of tip, if any, they would leave. They must have looked to her like hometown girls, not businesswomen, not quite housewives or mothers, already well into their thirties and out by themselves on a Friday night, poor things.

"Have you ever heard of Jallianwala Bagh?" Narika asked, taking a sip of tea and thinking about what she'd order for dessert so she could get Talinda to share it.

"No, Narika. I'm educated, not a nerd. And I don't have a big chip on my shoulder about a bunch of white guys, you know? In case you hadn't noticed, I married one."

"Haha. Well, this place I visited in India, it's a memorial now. Thousands of men, women, and children gathering unarmed, for a peaceful protest, were literally gunned down by the British army. It was unbelievable."

"Okay—I'm going to ask you something. Don't get offended, okay? I mean, why didn't they run? That's the thing about Koreans. We know when to get away and go think about revenge. Why were the Indians so passive? Answer that."

"But that's the thing," Narika said, cringing a little at the earnest sound of her own voice. "They couldn't run. The British sealed off all the exits to this compound where they'd gathered. They tried escaping. They wanted to get out."

"Oh."

"Terrible, isn't it?"

Talinda played with her chopsticks, staring at a spot just over Narika's shoulder. There was nothing there but the wood paneling.

"Well, I guess everyone dies," she finally said. "Can we talk about other things?"

"Isn't your mom worried about you? Especially with you being thin. You can't convince me George likes you this way. How could you possibly try for a baby at this weight? Your wrists are like matchsticks. I can see your veins."

"My mom is just glad I can fit into her stuff now," Talinda said, deftly ignoring the mention of babies. "Her silk *cheongsams* and her oldie-but-goodie Chanel suits. She's got a Pucci dress that would've been way too tight a year ago. It's great. If you just lose thirty pounds, too, I'll lend it to you."

"Tell me what's wrong, really," Narika insisted, refusing the insult, though she knew losing ten pounds wouldn't do her any harm.

Talinda sighed deeply and theatrically.

"I'll tell you once we're done eating," she said. "I want to enjoy my food."

Narika sat up, alert. "Wait, are you having an affair?" she asked, scarcely daring to believe it. "You're cheating on *George,* of all people? And it's guilt that stops you from eating? Or you're just getting so much exercise—"

"I'm not even going to dignify—" Talinda began, but Narika, dramatic, interrupted, closing her eyes and holding her forehead with both hands, as if she were a seer.

"And don't tell me—it's Bill. After everything, you're sleeping with Bill. Bill the jerk who ran off with one of your roommates during spring break, Bill the rich boy cliché, the trust fund baby who picked you up during freshman crush, who cried for you only after you were gone. Bill the screw-up whose only merit was his high-octane you-know-what."

"About right, except one major correction. He could barely get it up even in college. I doubt he's having any luck with his little thing now." Talinda laughed.

"But you're doing something that you haven't told anyone," Narika said, "and you're ashamed, and will tell me. Is it money? That big pharma sellout you got into? Tell me, dammit. You're driving me crazy. You know I'll support you, whatever it is. Especially if it involves indulging your vices."

"What vices?"

"Enough with the games—you need to eat," Narika said, serious.

Talinda signaled the waitress and soon the menu reappeared on their table.

"I'll tell them to add *bibimbap* to my order, just to shut you up."

"Hey—do you remember in seventh grade, when that tall Korean girl—"

"You mean Hannah, Hannah Eun. She had a name. You should do better. You never liked it when people called you 'that Indian girl.'"

"Hannah had this whole thing about how small your feet were. She called your loafers 'thimbles' and your mittens 'thumb-warmers.' She'd complain that she looked like a giant next to you. Remember that?"

"Narika, you're sad. You're the only person in the world who remembers that. I bet even Hannah has moved on by now. I bet she has tons of short friends and doesn't even notice it."

"Is that why you're so careful what you eat? Because you never want to be *both* short and chubby?"

Talinda shook her head. "Just that it takes me a while to eat these days. I feel nauseous a lot."

Narika's eyes widened in joy for a moment. "Oh, God! You're expecting! You and George! Great!"

"No. No, it's not that," Talinda said, her eyes filling with tears.

Narika stared, waiting, breath caught in her throat.

"Columbia Onc isn't sure yet, but they think I have cancer. Stomach cancer—the kind Asians get. If it's signet ring, my prognosis is laughable. Even if it's not, I haven't got long. But who does? You're the one proving that bad guys come and shoot people down. Isn't that, like, the thesis of your book?"

Narika found she couldn't move or speak.

Talinda rubbed her own cheekbones, smudging her rouge. "This is why I didn't want to tell you. I didn't want a scene. I didn't want to frighten you."

Narika nodded, grabbing a napkin and dabbing her eyes, clearing her throat.

"In case you're wondering, I was planning to tell George tonight, after I get the biopsy results. After I know how long."

"That's good," Narika said, too fast. "You have to tell him. But maybe it'll be negative. Maybe all of it is something else—not cancer. Not cancer at all. Like, isn't there this thing where you can be pregnant, only it attaches to your stomach and not in the right place, isn't it—"

"It's not an ectopic," said Talinda, cold. "Whatever this thing is, it's going where it will be able to grow."

Narika, chastened, could only nod her head.

Talinda, looking past her. "I wish I could feel the kind of childish hope that you can feel, I really do. The head-shrinkers who work at my clinic, they say denial helps at first. But none of that soft science matters now. Neither do feelings. 'Tissue is the issue,' like my pathology professors used to say. And if the tissue diagnosis supports the clinical and imaging? Including the weight loss, and my loss of appetite? George won't matter then. Love has no power in the place where I'm headed, Narika. Not even yours."

"Love is all you've got, you idiot. You're going to live. Even if the news is terrible, George will help."

Narika, expecting Talinda to say, "Of course I'll live, you silly bitch," or even "I don't need anyone's help," found it unbearable when Talinda bowed her head.

"Your mother," Narika said quickly. "You've told her, haven't you? She'll want to come and stay with you."

Talinda whipped up, alert and fierce. "Oh no, she won't know anything. She's in Korea now. Left just a few days ago for my grandfather's eightieth. Told me she doesn't see the point of coming back to the US, ever again. It's perfect. She's never going to know. After I'm gone, I'll get George to send her a telegram saying I died in an accident, suddenly. That I didn't suffer."

"You're not even going to—"

"No."

"But even if it's cancer, couldn't you have time?" Narika asked. "With my grandfather's cancer, he had years. He spent two years in India recovering. You shouldn't work. You should adopt with George. Love a child. You should do everything you can to live."

Talinda said, "If it's in the nodes, stage three or four, survival is a year or less."

Narika hid her face in her hands.

"Don't think for a minute I'm not going to fight," Talinda said. "I've got enough time to make a choice about chemo or not. They would do surgery in a few weeks to make the thing smaller. There's an experimental protocol at McGill. Canada. They freeze the balls off the cancer. I may elect to do that one instead. So far, some of the subjects have a higher survival. A year or two. One outlier even lived ten years, and trials are still going. NIH is so miserably slow."

"What's NIH?" Narika almost asked. And then she thought of more questions, so many more questions, down to the detail of what kind of nightgown Talinda preferred if and when she had to take to bed, but only because she didn't know anything, not because the answers would help anything now. Questions. There were more questions she could have asked, but now, choosing to be merciful, Narika shut up.

She tried to remember Talinda's favorite dessert but couldn't.

"Let me cry, okay?" Narika said. "I'll stop in a minute."

She put a hand on Talinda's cold, white one, noticing as she always did the difference in their skin color. But this time it seemed like a ghastly difference between a living and dying thing—Narika's rosy-golden-brown hand, unlined, against Talinda's pale one.

Talinda took her hand away and pressed it against her temple, massaging.

"You're not even forty. How is this possible?" Narika whispered in a fury.

Talinda's smile: self-deprecating, cynical. Savvy. Reminding Narika of just how much reality her friend had seen.

"Just lucky, I guess," Talinda said.

4.

I wish I could say that something deep and abiding, like love for Talinda, is what united us, George and me. That she will live on when we're together. That we will name our child after her—Kim Tae-Hyun. Her real, Korean name. But all of that would be a lie. What binds George to me is our years of baby hunger, real and plain. That little pirate, growing and greedy, in my belly—four months along now, his heartbeat softer but more regular than the gush of blood through Talinda's cancer—that little person is a dream.

Inside me lives a healthy, plundering group of cells that wants what it wants, like George's heart. Still I like thinking of me and Talinda having our dinner in Flushing, last year, before my son seized my affections. Even now, I enjoy replaying this scene, and the few weeks afterward, before I betrayed my best friend, remembering details like the texture of the dog's fur, the taste of the food before Talinda told me about her diagnosis—how much I enjoyed the evening, enjoyed being with her. How, looking at Talinda's lips as she mocked me, I relived the night in high school when she let me kiss her.

Then I think of the night I started with George, the first of only three nights that we fucked, hard, loud, and heavenly, before I got pregnant, as if I had been waiting all along, and I wonder if anything, anything at all, would have prevented what George and I have done.

Tonight—one year since she told me about her cancer, six months of me lying to her face—Talinda knocks at my door. It's past midnight. Nothing has announced her. My buzzer doesn't work, along with the stove and one of the windows in this apartment, a casualty of the landlord's smug indifference, a feature of this neighborhood.

I'm glad to see Talinda. Relieved that she looks beautiful, unchanged. I don't ask why she's come to visit me this late.

"The Canadian experiment's not working," she says. "The meds are shit."

She takes off her scarf and shakes her hair loose. If her treatment were working, she wouldn't have that hair, but as it is it looks exactly as it always has—lush down her back, black with red highlights, a dream-girl's hair, an illustration for *The Pillow Book*. George must have fallen in love with it. He never runs his fingers through my hair, which is a witch doll's powder puff, a mess of black curls that would be wiry if I didn't take care of them. But always he touches my lips, which are darker than hers and just a bit fuller. And traces my profile, whispering, "Nefertiti." And my dark nipples. Talinda's, I happen to know, are the lightest, most delicate and softest pinkish brown. When we were teenagers, it felt like a miracle when she revealed them to me.

Now it's nearly 4 a.m. and Talinda's sitting on my bed, me on the floor, and we're almost done watching *Dark Victory*.

"Wrong choice," I'd said when she picked it. "Trust me, you don't want to see that."

"You're making a pretty big assumption, aren't you?" she said. "Like—thinking because Keanu Reeves isn't in it, I won't have a clue what it's about?"

"I don't want you to see it," I said, feeling the tears. "Come on. Let's watch something else." I wanted to distract her from the things she'd said, about how she'd chosen wrong with the Canadian protocol, now it was too late for surgery and too early for hospice, how all this probably meant she had three months at most. How she'd been vomiting and couldn't stop. How the cancer has proven to be unstoppable.

But the movie Talinda chose plays on the screen and we're both enrapt, watching the handsome, stocky doctor tower over tiny Bette Davis, like George towers over Talinda. George said to call him again before I went to sleep, but I won't. I won't betray Talinda anymore.

Without George in the picture, Talinda and I are back where we were. We're eating popcorn. Talinda jeers, queen of it all on my pillows. Me sitting on the floor at her feet, unable to move, waiting for her to look at me. In thrall to her. Smiling at the movie's campy parts, loving the way she rolls her eyes.

It's not until the end of the movie that she speaks.

"I know about you and George," she says. "I know everything you've done."

I say nothing. If I don't speak, maybe she'll think that I'm asleep.

"It must be that you're pregnant, aren't you?" she asks, not waiting for me to respond. "It won't be long," she says. "It really won't be long. Just don't tell me about any of it. I don't even want to know if you're pregnant."

She must hear the sound of me crying, exhausted. Slowly, I stand.

"What can I do?" I ask, the way I should have been asking all along, the way I stopped asking months ago.

Talinda flicks on the light at the side of my bed, switches the TV off with the remote, makes room.

"Be close to me," she says, patting the place next to her. "You're what I've got."

I move closer. But I can't bring myself to sit on the bed next to her. Can't risk that what is wrong with her will pass to me.

"There's no way you have a cigarette, do you?"

I shake my head no.

"Then what are you reading these days, anything good?" Talinda says, picking up the book that lies on my bedside table. "Ah yes," she says, opening to a random page. "Sontag. Even I've heard of her. Good for you, starting to read people I've heard of. Not that Bakhtin or any of those names that sound like phlegm."

"Oh, look at this, perfect," she goes on, not looking at me. I'm holding the sheet against my front, even now protecting myself, keeping my flesh and the flesh of my flesh, the bone of my bone, separate from hers.

There is a baby inside me now, and without meaning to, I have forgiven myself.

"'Illness is the night side of citizenship,'" Talinda reads. "'A more onerous citizenship. Everyone who is born holds dual citizenship, in the kingdom of the well and in the kingdom of the sick—'

"An onerous citizenship," she repeats, now looking up at me. "I like that. Worse than the exam my mother took, when she became a US citizen. Once you're sick, part of you, most of the time, more or less feels forced to keep trying to live, even when you stop wanting to."

I stand, ready to move away and save myself. Save him. My little love.

"What now?" I ask. "What do you need? Is there anything that I—? Forget George. I'll break it off with him. It's not about him. I am so sorry, Talinda. So sorry."

Talinda stares at me, assessing. "You're not going to be with me, are you?" she says. "Not really. Part of you is gone. You're committed. You have become somebody's mother." Laughing now. "Congrats."

I stand there anyway, waiting. The least I can do is try to be the loyal dog. A small, pudgy dog, simple in its love. Ready to serve.

"Why don't you fucking let me sleep," Talinda says, rolling onto her side, but she doesn't slap my hand away when I come close enough to smooth my bedclothes over her. "In a little while I'll call my husband, and he'll come here because *I* ask, because it's right. And he'll ignore you. And you can break up with him then, fine. Sure you will. But meantime, Narika, let me sleep. I mean, really, can't you? Leave me alone to goddamn sleep."

A SHAKER CHAIR

1.

AT LEAST THE GIRL WAS NEVER LATE, thought Sylvia. Like most Indians Sylvia had ever known—actually, like most Asians in general—this girl Maya, this twenty-year-old patient who was over two decades younger than Sylvia, was conscientious, consistent. She paid for each psycho-analysis session, in Sylvia's chic Brattle Street private practice, with bedraggled wads of cash that looked like the contents of the cash register at some filthy curry restaurant. But cash was cash, and even the dirtiest cash would pay for Sylvia's two new, sturdy teakwood armoires.

Rosewood, bamboo, tropical breeds. *Comfort without indolence; luxury without opulence,* the shop's ad said. Sylvia couldn't stop spending her money at the overpriced Asian antiques shop because its aesthetic was so understated. The opposite of some Oriental depot palace that would have appealed to dramatic, beautiful Maya, who'd shown up for a few past sessions wearing pointed brocade shoes and carrying rusty old hookahs, one of which she'd offered Sylvia.

Whenever Maya sat on one of Sylvia's plain, gleaming, antique wooden chairs, she left behind a strangely sweaty curry smell, which Sylvia was too embarrassed about noticing to ever mention to anyone. As if it might in some way mean Sylvia, of all people, was racist, though the very thought felt bizarre in her mind, as if she were thinking like a white. Like a stranger. Or like one of Sylvia's own white relatives, not her maternal grandparents but her extended family who had grown up in the South. She didn't even bring up Maya's odor in her own psychotherapy, with the teacher she'd contacted when she acknowledged how uncomfortable Maya made her. After years of checking in with her old supervisor once every few months at most, Sylvia had recently begun seeing him once a week.

Countertransference, that was all—the way her heart beat so fast whenever she heard Maya's buoyant footsteps on the stairs. The way it felt to let Maya shake her hand, which sometimes she did before sessions, or stare at Sylvia's legs, or when Maya smiled instead of answering a question.

Countertransference was what had to be discussed. "Revulsion," Sylvia had said in a hoarse half-whisper to her old supervisor, now in his eighties. "Revulsion is what she makes me feel."

"I don't know what you're saying, I just don't understand," he'd said, forcing Sylvia to repeat herself, as if the act of repetition could teach her something.

"Ah, the revulsion," he finally echoed. It was a word he *would* like, for its passionate connotation, its confrontation, its elevation of what they were doing as psychoanalysts in this day and age— "Working for the insurance companies, wasting our time with paperwork"—into something necessary and elemental. "Revulsion. Finally, the smell of blood, of life," the old man said, leaning back with satisfaction in his chair, as if he'd confirmed that he was supervising assassins.

Not that Sylvia in any way lacked killer instinct. She made a point of being polished, calm, perfect. Prada bag hanging on the door of her office, delicate high-heeled shoes, silk blouse tucked inside a suit with good, clean lines. Revulsion, anger, and damn it, with Maya, something else—sometimes a pause, a quick breath held, Sylvia thought, as she turned the pages of a Ralph Lauren catalogue, a favorite Gold Amex credit card between her fingers. She paused each time a slender brown young girl modeled a pair of riding boots or a sinuous dress, a girl with hair the texture of Maya's. Sucked in her breath for girls with Maya's color skin, who wore lingerie

Not that Sylvia ever felt that way during session. Despite her loveliness, Maya managed to look slovenly. During the day, Maya was a research drone for some sort of web healthcare startup in Kendall, politely anonymous, as well groomed as Sylvia for the white folks she saw day in and out. Maya only showed up disheveled for black, biracial Sylvia.

From the beginning, feeling that things were sure to turn around, Maya denied that anything serious brought her to therapy. Therapy was just *"covering her bases"* or *"taking advantage of how Boston had so many shrinks."* It was something Maya's internist, a real doctor, not just a psychologist or "a mere social scientist" like Sylvia, had pressed upon her, even writing Sylvia's address on a prescription pad.

The internist diagnosed Maya as being *"a little depressed."*

"But it's not like I'm having a nervous breakdown, you know?" Maya had said. And anyway, these days, for patients like Maya who held down jobs and weren't doing drugs, big-impact nervous breakdowns went in slow motion if they happened at all, like young leaves quietly fading into brown before they curled up and, disintegrating, disappeared.

Maya was already a beautiful shade of brown—a much darker shade than Sylvia herself, though, in the political color scheme, it was Maya, not Sylvia, who was considered nearly white. White enough so that there was an Indian-American governor in Louisiana nowadays.

Sylvia had read about the Christian-converted Indian-American Southern man while sitting in her mother's warm kitchen at home, turning pages slowly and halfway listening to the perpetual sound she knew she'd never get away from, her father talking back to Rush Limbaugh or some other right-leaning blowhard on the air. Daddy ranting from his room during commercial breaks, about how disgusting it was that now the KKK white folks and all their un-righteous brethren could call on the monkey immigrants, the curry-smelling, greedy Indians, the fucking Hindoos, to do some of their dirty work and call it "diversity."

Sylvia's mother hadn't grown up hearing language like that about Indians. Sylvia's grandmother was an old white Democratic fund-raiser. Sylvia's Virginia-born grandfather was the descendant of slaves who'd escaped. Sylvia's mother listened carefully to Sylvia's unchar-acteristic condemnation of affluent, educated Maya with her Indian doctor parents, listened to Sylvia say "this patient" in an irritated tone of voice. Listened to her complain about how offensive it was to have cash dumped on the table every session. About how Maya must think of Sylvia as being a black cleaning lady, to pay her that way.

"But what is it about the poor child that bothers you this much?" she'd wanted to know, the last time Sylvia vented—prompting Sylvia to refrain from telling Mother anything else about Maya.

You can't become a therapist by being nice, Sylvia would have said, if she were still sixteen, or twenty-two, and not age forty-seven, and therefore past debating with her mother. But Mother's empathy rankled. Fine to have empathy, if you didn't have patients seeking to devour you. Fine to have kindness, if you couldn't be ruined.

Any decent therapist knew that being too empathic got in the way of *being* a therapist. You couldn't be soft. You had to fend for yourself.

Sylvia had wasted enough time, earlier in her career, on rumina-tion and compassion for difficult patients. In her ridiculously de-tailed care for others, she had missed out on her own life.

Acknowledged or not, in psychoanalysis there usually was the smell of blood—people were brutal when exposed and vulnerable. People could hurt, especially when they were trying to take from the therapist what their own parents had not given them. They'd strike out if you didn't watch. Keeping up your guard while smiling warmly—that was the ticket.

Sylvia's mother had never had to keep up much of a guard, Sylvia's father always said. Eugenia resembled her little white grandmother, for one thing, with very soft stick-straight hair. She had the hair of a Sicilian girl who had been fed well, treated kindly, led to expect a comfortable life. Sylvia herself hadn't inherited hair that both black and white strangers referred to as "good." And Sylvia's mother, in addition to having a near-encyclopedic knowledge of French wines, early American furniture, and antebellum history, was, unlike Sylvia, a poet. Not an analyst of any kind.

"These are my other children," Sylvia's mother would say, gesturing at her eleven published books, each of which had mostly been written (she would admit, but only after Sylvia grew up) during long afternoons and entire weekends spent alone, instead of being a mother.

In addition to the slim, prize-winning volumes of poetry that were proudly displayed in a mahogany bookcase, built by Sylvia's father, that sat behind the antique Shaker rocking chair in her parents' living room, Sylvia's mother had quietly pulled off another accomplishment: she was known in Boston for her annual seminar, one for which she accepted only three poets. The culmination of the seminar was an evening at which her annointed young poets were invited to read the best poem they'd ever written while seated on the Shaker chair, fashioned for someone hardworking to rest in late at night. Everyone held their breath while each poet squeezed in. Praying their weight wouldn't break the wood. Savoring that seat of distinction while they recited lines from memory.

Sylvia's mother inherited the chair from ancestors who had been taken in, more or less rescued, by the splinter group, the serious men running a Shaker homestead on the Underground Railroad. Blue-eyed men like Sylvia's old supervisor, wearing heavy black shoes, had once smoked pipes and stroked their beards while discussing the fates of fugitive slaves huddled in their Hancock barns.

While her mother entertained young college acolytes, the students and audience sitting in lotus position on the floor of their living room—

nobody daring to touch the Shaker chair, of course—Sylvia's father was a silent, skeptical presence, moving in and out of earshot, nodding politely, keeping his own secrets, some of which Sylvia knew but wouldn't tell.

During these special events, Sylvia the child was relegated to her room. Told to take her milk and cake upstairs. Told above all not to make a disturbance, to stay at the periphery.

Her father would always come upstairs to her, whispering family stories. Sylvia's daddy was a banker whose own father had come to America as an engineering graduate student from Kampala, Uganda. Soon after taking his degree, Sylvia's paternal grandfather quietly married a white woman from Kentucky whose family had once included Klansmen. The couple settled in suburban New Jersey.

Efraim Nuwagaba, Sylvia's father, who'd met Sylvia's mother in Cambridge when both were at Harvard, had grown into a man who wore the mask that grinned and lied in all social and professional settings, except his house. A man whose anger was simple, and often effective. Wise anger he said he learned from his father, whose Lugbara family supported the Amin regime. Whose family acquired fabric stores formerly owned by Indians, when in the early 1970s, around when Sylvia was born, thousands of those smelly dukawallas were kicked out of Uganda for good, their properties seized. A move cheered by black nationalists in the U.S., her father always reminded Sylvia, for whom Idi Amin was like the second coming of Marcus Garvey.

Sylvia would have felt ashamed of the Ugandans' pride in killing and exiling Indians, except that the Indian men she'd met in college, even the ones with whom she'd listened to music far into the night, confessed they'd never be allowed to date a black woman. Told her that she was beautiful, sexy, but that they didn't want to lead her on. They wanted to find a woman they could realistically have children with.

Her parents' neighbors in Lexington, Asians for the most part, Indians and Chinese and Koreans, kept their distance. They couldn't fail to notice her father's scowl. Sylvia's might have been the only black family in the neighborhood, but there was never any garbage placed on their lawn, no messages in egg yolks or shaving cream, no stomach-turning graffiti.

The Lexington neighbors also kept their distance from Sylvia and her mother. With their sweater sets, designer suits, and creative ambitions, Sylvia and Eugenia never had much to say to the Asian women drones who worked for big pharma and always looked harried, shuttling kids to soccer games. The stay-at-home Asian women in their tight-fitting designer sweats were usually the wives of rich white executives, the women in lumpy pantsuits much better educated immigrants. Like those who'd come from India. Like Sylvia's patient Maya.

"It's a matter of getting respect from Indians. You see, they've never really had respect for their black counterparts, Eugenia. They've never even *seen us* as equals," her father told her mother, after the first and only time Sylvia complained about Maya, and Sylvia nodded with relief at being understood, being allowed her revulsion—thinking of Maya's nonchalance, her strange ways of communicating, her dirt, her lank hair and unwashed smell. A smell of dark earth. Intoxicating, in a way. But sickening too.

🐘

With only seconds left before the therapy session was due to start, Sylvia shuddered in the refuge of her office, finally hearing Maya's step. *Revulsion*, Sylvia thought again. But maybe the patient, like other patients, would improve. Maybe there would be a transformation in the weeks and months ahead, and Maya would come to a session smelling clean, face scrubbed, hair pinned up sleekly, wearing the high-quality pressed skirt suit she wore for her job and taking a cool, discreet credit card out of a designer wallet. A wallet good enough for Sylvia herself to carry. Smiling at Sylvia without an intention to provoke. Taking for granted that both she and Sylvia belonged. That they could support each other. Brown girl, brown woman solidarity. A dream.

And maybe then Maya would get real. Would show herself, instead of one of any number of pretenders who, like the faces of Eve, could show up on any given day—the torn-up little girl, a helpless and huge-eyed waif asking for Sylvia to please please please rescue her; or Maya the shrewd-eyed seductress; or, worst of all, the fake Maya who got herself up like an unkempt, pathetic Third World whore, without sense or respect. Standing there on garish rickety heels as a humiliation to all women of color, the bad smell of Maya's body magnified by glaringly cheap clothes that were ill-ftting, too short and tight. Her makeup smeared-on, her hair matted.

Today Maya arrived for the appointment in subdued, almost neutral garb. She wore an androgynous black ninja hood, loose pants like the white boy skaters around the Harvard T—but when she lifted the hood, an ugly metal piercing linked her nostrils, as if she were a yoked animal, and in her tangled, wavy hair was a wide streak of pinkish-red. Maya as punk. Statue of a Hindu goddess defiled.

"You like?" Maya asked Sylvia, smiling her gorgeous smile, dumping cash from her pockets onto Sylvia's orderly antique desk, then slumping onto the edge of the analysand couch, saying nothing and refusing, as usual, to lie down.

Sylvia nodded, also saying nothing. *Let her be the one to begin,* her trained internal directive. *Let the patient tell you where to go.*

But the silence went on, broken a full minute later by Maya's rough laugh. Maya's voice was pitched lower than her age and looks made one expect.

Sylvia persisted, not saying a word.

Maya sighed and blew a raspberry, scratching herself under one armpit, snorting as if her nose ring itched.

All dyke again. Sylvia herself wasn't gay—just sort of a secular Buddhist meditating on a round silk pillow in a hushed candlelit room in western Mass, going on weeklong retreats followed by spa treatments in the Back Bay, disdaining public and excessive gatherings, like the People of Color sitting in Cambridge that gave black and Latina Buddhist lesbians an easy way to find each other.

Sylvia was more curious about those lesbians than she ever let on. But her parents, her father in particular, was always saying he was afraid she would be swept away by some alpha male banker or international lawyer—some former fraternity president—and move out of Boston suddenly. Away from her parents. Far from her daddy.

"Don't worry about your parents, they'll be fine if you leave Boston," her most recent boyfriend (though she was too old for boyfriends) had told Sylvia, after listening to her complain about her father, how exhausted she became from worrying about him. The boyfriend's name had been Ken, like the doll, and he was white. He'd admired her tiny but tasteful Back Bay apartment, her Benz. He'd shared her taste in furniture.

Ken was too kind to ever mock or judge Sylvia for how many weekends and evenings she still spent at her parents' house, as if she were a child, letting them do her laundry, being cared for, never contradicting her father though now she was nearly fifty, and soon she would have to think of hiring nurses for them, of maybe even selecting a nursing home.

"Just think of it: Santa Fe, New Mexico. While I work on the rez, you set up a community mental health clinic. They need that too, Sylvia. They'd make you director. Psychology, all comers. You'll have a flourishing clinic in a week. It would be important work. We could even adopt a couple of kids, if you wanted."

A couple of Latino or Native American kids, Ken meant, or even black if there were any in New Mexico foster care.

Ken would never intentionally be selfish about race. He was sincere. He'd never think of Maya as "that smelly Indian," like Sylvia did. Conceding that she herself was nothing like Ken, Sylvia conjured up Maya all the time, hoping for revulsion.

In bed, on their final night, Sylvia had kissed Ken on his bare, dark blond hair-covered chest. But that had been six weeks ago, and she'd said no to coming with him, knowing he'd leave Boston anyway. He hadn't consulted her before accepting the New Mexico job, after all. She couldn't imagine leaving serious psychoanalysis—because that *was* what it would mean, leaving her entire world—to go and live in godforsaken Santa Fe. And the isolation of it all, how Sylvia would feel being a black woman in New Mexico, so far, way too close to a border for her to ever wear her hair relaxed or walk around in less than formal clothes for fear she'd be mistaken for a kinky-haired, illegal Mexican—well.

At L'Espalier, Sylvia and Ken acted like parting roommates, resigned and openly happy to be moving on. "Remember me," Ken sang out once he was drunk, a baritone version of Sylvia's favorite aria from the Purcell opera. Then Ken kissed her sweetly, patting her neat dreads as awkwardly as usual. Added, "I shouldn't have asked you to leave your parents. They're getting old. You wouldn't have left them. Especially your dad, you're so attached. And all your work in the community. You have transformed so many lives. You're an incredibly engaging and committed therapist."

But here was Maya, hardly engaged in treatment, not yet committed.

Still hoping Maya would talk freely in today's session, Sylvia pictured the girl walking outdoors in New Mexico. Maya offended at being mistaken for a Latina cleaning lady. Maya looking like she did right now—a drugged-out rebellious little girl of indeterminate brown ethnicity.

What if Sylvia had run away with Ken to Santa Fe, without telling her dad? That same day, her father would've been on a plane to bring her back—to rescue her from "useless Ken," a white stranger. To save her brilliant academic career. Daddy would have offered her a lavish trip to spend some time with great-aunts and great-uncles in northern Uganda, so Sylvia could better understand how hard her ancestors had worked to create her. How much Daddy had sacrificed to make sure that even the concept of Sylvia—Harvard psychologist, nearly tenured analyst and scholar, antiques collector—would eventually be feasible.

Maya was staring at her, starting to look amused. "Do you ever find it hard to be with me?" Maya asked. "I mean, does all that money not seem like enough?"

Waiting a beat, Sylvia said, "I'm interested—and wonder if you also are interested—in why you bring up money now."

Maya laughed again. "Well, it's a lot, and I spend a lot of hours earning it. Who could forget?"

Sylvia nodded, trying not to look overeager.

"And I dunno, I could buy shoes with it."

"You could," Sylvia said, in an even voice.

"It reminds me each time," Maya paused, watching Sylvia carefully.

Silence again.

"Yes?" Sylvia half whispered.

"It reminds me that I don't *have* to come here. That it's money in the end, money that pays your rent and buys your boots and whatever, money that drives you, just like it drives everyone. You don't care about me as a human being. I could jump off a building and it wouldn't change a thing, except you'd have to fill my spot somehow, with someone else who'd pay."

Sylvia tensed. In all her sessions, Maya had never once referred to suicide. What had changed now, for her to up the ante in this more primitive way? She swallowed, making an effort to relax and sound merely *interested*, instead of alarmed. She told herself that at least their real work had begun.

"Jump off a building," Sylvia said, her voice neutral. "Why don't you tell me what you mean."

Some of Sylvia's former supervisors, old women she now saw at the invitation-only soirees of various professional societies, might have leapt more quickly to the type of "combat with certain borderlines" they greatly enjoyed. "Is that a threat?" they would've asked, sounding like threateners themselves—working-class fixers, team-sters, the most senior of Whitey Bulger's boys.

It wasn't that Sylvia thought calling Maya's bluff could make her go and hurt herself. If Maya were like other borderlines—if Sylvia were even confident of the diagnosis. But she wasn't. There was no proof that she'd experienced abuse, only the odd phrase here and there—"always watch-ing me," "too close," "I didn't like the way it felt when my father hugged me"—and then Maya would sit silent, and not cry or even seem angry.

The likelihood that the girl had been abused made Sylvia regret her impatience. But Sylvia wouldn't confide her feelings of guilt to anyone. Being immune to emotional manipulation, for a psychia-trist, was like being fearless about blood, for a surgeon. "The shrinks with too much loving-kindness are the ones who face the board," Sylvia's classmate, who was now on the board of psychology, had said. "The ones who can't draw boundaries, who take the world's suffering straight onto themselves."

The psychology board of overseers, the girl's long, provocative silences, her cash, her hair, her smell—these thoughts exhausted Syl-via. She decided, just for one session, to depart from active listening as her main strategy.

"Maya, if you're thinking about hurting yourself, I need to know immediately," Sylvia said, making her voice firm. "Stop playing games. Just tell me straight out. Do you need to be admitted? Do you need to be put somewhere safe starting tonight? Do I need to send you to an ER? Is that why you've suddenly brought this up to me?"

Maya looked by turns stunned, afraid, then mad. "You'd fucking lock me up?" she said. "Just for saying 'jump off the roof' one single time? That's it?"

"You used a phrase that connotes suicide, and you won't tell me anything more," Sylvia said. "I could get someone to lock you in, yes."

"But you couldn't lock me in if I left now," Maya said, standing up.

Sylvia shook her head. "I still could. In fact, your leaving sud-denly would make it more likely. I'd have to tell the police I couldn't keep you safe because you wouldn't talk to me and fled. And then they'd take you to the Mount Auburn ED. If I called them right now—" Sylvia said, hating the way her gut twisted at the sight of Maya's frozen expression, "—yes, Maya, if I called them right now, they'd come for you."

"But I didn't make a threat," said Maya, sounding serious and hurt. "I was just saying how I felt. That I felt you didn't care for me."

"But I do care," Sylvia said, too fast.

Maya, still standing, closer now to Sylvia than usual, stared at her with a perplexed smile.

"You mean—you never told me. Not married. No kids. Holy mackerel, Dr. Uwagaba. *Girls?*"

Sylvia shook her head. "Don't take a step back when you've taken steps forward today. Don't start acting out. You're doing excellent work today."

"I knew it, you don't care," Maya said. "You aren't attached to me at all, not even as my therapist. You just don't want to be perceived as not caring. *That* was why you answered so quickly."

Sylvia didn't move, sensing more to come.

Maya laughed. "You're basically disgusted by me, aren't you?"

Sylvia raised her eyebrows but didn't speak. Some impulse or habit made her check the clock at that moment. It didn't lie.

"The session's up," Sylvia said, "but I need to know something."

Maya sat down again. "You're keeping me over?" she asked. Sylvia winced at the bare hope in her voice. "And you're not charging me for extra minutes? Wow. You're like a really generous hooker." At Sylvia's silence, Maya laughed. "It must mean I'm your regular."

Sylvia stayed focused, not breaking eye contact. "I want you to check in with me by phone once a day for the next couple of days."

"Check in about what?"

"I want to know if you have any thoughts of suicide. Do you, Maya?"

"Well, it's not like I'd tell you now. Knowing that you'd call the police."

"Telling me decreases the likelihood that we would need to go that far. But I have an obligation, you know. Since you said that. To have another doctor examine you."

"Examine me, like a corpse," Maya said. "Morbid."

Sylvia leaned forward, sustaining eye contact.

Maya spoke first. "Okay, fine. I'll play your game. I do think about being dead sometimes. Not killing myself or hurting myself in any way. Just having everything be done so I can't fail—like I would be exempt from being judged."

Sylvia nodded, listening.

"So now your turn. Do you ever feel like that?" Maya asked Sylvia, moistening her lips.

"Fail at what, Maya?" Sylvia asked, sidestepping the question. "Fail in what way?"

"Fail at everything," Maya whispered. "Fail at being married off in time to the right rich, good-looking Indian guy. Fail at maintaining the one or two friendships I have with good-enough guys who aren't the right ones and I could never marry—but might someday, if I had to. Fail by losing even my good-enough backup Indian guys. The ones who come off as...durable."

"But why do you have to get married at all," Sylvia almost asked, but stopped herself, not wanting to betray the irrelevant feeling of panic that came over her at the suggestion of Maya marrying someone. She settled on saying absolutely nothing, remembering her technique. *Let her open the next door*, she thought. *Don't assume you know which one it is.*

"There's no way I'll ever escape my parents if I don't get married," Maya said. "It's that simple."

This time Sylvia didn't hold back. "What is it about them that you want to escape?"

Maya stood up. "Isn't the session over? Don't you want me to go?"

A loud knock made both of them turn toward the door.

"Next patient," Maya said, starting to go. "I get it. I'm out." Flipping her hood up, she skulked toward the door. "And by the way, I'd never kill myself. Too proud. Too young to die. Also—I would miss sex."

Sylvia didn't move from her seat as quickly as she normally would, to jot down her progress note before the next patient. There was no time. Patient after patient came in, each one in general admiring and respectful of Sylvia, with only one other patient, the one whose session began late, just slightly irreverent, probing for some sign of weakness, asking when Sylvia was "going to get married, have kids, be normal, or else what's the point of even being a therapist, seeing as you can't fix yourself."

The patient who'd said that last bit, an Italian man in his sixties, someone whose affluent adult children were paying his bills, paying quite a lot, had always been challenging, but until today, Sylvia had felt invulnerable to those moments when his working-class assumptions—that a woman needed a husband and children to be "normal"—came out. The minute she closed the door behind him, Sylvia wondered, really deeply examined, why she hadn't called the police as soon as Maya left the room. Why she had stood there bargaining with the girl. If Maya betrayed her by hurting herself—if something terrible happened—

She left a message for Maya, reminding her to check in before noon the next day with a brief call. "Hope you are well," Sylvia said, wincing at how stiff and formal she sounded. But at least she didn't sound intimate.

It didn't occur to her until nearly six, when there was a two-hour gap between her day patients and the few who came to her sessions at night: How could any patient—not just Maya, but other patients, know for a fact that Sylvia was unmarried, without kids? Sylvia popped open her laptop and Googled herself, looking forward to seeing the listing of accomplishments, degrees and articles, that would appear under her name.

Sylvia Uwagaba PhD, Behavioral Partners. A long list of articles, the prize-winning essay she'd written for a journal years ago. Nothing about children, family, marital status—but there it was, the deed to Sylvia's parents' house on the Mass Registry, and listed next to her name was "No Spouse" and also "Dependents None." The fact that she slept alone at night, after her various boyfriends had sexed her and then gone home, was knowledge anyone could get, along with precisely where her parents lived in Lexington.

Using Google Earth, strangers could look inside their bay windows. Could even see Sylvia, and Sylvia's father, though he'd always been fiercely private.

Sylvia closed her laptop, feeling sick. How many times had she walked semi-nude and careless behind those windows? How many patients had looked through those windows and seen her?

Before leaving her office that night, Sylvia documented in the clinical chart religiously. Risk and so on. The respectable and recognized steps she'd taken and would take as a therapist, to lessen the risk of Maya committing suicide. But nowhere did she write the truth about how she felt—how, when she was by herself, Sylvia recognized her revulsion as desire plus fear, and relived dreams, with exquisite detail, in which she and Maya were naked in bed.

Sylvia didn't really want the dreams to go away or be explained. She'd never told her former supervisor she'd been having them. They came to mind sometimes when she was waiting for the start of Maya's sessions, twice a week. Instead she determined that she would never see Maya again, not in this lifetime, except in the presence of a second therapist in the room with them, and not just any therapist. A trainee to witness how Sylvia behaved with Maya. A trainee who'd never read Sylvia's thoughts.

2.

Asking someone to tag team the treatment ended Maya's interest in being treated, but Sylvia was too relieved to care. Now they were nearly six months along, well into the spring.

Initially, Maya had made some comments here and there.

"How the fuck can you live with yourself?" Maya had hissed, refusing to make eye contact with Abner, the trainee Sylvia had selected, refusing even to acknowledge he was in the room at first. The girl had come in and barely glanced at him. Maya even, on one occasion, reached out to touch Sylvia on the knee—only to pull her brown hand back, looking ashamed, when Abner's high, surprised, refined voice intruded, cheerily asking her if "you as the patient have any questions, any questions at all, about how therapy works and what we're all *about*." At that question, Sylvia looked at him askance, wondering if the young man realized what he was implying—that Sylvia, an analyst with thirty more years of experience than he had, had somehow failed to educate Maya in the basics of therapy.

Sylvia marveled at how quickly he said it, how confident he was. That he could so readily believe he knew something, some clinically essential and salient detail, that Sylvia, though she had four degrees and he had one, hadn't thought of.

A week later, after that first, seemingly impossible session, Maya had made a cryptic threat. Used words that worried Sylvia. Later, Abner insisted it was all benign.

"What if I had a way to burn it all?" Maya had said, staring at Sylvia, flicking her lighter on and off for a few clicks, till Abner, polite, asked if she minded him holding it for the session. She'd laughed while passing it to him, still looking at Sylvia, chuckling and saying, "You know that white boy's keeping it to light his weed. You know it, right?" Abner smiled back.

"A way to burn it all," Sylvia repeated slowly, interested, alert to what this meant.

But Abner, cutting off Sylvia without seeming to notice, turned to Maya, saying, "You're referencing Fear Factory, aren't you?" he asked, chipper for what Sylvia assumed was talk about a horror film, but then learned was a punk or metal band, the type of music for which Maya's nose ring did make perfect sense. "Burn It All" a new album title. Their following banter—friendly, casual—made Sylvia relax just a little. Maya had never burned herself. She had no history of arson.

Perhaps the instinct had been right, to find a young trainee, a younger therapist in the peer group of the patient. After all, with only a few sessions of being permitted to see Sylvia only with Abner, Maya stopped dropping any hints of suicide.

To make sure Maya would never guess the truth, Sylvia also took to wearing rings, multiple, eye-catching, two or three chunky things flanking a wedding ring. Different ones on each finger—Lucite, silver, a turquoise one Ken sent from Phoenix—but always the same one on the ring finger, a classy platinum wedding band. With Abner sitting there so vigilant, taking notes, scarcely breaking eye contact with Maya, the girl never asked Sylvia about the single ring, though she stared at it in every session. Not that Sylvia was engaged to be married. Sylvia wasn't planning on a husband and kids—not when she was younger, and not now, with tenure so near.

Frightfully near, and she was still so young. The first woman of color to make tenure at the academic hospital only half-jokingly known as Man's Greatest Hospital, and before age fifty, no less. The same hospital where she had once been the first black woman psychology intern, object of obvious scrutiny and condescending warmth—like her father when he'd integrated the bank where he'd been hired out of business school, Sylvia remembered, moved. Daddy's girl. Sylvia now also knew what it was like to be courted by the higher-ups, with several months of meetings, smiles and promises, and rich dinners in clubs, after having been slighted in subtle (and not so subtle) ways for many years.

Sylvia's trainee, the technologically adept Dr. Abner Stein was a very nice, allergy-prone, skinny white man who'd recently been assigned to Sylvia through his number-one-ranked internship. His enthusiasm for social media, and for his smartphone even during therapy didactic meetings, Sylvia had been meaning to talk to him about, but he was otherwise a terrific young clinician by all accounts, and maybe someone (Sylvia hoped!) with whom Maya could build alliance.

In one session, the one that ended up being their next to last, Maya put a hand up, so Abner wouldn't talk, and then asked Sylvia: "Do you think you might have already forgotten me?"

Her voice was so plaintive, so direct, that in that moment Sylvia almost was transparent. If they had been alone she *would* have disclosed, she realized then. Told Maya, no, that she expected she'd never forget. Confessed to Maya that she would always think of her.

It was a *blessing,* Sylvia thought afterward, a *blessing,* really, that Abner, true to form, had prevented Sylvia from answering. "I'm interested, and wondering if you're also interested, in this notion of *what forgetting means,*" he'd launched in, ignoring Maya's hand in his face, and starting a canned talk on trauma, memory, and the media that Sylvia didn't listen to. Was glad she didn't *have to* listen to. It was the tone he cultivated—friendly, professional, and just a tiny shade condescending—that diverted Maya. That made her look at her lap in what Sylvia could have sworn was shame. That made her, in fact, never, in session, look directly at Sylvia again.

Yes, between Abner being as friendly as a well-meaning Quaker town hall leader even when Maya ignored him, and Maya's inexplicable cleanliness nowadays, hair neat and combed, clothes fresh, even her shoes professional, and Sylvia's own pleasant absorption in matters of career, of her true heart—life was *all right.*

During the last week of April, right before the big departmental meeting on tenure, Maya stopped coming in at all, just leaving one voice message: "I'm done with therapy. I'll see my PCP for meds if I need them. Don't try to call me. Don't bother." Of course, Abner's documentation of his follow-up, his phone calls and messages to Maya, his coordination with her primary care doctor, were all impeccable, reflective of the impeccable training Sylvia provided him. Everything had been tied up.

This warm spring day, the clear and exciting Monday of the critical tenure meeting, when the weekend hadn't brought any ominous news, not about Maya, not about any patient, Sylvia was driving home in fine spirits, waiting and not minding the wait.

Vivaldi was on her sound system, turned low so she could easily Bluetooth to her phone when The Call came. Deer raced safely in the woods next to her road, away from cars; Lexington was lush but well controlled, Minute Man Park as lovely as ever, and Wilson Farms had an especially large shipment of Sylvia's favorite red plums. She'd bought a whole crate.

They were so sweet and so cold, she was thinking, trying to recall the exact words of the William Carlos Williams poem, the one Maya had recited in a session once, without Sylvia commenting, at the time.

At 4:25 p.m. that afternoon, when she was only half a mile from home, an unexpected call came to her cell—but it was fine, her favorite senior faculty ally at the medical school, not on the tenure committee and therefore free to talk to her.

But maybe something had happened. Stopping the music, Sylvia panicked. "A patient?" Sylvia asked, praying it was not. "A suicide?" Instantly, she feared for Maya.

Her friend paused. "No Sylvia, dear, not a suicide. Just a weird incident. They're looking into it, okay, it's nothing yet, but I wanted you to know, in case. The meeting that they'd planned to have, to do the vote, has been indefinitely postponed. You know, in case there's anything…" Sylvia's old friend repeated this word, "anything" again.

"Anything like what? More papers?" Sylvia asked. "More evidence of my scholarship? What do they want? *What* else?"

"No, no, Sylvia. No one doubts you as a clinician and scholar. It's just this young woman—"

"Maya." The name came out before she could help it.

"Oh, so you know?"

"I only guessed," said Sylvia, grim.

"The girl has posted an obscene video on the Internet, and she's saying that somehow you sponsored it, and knew about it. Good heavens. That you orchestrated it. That you gave her keys and all sorts of access to your things and even to your family? That you gave her a credit card, somehow? It's quite obscure. Abner Stein was the one who brought it to my attention. He came across a link or something on YouTube? MeTube? Some kind of Tube I've known about only for the past hour, so forgive me. A video, and not just an image—"

"Image of what?"

"Not just a—well." Her old mentor paused, clearing her throat. "You'd better see it for yourself."

"Do you think I should? Isn't it better to—"

"Sylvia, you need to decide if lawyers are warranted. The girl looks like she went into your house. And the man with her. Whoever it is. An older African American man. He could have been intoxicated and a burglar too, for all I know. They're saying—ah, but I don't know who he really is. You can fight this. She's saying you knew and set this up. That you and she were intimate. All defamation, we expect. But still, your case records—could there have even been some small impropriety, explaining how on earth she gained access?"

"No."

"This young woman seems to have gone inside your parents' house—I've been there, it really does look like the house, it's so distinctive, is the thing. The antique chairs, the lovely furniture."

"Impossible. But what did she do? I mean, did she break something?" A memory. "Did she set a fire?"

"Oh, my, good heavens, my dear. Just look at it so you can determine what to do. Lawyers will likely be involved. Courage, okay?"

Sylvia, too frightened to do more than end the call, pulled over in a no-longer-bucolic clearing. Whatever it was, she would face it. The Buddhist word from that long-ago meditation class. Upekkha. Equanimity.

She Googled Maya's first and last name on her smartphone, something she'd never done before, out of respect but also because she'd never wanted to see pictures of Maya with lovers. Sylvia clicked YouTube and waited.

Then Sylvia heard Daddy's voice, angry and aroused.

Slapping bare skin, shouting loud curses.

And there was Maya's full face on the screen—beautiful up close, watching everything, looking out of the phone surface as if she now saw Sylvia. *You like it like this?* she asked the camera, looking out with immense eyes. *You like it, Mr. Uwagaba, father of Sylvia Uwagaba, renowned professor?*

Yes.

More slurs, familiar words about "fucking Hindoo bitches," the sounds of which literally made Sylvia sick.

And then the white rolling text, which Sylvia assumed Maya had written:

THIS ADULT VIDEO CONTENT, APPROVED AND ORGA- NIZED BY DOCTOR AND ESTEEMED PROFESSOR SYLVIA UWAGABA, WHO GAVE ME THE KEYS TO HER PARENTS' HOUSE AND INSTRUCTIONS ON PLEASING HER FATHER FROM HER OWN EXPERIENCE. LOCATION: LEXINGTON MA. EXACT LOCATION: SYLVIA'S PARENTS' HOUSE. EXACT LOCA- TION: THEIR EXPENSIVE SHAKER CHAIR, NICE ANTIQUE.

WHO SYLVIA'S FATHER THOUGHT I WAS: A CLEANING LADY, JUST ONE OF THE ASIAN GIRLS TURNING TRICKS TO MAKE AN EXTRA BUCK.

WHO I REALLY AM: THE GODDESS KALI, YOU MOFOS, AND DON'T YOU FORGET IT. NO JUSTICE, NO PEACE.

The call from Maya to Sylvia came minutes later, before Sylvia had had a chance to react, or even restart her car.

"Performance art. Your father enjoyed it."

"You're severely ill," Sylvia said. "You need treatment."

"You were supposed to be giving me treatment. Not covering your ass."

"Where are you?" Sylvia asked. Parked along the side of the road, a few miles from Hanscom Base, she could hear the military planes taking off from a vast airfield.

"Where am I going's the question," she said. "I'm thinking New Mexico. Don't you think Ken would enjoy me?" Maya laughed.

"You stay the hell out of my life," Sylvia, throwing aside technique.

"Just so you know, I booked two plane tickets to Phoenix in your name. For you and for me. Your cute little gold credit card was laying on your desk one time, next to one of your catalogues. During a session that turned boring—yes that's right, boring for me, boring for you—I realized I could read the numbers on the card. I memorized them in a flash, something I'm good at. Like all Indians, right? We're monkeys, so good at math and computers, aren't we?

"I booked the tickets for us with a nice hotel, spa treatments included, just one room. I bought them a month ago and you didn't call your company or block the charge. People will believe you planned this. But just to make sure, I hacked into your email account. Poor password selection on your part! And naughty too! Doctor Uwagaba, a.k.a. 'doctorSappho'?

"Anyway, once I had sent myself a bunch of friendly and erotic messages from your address—messages I'm planning to print out and show the board of psychology—I sent a bunch of emails to Ken and made it look like you were going to pimp me out. In the emails, I wrote about all your fantasies and the times you kept me late, alone in your office, mentally and physically undressing me. I told Ken things, all kinds of things, and he was so 'honored' by you confessing to him. You let a good one get away there, I think. He said all the right things. *Seek supervision on the case. You really need treatment.* I can't wait to meet him. But your romance with Ken is done, and you are too, *Professor* Uwagaba. You wanted me, didn't you? That's why you ended the treatment. Except you only thought that I would endanger myself. You will be lucky if they let you keep your license. But don't worry, your father's a real sweetie. He'll support you, I'm sure. Even though he really does seem to hate not only Indians, but queers.

"And your mother—it won't surprise you. She wasn't home when it happened. She was off writing. I would bet cold cash that he's done it before. With other young girls. Maybe boys too. When I explained I was with your cleaning service, he let me in, grasped my hand a little too tightly, then shadowed me all through the house until I began unbuttoning, and instead of acting all outraged, he smiled and started undressing too. But you must know exactly what he does. What he has done. Maybe that's why you couldn't bear to continue treating me. Because we had that in common. What we know. What he did."

Uselessly, Sylvia tried pressing the record button on her phone. But it was too late. Maya was gone, and there was only a tone, loud in the space—the sound, Sylvia sat there imagining, of bugs in the desert. The desert like the one that Maya might soon be flying over, sitting on a plane with an empty seat next to her. Sylvia's car was empty too, no longer full of possibility.

But Sylvia didn't want to fill the space. She didn't want anything now, not even lawyers. It was an indulgence, like her dreams about Maya had once been, but Sylvia just wanted to think. Of vast and quiet areas where one could sit, in the desert, out in a simple metal folding chair, and contemplate phenomena never seen before by anyone. Of Maya, her desperate, outlandish behavior. Of her need for revenge, which Sylvia recognized and understood, and of Sylvia and her father, long ago, when Sylvia had just turned eleven, and had been pulled into the Shaker chair. Pulled onto her daddy's lap, naked, afraid.

JAGATISHWARAN

IN THE BACK OF THE HOUSE there is a corner room that does not open onto the lush and well-tended garden. Its shutters are indolent eyelids opening and closing with the wind. Light comes in small beams from the courtyard where pots are being washed. A woman is sweeping dirty water away from the steps outside the window. At a certain spot behind the empty teak wardrobe that barricades the door, all noises from the courtyard and the kitchen it adjoins are muffled by thick wood. Crouching there, it is not possible to hear the women shouting at each other, mistress to servant and back again, scolding and fretting, cramming the small house full of nervous life.

Flat on my stomach, facing the wall, I can look at my paintings. They are vivid miniatures, set low, near the molding. Their tiny faces sport green Kathakali dancing masks, leering with painted lips and yellow hair like aging American starlets, their glossy eyes faded. My paints have dried in large, expensive tubes littered on the floor, strewn in the dust along with tiny sable brushes that were once a woman's accessories. The mirror on the wall is British, cracked and decadent looking with too many faded gilt curlicues around it. Amid old newspapers and combs black with hair dye, I keep my shaving kit and my traveling case. The mirror, like the room, is dark. When I look into it I see the sweat on my forehead and chin and wonder how it remains in the air-conditioned coolness.

I shelter myself from the house with second-hand screens, four of them, made of wood that looks better for the dust on it, less costly and more secure. I write after the others have gone to bed, hiding my diaries and papers during daylight. Sometimes their faces flash by me in the darkness, as if they were peering in rudely through a space between the screens. Only the visitors are overcome by curiosity. The niece from the States who looks at me with her little cat face, jeans curving around soft plump hips. My sister the doctor, talking about leper colonies at tea, bringing medicine and a fancy new toaster when she comes, making the house smell of Ben-Gay and bread. Even the trees in the garden move away from the house, as if in disgust. The living room is brightly lit behind embroidered cotton drapes. On each evening of her stay, I hear the news on television from where I crouch behind the screens, and listen to loud, excited voices talking above the announcers, nearly drowning them out. The niece is always quiet when her mother and my father shout about corruption and bribery or point to picket signs and angry crowds when they appear on the old-fashioned screen.

No one in this house knows that I listen to a radio hidden in my room, and that I read imported copies of *The Herald Tribune*. Or that I spend the money given to me by Father on tobacco, and go to the same place almost every afternoon with my pockets bulging. Nixon, Watergate—my sister doesn't know how much I know, how much I hold fast in my memory from those times. Imprisonment, Emergency. Who wouldn't have been paranoid then? But it's my sister who's the smart one, the doctor lady. She thinks of us as dull-witted rice eaters waiting for her borrowed Anglo china plates and blue jeans, silk ties and pantyhose, perfume in fish-shaped bottles, white linen napkins and forks so we won't eat with our hands, expensive bolts of brilliant cloth—smelling slightly of glue, precious…"The exchange rate is wonderful," my sister remarks, at least with the grace to laugh uneasily. Once she brought paints on a visit—"Padma picked them out specially," she explained, handing over a shiny gift-wrapped box. Padma's gift. They are beautiful and useless now. Exotic.

I don't voice my opinions anymore because I know they only pretend to listen, looking at me as if I still ranted and raged as I did in the early days of my illness. Breakdown. Maybe schizophrenia, ranting…I can hear them whispering it, concerned. The cleaning woman who goes everywhere, poking into wardrobes for silk pieces and loose change, cleans carefully around my teak screens, never daring to touch anything behind them. On trips to the kitchen to fill my coffee mug, I watch her slowly moving and she peers at me, afraid. That's what the barricade is there for.

From behind the screens I can smell food from the kitchen, the smell cleaving to the carpets, damp, stronger than the scent of leaves and sweat from the courtyard. The old man calls me "demon" when he sees me eating, muttering as if I were still a young child and he were bending over my pillow promising candies in my ear. I am his youngest son; years and years ago he called me "eyes" in Tamil, which meant I was the dearest. Then in school I didn't turn out like his nine good children, neither physicist nor lawyer, neither doctor nor engineer. I got sick, I remind him often, just before my college exams. I got very ill, it was terrible. First tuberculosis, then something else, something in my head. I was in pain, for pity's sake. It became too late, impossible to work. To do anything but sit or stand very quietly, in peace, left to myself. I've tried to explain. "But you're a grown man now," Father says in disbelief, "and that was years ago." He talks about my hair and the sweat on my face, jabbing at my clothes, fuming, gesticulating, until my mother stands between us, the veins bulging in her frail hand on his arm.

Mother used to come at night, years ago, before I put up the screens, to ask how I was, but now she's afraid. Once I pushed him hard, not her, never her, and I felt disgust at his shriveled skin, his nasal voice, always skeptical, his tiny well-read eyes like an elephant's, nearly blind but remembering everything.

On some evenings when the house is empty my father and I sit in the library pretending to read, not looking at each other, crickets caught between the pages of old books, gray moths appearing from the bare bulb on the ceiling as if by spontaneous generation. He taps his cane as he turns the pages, licking his soft, wrinkled thumb as he lifts the corners like a toady hidden in reams of office paper, calculating newborn deaths and taking bribes. I stare at him first if he's been bothering me that day. "Have you taken your medicine?" he asks in English. Patrician, concerned, I am silent. In the dim light he can see the outline of my face, my bones almost his bones, my hands threatening. "Don't hit me," he says, as a warning, though I never do, and he knows it. It has become an evening ritual, more honest than prayer.

When my sister comes in the summers there are annual rituals—special prayers, more sweets, more garlands lying on the puja room floor or strung up around glossy pictures of the gods. She calls for the barber to come in the evening. He does his work squatting on the steps leading out toward the blue main gate of the house, never coming in the house. He squints up at the dimming sunlight and tells my sister's son to hold still—he uses scissors and a gleaming old-fashioned razor. The little boy shakes his head no, rubs his soft, protruding belly and laughs. Once I watched from the doorway, making him laugh even harder by imitating the girlish, feline sounds of his voice, until my sister stood in front of me and edged the door nearly closed. "Leave him alone, he'll get himself cut," she muttered quietly, not looking up at my face. I stared at her as she turned away, aware of the fresh smell of her hair and clothes. "Why don't you take a bath," she advised, watching the boy, her shoulders tensed until I moved out of sight.

The large bookcases in the corridor between my room and the puja room are opened in the summers for my sister's daughter. Her back pressed against the wall, eyes fish-flat behind thick glasses, she reads old books, like Omar Khayyam's *Rubaiyat,* in the opium-den light. "Conserve your eyes," my father says when he passes on his way to prayer, rapping on her glasses with a finger. He adds, sounding like my sister, "Near-sightedness is a reading disease." She puts the book down, covers her face with her palms for a moment and laughs, as if pretending to put her eyes away.

When she was younger, she asked me all kinds of questions about Indian politics, Shakespeare, the price of sandalwood soap in villages, why I had painted on the walls. She would nod calmly at the answers and say little. She would lean against the door of my room near the bookcases, staring like a pretty cat with blue-black eyes and secret thoughts. "Don't bother uncle," my mother began to say, when the girl grew older, and she nodded as if she understood. "Leave Padma alone," my father said once, stopping me on my way out from taking salt from the kitchen. Now with her large feet in new American tennis shoes, with her hidden breasts and her delicate neck, she only glances at me now and then with that same mute questioning look, grown-up ivory jangling at her wrists.

When my sister comes every summer, Father comes out of his room to talk to her. My niece and mother smile and whisper to each other as my sister talks about San Francisco, New York, Santa Fe, the old man repeating the names, drawing them out with his proud camel lips. My sister doesn't know that I've seen the names in books, in the paper. I've heard them pronounced properly on my secret radio. They talk about the days she has left in India, counting up the brief nights and muddy afternoons watched from the window of the genteel Ambassador car, traffic stopped for thin men driving even thinner cows across the road and being photographed by the niece's new expensive camera. I listen to them without hearing words, staring from behind my book at the faces. I am quiet in my dusty chair, sitting away from the soft light that hangs over the center of the room. Crickets chirp near my ear on the window, the light bounces off the limbs of a black dancing Shiva that has been placed on top of the television set. I watch their faces as they think about the tiny airport, old man and woman pressed against a large window with other damp cotton cloth-wrapped bodies, looking out at the plane with tiny windows about to take off. Men in white, Western uniforms will dot the runway, red English and Hindi letters juxtaposed on glossy white wings. Before leaving the house they will pray, jeans and mustard seeds packed, my niece and sister looking awkward in new saris. They will mix languages in a sad babble of exclaiming. When my parents cry they look like blind newborns, skulls soft and nearly bald, features melting so that the sharp creases of age grow mild and nearly invisible.

In the early afternoons, after lunch has been cleared away, I sit in the dark room near the door, listening to the servant wash pots outside; my travel kit propped on my knees. The women sleep lightly in a cool room, the door closed, the light soft on their thick eyelashes. I close my eyes, waiting, wondering if the old man is too tired to watch me. He asks me questions like a child. "Where are you going? Where do you go in the afternoons?" When he has not eaten well he demands, "Why don't you go get a job, demon, if you feel strong enough to go out every day?" He combs back his few strands of white hair, crackling them with static and impatience.

He follows me to the main road only on dry afternoons. I sense the gate swinging open again behind me. I hear my father softly complaining to stray dogs. "That man shoveling dirt over dead bodies is better than you," he said once, when he saw me stop to look at a young man with dirt on his teeth. "He's working at an honest job." I made no answer, walking on as if he were a beggar I heard whimpering in the street. My father continued. "He isn't draining the life out of his parents." I took longer strides that day, aware that my breathing was strained, aware of the wind pressing against my back.

In the afternoons, I lose him easily in the crowd, when we get to the rikshaw stand where drivers are always waiting. He follows me only to demonstrate that he can, I suppose. The effort of the gesture is enough. He turns back without running after me, wiping his high forehead with a white handkerchief my mother ironed herself, and slowly starts the walk home. Chewing *paan* and leaning on his auto-rickshaw, the driver watches the old man as I climb into the back. The driver is a young boy who comes to the big house in his rikshaw on some evenings, waiting by the blue gate to take my sister and niece to the bazaar. He notices the flowers in my niece's hair, glancing down at her soft brown fingers gripping the bar against his warm back before asking where to go.

The driver doesn't need to ask where I am going. Like all auto drivers he is careless, even dangerously fast. I can barely see the road from the tear in the plastic sheet that serves as a door. I grip the metal bars tightly, knuckles showing white, tasting the potatoes and rice I ate before I left. I am thrown forward when the driver stops for a person or an animal. I swallow the different tastes in my mouth, remembering the salt hoarded in my room from the kitchen in news-paper packets. I imagine the peppermint taste of the crushed medi-cine my sister bought for me this time, which my mother will soon start mixing in with the salt. When I fell ill again last year, Father cried on the phone to my sister long distance. No doubt the connec-tion took hours to get, with long silences and wrong houses woken up somewhere in the middle of the night by a sudden ceaseless ring-ing. After the phone rang in the right house, darkness here and light there, Mother excited and barely whispering, "It has come, it has come," in girlish Tamil—I could hear my sister loud and soothing, yelling calm assurances through the static.

The women stand in the doorway as the rikshaw pulls up, watching for me and tittering slightly. They've never asked my name, but they know who I am. I wear dirty orange *kurtas* like scarves around my neck and knotted around my waist so they will set me apart from other men. They speak to me in more measured voices. I pay them well with Father's money. They don't smoke ciga-rettes in my presence, though they accept the tobacco I bring for them with gentle smiles and nods, hiding their eyes. I have seen each one of them with mouths wiped clean of paint, hair loose and smelling of hibiscus, laughing at their children and stroking black *kajal* on their babies' eyelids. My face is dry when I lie on their cotton sheets, gather up the hems of their thin embroidered saris in my hands. The sweat disappears from my chin and my cheekbones, though the rooms here are warm and the breeze is barely stirred by low ceiling fans.

At times I stay past the late evening, missing dinner at home but not needing to eat. I stay for the morning, sensing the presence of women waking and stretching their smooth, bare arms in flats above and below me, hearing children fighting downstairs as if they whispered in my ear, and the dogs from the street below as if from a great distance away. I hear bangles jingling from downstairs where sugar in coffee is burning, the smell stronger passing from the downstairs windows to where I stand on the sturdy balcony, waiting for the night to pass into morning, listening to the woman in the room behind me as she unwinds the sari from her slender hips.

The balcony is made of slate gray concrete that, where chipped away, looks like the softened surface of stone dancers in northern temples, with faces torn away by harsh, factory-polluted wind. There is a thin black railing that stretches out in a winding pattern of water snakes around the balcony, with the thick slabs of concrete rising up from the base like graceless fingers pointing up much higher than a small child's head. I have seen the children often play up here; I have heard their laughter as I stood waiting. There are spaces between the thick slats for their small brown faces to look out.

But there is nothing at all to see at night but night itself, when most people in Bombay and all the big city-villages far from here throw dinner parties, and use their balconies to hear moonlit fake-American music with evening-gowned, light-skinned ladies beside them. Here the smells below the balcony predominate: corn cooking in street fires, pigs nudging garbage, incense burning in a window, cows leaving holy excrement for fuel, autos letting off fumes while drivers gossip, smoke and count money. But there is nothing at all to see on the urchin-abandoned street until just before the sun rises.

The paint on the railing is chipped away in places, showing metal that glows underneath in the dark like sudden fireflies. The rest of the railing is slowly revealed by the dim progress of morning, until the full, unblanching sunlight hits it, is seized by it, and is made burning black. But there is no hint of that when the early morning buses approach the street empty, pausing until the motor scooters have passed and the factory workers have disappeared inside, five to a bus seat and some hanging on the railing above, peering through small windows. Their faces can barely be seen from the balcony, but when they smile their betel-stained teeth gleam.

For an hour between the departure of the buses and the appearance of wobbling rice-flour faces and flower design on the ground of the balcony, new smells of clarified butter and talcum powder twist out from the room inside, lingering after those smells have been replaced by cooking green beans, tiny pickled mangoes, and saffron-flavored rice. A woman's acrid sweat tinges the stone as the seven o'clock sun approaches. I avoid her eyes as she moves about next to me, hiding my eyes with a hand, staring down at the loud crows beating their wet wings below to drive the garden awake.

There is a child's school uniform draped over the side of the railing which never dries completely. Several small pictures have been inserted in the slates of the balcony; the expectant face of the goddess of learning, a bubblegum wrapper full of salt, and a much-handled picture of an erotic couple on the porch of the Temple of the Sun torn from a tourist magazine. At times, I finger a worn Vishnu prayer book with doodles that blind the serpent upon which the god is resting. I picture the old man praying under his breath at the tea table. The balcony is an unsmiling witness, uncritical save for an occasional blast of wind or smog which ruffles my hair suddenly.

And the trees outside the balcony, not whispering like pines in a Canadian forest, not readying themselves to scatter and blush like New England trees after the first spring respite from the cold? There may be trees like that in white winter resorts at hill stations, modeled after slick postcards, but here the trees are lush and solitary. There is one great and rustling tree, tropical, green, shimmering and wild, never cut back from the balcony so that on certain nights it sweeps drying cloths with branches like fingers gesturing and rolling a cigarette. "Isn't that a banyan? Or perhaps a neem?" I imagine an American accented voice saying, pointing at it, as young hippies stand on the balcony and marvel at the rustic charm of the street. A washerwoman stricken with typhoid in some rainy night has been seen crouching down next to the trunk outside the main gate, looking up warily at the balcony and the people.

I know there will be no dinner parties here, and music that issues from the room opening onto the balcony—a woman singing in Hindi about a god being mistaken for a deer—is often quickly and abruptly ended. But there will be moonlight. Peace in the leaves of the tree and the awkward protective slats of the balcony after screaming fights about men, the price of school books, the length of a child's new frock and the rust on the body of a new black bicycle. Its wheels are closely entwined with the circle designs of the black railing of the balcony. Leaning forward in my seat, I remember my father named me *Jagatishwaran*, "lord of worlds," holding me aloft.

In the darkness approaching I look at the ground, peering down through the slats, seeking out the sudden fireflies, the lighted tiny lamps in the windows, roadside meal-fires in the street. But there is nothing to look at in the twilight but the feeling of night itself in the slammed doors and fading child-shouts on the street below. The promise of moonlight contains the promise of the burned incense and rice-flour tracings that I will see there again in the morning, after the view and the objects of the street calmly and fatalistically appear.

One evening when I return to the house it is the end of the rainy season, nearly time for my sister, who is so adept at comforting, to leave here for her American city. They have all gone to the market again. A pink carnation has budded, tender, in the box of green placed outside the front door. I crush a few petals underneath my tongue, wondering why they are not sweet, sucking them like candy, resisting the dank smell that permeates the unlit rooms. Even the maid servant has finished for the day. She will return in the morning to clean pots and *thalis* piled high in the stone sink in the courtyard, excavating soap and dishrags as if they were moist treasures.

I sense dust on the covers of old books in the corridor, their pages crumbling—a good wind would blow away the words, the fine English print. I wonder if the old man would even mind that only husks were left if every one of their pages were gone. I run a hand along the old curved spines lined in neat rows before opening my door.

It's darker here than in the rest of the house, though there is a small kerosene lamp burning. "You'll set a fire," the old man always says to me. "Use the good American fluorescents." I can see my niece's hair gleaming in the light, near my paintings, her head bent forward. She sits cross-legged on the floor, old books lying open all around her. Her back is to the door, her wide shoulders relaxed. The room smells of turpentine. "Near-sightedness is a reading disease," I say, in my best grandfather voice.

She turns quickly, her eyes solemn, hiding something in her hand. The dust makes her cough. She smiles when she recovers herself. "Look," she says, opening her hand. I look away from her, afraid. There are pictures of stone Chola maidens in a few books left carelessly open, revealing contemplative moon-faces, wide hips and shoulders, girl-breasts, gray and perfect in relief. "Please look," she says again. I see the brushes in her hand. There are caps on the clean tubes of paint now, a water jar on my dreams, a tiny palette made of wood. "It's carved," she says, smiling. There are drop cloths on the ground, as if my work could begin at any moment. She is silent, drying off the last delicate brush with her long fingers. "Why?" I ask, not exactly unkind.

"They are gifts from me," she says. The teak screens are closer together than before, as if they have been gently moved aside and then carefully eased back into place, order preserved. She drops the last brush into a child's pencil box on the floor, probably her brother's. The paintings are brighter in the lamplight, the smiles on the mask still lewd and masculine. The wall above them is blank, expectant like Padma's face. "Please get out," I tell her. She takes off her thick glasses and wipes the sweat from the bridge of her nose. Her eyes are distant, as if she were listening to crows settling on the roof for a moment.

"Have you seen this?" she asks, holding up a book and pointing. A woman smiles in black and white, her hips exaggerated, legs strong, arms bent with hands pointing upwards, fingers curled. We stare for a few moments, meditating. "I know all the hand gestures mean something," Padma says, her voice soft. She adds excitedly, "Some of the dancers in this photo are wearing Kathak masks like the ones in your mural." I look away from her at the dresser, at combs and open bottles of hair dye and smile furtively. The book in her hand was once before in this room, on that dresser, open to the picture of a woman balanced on a tiny demon's back, vanquishing greed with her graceful stomping feet. I had made marks on the pictures of the dancers. In a notebook hidden under the bed there are line-drawings of masks, of temple-dancers—all useless, exotic and beautiful.

She stands up, the book still in her hand. I gather the others, shutting away the orange-colored abstract Ganeshas, Rajput miniatures with black staring beetle eyes, Nataraja dancing on the top of a temple, trapping gaudy life between the fading covers of old books. She takes them from me, brushing my hands with her smooth child fingers. Her hair has come undone from the effort of the afternoon; suddenly I feel ashamed. I promise to work on my paintings again, and her eyes open wide with pleasure. When she smiles like my mother I look down, unable to thank her. "You know, I may be in love," she blurts out, pausing at the door and balancing books on her hip, trembling slightly. "Uncle, please don't tell." She disappears behind the screens. In the dark somewhere the town is closing, and my sister will come soon.

In the morning, I watch my niece, waiting for clues. She is quiet as usual, setting off on long walks when the women are bathing or asleep, or hiding by herself in the garden, reading secret letters. "When she was small she was afraid of snakes," my mother says fondly, waiting for the vegetable seller with his cart and watching Padma move a chair behind the trees. My father retreats to a back room with a book, preparing for abandonment as my sister packs and talks to her husband on the phone. She does her packing everywhere as usual, suitcases open on the floor and in the landings, saris and scarves mingled in radiant profusion, lists made on crumpled envelopes and pieces of newspaper. Sometimes Padma swings on the gate with young children or waits while they play, serene and maternal. "Only one more trip to the market," my sister promises, when she sees Padma waiting at the gate for the auto-rikshaw. When he finally arrives, her smile is pure and flushed, the twilight settling on her neck. Her mother waits in the rikshaw as Padma slowly gathers up her full skirt using both hands.

"Don't forget to lock the front door," my sister tells me, and I nod, dutiful. Padma's hair is loose and long enough to fall in front of the cold metal pole that separates the driver from his passengers, her black curls helpless, streaming down as the rikshaw jerks forward. Strands of Padma's hair are crushed between the pole and the driver's back, tickling his bare skin through the white cotton shirt. "You're imagining things," my sister would say, if I described it. Her voice would be angry. On trips from the square with the driver I say nothing, watching him in the rear-view mirror until he turns once, his eyes full of laughter, stopping for an old woman who's wading with difficulty between animals and bikes. He is young, I realize, like my niece. We wait. "My name is Ramdas," he whispers in Hindi, like the medieval bard by the same name. Then he looks ahead again, lurching forward quickly before anyone can cut him off, because the old woman is safe now, after all. He resumes hurt-ling onto my usual, my only, destination.

Months later, standing on the balcony in the early afternoon while there is still light, I read Padma's letter. It is the first time she has written to me since she was young, when she held onto the gate like a child, waiting only for her mother. The letter is new but is already faded, crumpled, sent by airmail on cheap blue aero-gram with wispy ballpoint pen handwriting like mine. "Uncle," she wrote, after some grown-up pleasantries. "I thought of you when Ramdas told this to me."

'*Wild-eyed, blacker in your brows than crow-black nights, your legs are twisted into heavy branches, rivers fallen in your tangled hair. You take me up into the dance, your arms taut with the tiger-tooth bracelets. I was silk-clad and pale in the incense-burning light. Bells and gongs clamoring, emptying my mind of fear, I forgot that you had burned the body of the god of love when he teased you with his beauty.*'

A man puts washed clothes on the balcony, nodding politely, cutting the cloudless sky into dark, wet shapes. A bottle-green sari mingles sinuously with the shining body of black lattice. The dark green is flecked with gold crisscrosses and flanked by deep yellow borders of crushed silk ending in tangled threads. It is faded with many washings, a pleasure gift when there was no chiffon to turn the eye away from grandmother cloth. I put my face up against it, as if smelling my mother.

The day Padma is scheduled to leave, I stay at home, away from the women. There is no time for argument or recrimination—every member of the household strains in silence under heavy suitcases, loading two taxis. The taxi-drivers are fed, given tea, made to engage in small talk and polite price-negotiation. Sweating, I look in my room and see that the paints are just where Padma has left them. I wipe my face with a damp cloth, staring at the mirror and feeling impatient. To go to the airport, I will have to bathe. My face is dry in the bathroom mirror, even with steam rising from the walls. Turning from her post beside the window, Padma smiles when she sees that my hair is washed and combed. There is a red tear-drop in the center of her forehead. Her hair is bound in rose and daisy petals like a bride's.

Padma's hands are soft, pressed together. She prostrates herself before the old man, then the old woman, her mother looking on. They touch her smooth hair with approving, wrinkled hands. She eludes them by promising to be back in half an hour, walking quickly down the street. Her mother sits on the front steps, saying nothing as Padma's younger brother plays in the driveway. He giggles, imitating me as I describe the route the taxi-drivers should take with my hands. The old man stands behind my sister, hands resting on her shoulders, little eyes squinting in the light.

In the taxi I sit in front with the driver, next to my father. His elbow is sharp in my side when the driver makes a wrong turn. When we reach the airport early he wilts, no longer angry. He waits before opening the door, trapping me inside the car for a long moment. My mother's voice is unnaturally bright as she adjusts the back of my shirt collar, her hands shaking a little. "*Appa,*" my sister says softly, when she helps him out of the car, easily bearing her weight.

The airport is crowded, hot, inefficient. There are nuns everywhere. "Oh, don't sneer at everyone," my sister says, her voice matter of fact, before she takes her place in line with Padma. I help the taxi drivers load suitcases onto a cart, which is then wheeled to the tiny airplane and loaded on by men who soon become tiny dots in the distance. I put change in vending machines, buying copies of the *Times*, bottles of Limca soft drinks. My father, rooted firmly to the earth like some ascetic waiting for a boon, says nothing. He stands in one spot as people push past him impatiently.

Padma and her mother become dots too as the line of passengers moves toward the runway. We wait at the large glass, looking out, old man and woman waving, bodies pressed against tall windows, straining hard to see. Long after Padma and her mother are hidden from view, we stand there and move into ourselves, imagining trays of candy and bright-painted stewardesses, hearing the canned Ravi Shankar music, breathing the sweet, stale pressurized air that must be coursing through the plane at that moment.

Later, standing on the balcony with Padma's letter in my hand, I breathe easily, wondering at the purity of polluted air.

"Ramdas said you were named after Shiva. I miss you. Please write soon, and paint. Your loving niece," she has written, printing her name at the end in round childish letters. I turn the blue leaf over in my hand, looking at the address of my father's house...*Jagatishwaran,* Padma has printed before it, with no last name, only *lord of worlds.*

A woman stealing up soft behind me, having first turned to the radio in the room below, places her hand on my neck, her lips soft on my cheek. I put Padma's letter in my pocket, thinking of how I stood in the airport, watching the old man and woman stare out the window as the plane began to move. As we watched it take off I had moved close behind my father, bracing myself against his sobs, my hands steady on his bony shoulders. "Let's go home," my mother said, fumbling for a handkerchief. They looked up at me as if they were children, Father's eyes almost erased by tears. "Please get the taxi, *Bhuvan,*" he had said, calling me by name.

Now, here on the balcony, I feel bare female arms around my waist, woman-soft while a radio plays a song below. My hands on hers, flat against my stomach, we brace each other gently, waiting for dark to settle on the street.

THE BANG BANG

MILLIND COULDN'T EXPLAIN WHY, of all days, he chose that one to duck inside the bar. He didn't drink and wasn't looking for a drink. He would have had ten if he could tolerate them. But thirty years before, by age nineteen, he had already known, from sneaking drinks out of a dissipate uncle's grasp, that he would never find much comfort in liquor.

Sound from the basement was what moved him inside. Loud voices reading words stretched tight. Occasional shouts of laughter but, more than that, big grand compelling silences, human breath caught and talk quieted, as just one single voice spoke. The quiet in the basement seemed to be absorbing sound from outside, and also exerted a gravitational force, pulling Millind, who was timid like an old man, yet still graceful, down a dark set of stairs, to a place where over a hundred people might have their eyes fixed on just one, making Millind less afraid and more eager to get down there than if there'd been music and steady conversation, the sounds of tinkling glasses full of wine that didn't interest him, forks clattering on plates of food that he could not afford.

With a slow, deliberate push, he opened the black door. He was at the foot of the stairs, grateful no one was standing watching guard either in front of or just behind it. In other places, there were hulking pale-faced men, thick around the collars, angry even before they caught your eye, their huge hands constantly adjusting, cracking, smacking, punishing, the sheer size of their grip on a man's shoulders humiliating to him as a man.

Before he'd come to this country twenty years earlier, Millind had never come to these places, because of men like this, whose light-colored eyes would narrow in malice and satisfaction at his wrinkled-brown skinny man's fear. "Worse than police," he warned his daughter and his son.

But in this basement, there were other men who were equally strange but in no way terrifying. They were as thin as Millind, and though there was no food now on the tables, none of the young men looked hungry. Their faces, though pierced through the nose or lips or even cheeks in ways that struck Millind as deeply cruel, turned toward Millind, nodded and welcomed him.

One of them pulled out a chair for him, perhaps respectful of his new and stiff black suit, or else his age, which might have been closer to sixty from his appearance. These men were the same age as Millind's son, who was twenty and the reason Millind had come to the U.S. with his pregnant wife, so their first-born child could be American.

Millind listened closely. Someone was reading about fire. Another person on the stage, a very light brown girl with green eyes like a snake's and huge curly hair, kept repeating some phrase in a language he suspected, but wasn't sure, was French. She must be Arabian, Millind thought.

From somewhere, other words configured in his head. His own. When he stood up, thinking to leave and maybe write them down, a young woman, physical sister to the men, with the same piercings and thinness yet kindness, the same lack of hunger or animosity, tapped his shoulder and asked with a gesture toward the mike, "Would you like to?"

Soon, flanked by the woman and a man, Millind was up on the stage, in front of a mike. On some impulse, he would say later, he closed his eyes and began speaking in Sanskrit. Just a few words, invoking blessings from the goddess of learning. It was 1981. People were angered by politics, completely certain that the world was getting worse. Yet there was Millind, praying with an equally certain confidence that if Saraswati blessed him then, right there on stage, everything would only get better.

His poem composed that night wouldn't be one that got published. But when he opened his eyes, reciting phrases like "diamond miners shafted" and "lone bird with the power of aeroplanes," people listened, visibly deciphering, their attention clear on their faces, clapping when he finished suddenly, wanting to know when he'd be back.

Who wouldn't want to be happy for him? But if I'd been there, sitting in the audience, watching Millind become a new person, I couldn't have been.

On the same day our father discovered poetry, my only brother disappeared. As if the incantations Dad dredged up could hurt the two of us. As if, because our father had found joy, my brother and his quiet sadness had to become invisible.

By the time Millind found the Bang Bang Poet's Café in the Village, on Charles Street and Greenwich Avenue, he had been in the US for twenty years, not leaving once; not driving to Canada as his brother did, to flee the draft for Vietnam, a war Millind was too old to fight by then; not even leaving New York to go home to Tamil Nad. Millind, at forty, was trying to make a house for his two children while his older but pleasant wife worked full-time as a home health aide, only five blocks from where they lived on Union Street in Flushing, Queens, precariously close to a city sewage processing plant.

Maybe Millind wanted so badly to make a house that was cozy because his ideal life meant always staying in the house. He'd sit for hours in his "study," smoking and pondering something. This was a closet his motherly wife had converted to a puja room-slash-sewing closet. It smelled of camphor and darkness in there, but he protected it, annoyed to the point of making real threats when his daughter and son pretended to be royal knights, crashing the gate of the castle that was Millind's rightful place. The children didn't care. Squealing at how it provoked his anger, the boy and girl kept trying to get in, until Millind pushed a cabinet against the door so that, hard as they battered it, and him, from the outside, there was no movement inside, where Millind, soundless, did *something* besides smoking, became someone they didn't know, but desperately wanted to see.

Whatever he was doing in there, it couldn't be work-related. Millind had not done well in school. His immigration history was spotted with failures—leaps across continents in search of places where he'd start over. "The right start is all I need," he muttered, wandering through the house, instead of paying bills. In fact, sitting in his closet alone, Millind was not writing poems, as his being so pulled in by a poetry "slam," a word he'd never heard used in that way, might suggest.

"What do I know about that," he'd muttered resentfully, when, at age nine, long before his own poems came, I showed him my handwritten essay on *The Odyssey*. Years later, he'd break a clean plate in the sink, shouting, "What do *you* know about writing a play?" when I joined a preteen playwriting workshop, when I was twelve and he was forty-two and hadn't yet been to the Bang Bang.

Long after, when he was seventy and we weren't speaking, I read in a famous and elite culture magazine that several of his poems were adapted for the stage.

I thought of writing the magazine a letter, explaining my brother's and my family's history, but never did. After my father's death, that was the magazine that hired me, made me a regular writer, partly or even mostly because I bore Dad's name.

🐘

Millind, though only newly literate in English, wasn't a man of the dark soil. No, he wasn't some "I'll dig with it" kind of farmer father who could be observed wistfully by a poet-child who'd once pledged fealty to the pen. Millind had never been a farmer, period. His hands were always clean and carefully kept. He had been trained as a bookkeeper since boyhood. There was some sort of scholarship? Where he was supposed to use it to turn into a financial expert? But according to Millind's younger brother, a drunk gossip before he disappeared to Canada, when Millind presented himself, on the first day of class at Pace University, for Finance Wizardry, he with his dry dessicated skin and thin aging face, throats were cleared, white faces lowered, and Millind was quietly shown out, advised that he should not have lied about his age in the essay, in which he'd said that he was twenty-five.

At that time, he was only thirty but looked fifty at least. Over half his teeth were yellowed and weak from chewing *paan*. Given his skin color, those benefactors might have assumed he had bad teeth from smoking crack. Millind swore that he was born very handsome and fair, but he had gotten dark and thin, as if a faint curse settled upon him, when in his youth he was sent to live with relatives who wouldn't buy him milk or shoes. He swore that drinking dirty coconut water and living on leftover rice ruined his looks. Either way, he was no match for the people who, sight unseen, on the basis of a competent letter he had asked his wife to write, awarded him thousands of school fees to study finance in the US. They'd gotten visas, on account of his wife being a nurse, in the days when Vietnam took hold of young doctors and nurses, forced them to remove the boots of soldiers who had had both feet blown off, pinned these doctors and nurses to makeshift medical tents where they hid from mortar under their beds.

Yet Millind and his wife were not afraid of failure, not afraid of Vietnam.

"It wouldn't be worse than Partition," he reasoned. So he was not demoralized by losing the scholarship, or even by the fear that if he was not at a university, the government could decide thirty was not too old to fight and send him to Southeast Asia. Millind's jewel of a daughter wasn't born yet, and the princely boy was still suckling at his wife's breast, the baby tiny and content. Instead of studying finance, Millind got a job driving for a rich Indian family on Long Island. He was able to look reassuring yet not understand a word they said, since they were Sikh and spoke Punjabi. "Thank God they aren't Hindu, or Brahmin," his wife whispered to him, comforted that no one whose opinion she really cared about would see or indeed ever know how Millind had become a servant, despite his noble but poor Brahmin origins, in spite of them making it to the U.S.A.

Millind couldn't complain about his job. No drugs or shouting or late nights, no illegalities. Generous with food. Polite to each other. Regular about going to *gurdwara,* visiting elders, taking care of properties they owned and rented to Americans. The father also had some sort of import-export clothing business. The tall, imposing daughter of the family, though no one knew it at the time, would marry a white man when she grew up, convert to Christianity, and become a U.S. senator.

Comparing himself to taxi drivers who smoked pot and crack on the highway, weaving and cackling like despots on their way to LaGuardia, Dad rightfully ranked himself as superior. And anyway, it was much easier to drive than keep track of many narrow columns of numbers, or be a clerk in the post office, or, God forbid, train to be a priest. If he had gotten admission to a good college in India, things would be different. But those sorts of colleges were for his brothers, the two older ones who had been kept at home while Millind was sent away to richer but mostly indifferent relatives, who barely fed him.

My dad, a reasonable father—an employed driver with a small nest egg built up by a stable family who had started a business, who reassured him with unfeigned affection that they couldn't function without him—could not understand the discontent with his own life that started long before my brother was born.

But then my brother came into this world, imperfect, smiling though there was nothing to smile at. Repeating himself, unable to stop eating, unable to stop being anxious. Afraid, and rightfully so, of my father. From the beginning, my brother was strange, with his body and his face and his hard voice that seemed to have changed earlier and faster than normal. My brother, playing at knights with me while our father locked himself in a closet. My brother, sitting next to me at the piano in the Unitarian church on Bayside Avenue around the corner from us in Flushing and banging out jarring melodies, indifferent to the cold stares of white women who wanted to say we didn't belong and that we didn't deserve to make a noise, but didn't dare say cruel words in public to a young man who was so obviously handicapped.

Millind's wife didn't object, once she learned of the poetry. Here was the routine the two lived by. Number One, get everyone ready for school in the morning. Number Two, give her son all of his medicines, fretting and throbbing over each of them, holding her head as if the grey capsules had penetrated her own skull. Number Three, prayers and flowers, filling the closet where, eventually, great books were composed. Millind's journeys through Samarkand, his musings on forgotten peasant revolts. Images of famines and of wars. There were other stories, moments, in Millind's poetry that his wife, though keenly listening, never did understand, though she had read his book in the bathroom, the only place she was alone. She tried reading his book on a public bus with all the ladies around her reading fat, indulgent, sexy books, or else sleeping.

But other people understood his work. They were the ones who counted, not his wife. Slimmer ladies, ladies with frizzy and unfashionable hair but intense, inhuman eyes and townhouses. Women who would have been insulted by the word "ladies," unless they used it themselves. Ladies who lunched and, through their lunches, controlled publishing. They championed Millind, who was thin, frightened, mysteriously asexual and sage-like, whose home life no one knew or asked the details of, who existed, in 1981 and beyond, as a reminder of "other voices," "from the margins,"and all sorts of phrases and symbols that Millind himself, not through shrewdness but just luck and ignorance, succeeded brilliantly by completely ignoring.

It was as if they could see, and anyway already knew, how uncertain he was of even standing before them. How reluctant Millind was, to dare to aspire to be anything but invisible. How fearful he remained for years that all the thin women and vigilant but kind men, the same ones who had welcomed him onstage, would suddenly turn away from him, look at him with incredulity, contempt, even anger, for stepping on his own into the light, up there on stage. For daring to believe had something to say.

But he was never invisible, my dad. Even at temple, while he was praying, people came to him asking for advice, or simply wanting to hear his voice, mellifluous and full of conviction. He never revealed how, having barely passed the class in middle school, he didn't know very much Sanskrit, only verses he'd memorized. He recited each prayer like the poem it was. He made me love poetry, though it makes nothing happen—that is the truth.

My brother, at twenty, left a note before he disappeared. My parents searched for him half-heartedly. He might appear, my father said, on the book tour my father's generous publishers had set for him through major towns in the U.S. and Canada, Britain even, where Dad stayed in a small hotel with tubs in the living rooms. Dad said he'd look for him in the back of each auditorium, walk around each town searching for him.

By then my brother was gone nearly two months. The police had exhausted their searches. My mother couldn't quit her job but came close, taking vacation and sick time to search for him. She faithfully prepared food for his return. There was no clue in his letter to us, only the promise, "I am going." We knew he didn't mean for only a short time. All of his clothes and the toys he still played with, Legos and figurines bought for a younger child but still vital to him at twenty—he'd put them all into a knapsack, along with the money he extracted from the dresser where I hid my wealth. Four hundred dollars, all in twenty-dollar bills, folded and stuffed neatly into the Superman wallet he'd begged Ma to buy for him when he was ten.

On a night my father was away, at a reading, my mother asked if I thought that we should do *sraddha,* death rites for a beloved, to prevent my brother's soul, if he was dead, from wandering unloved. She never would have asked me such a question years ago. Ma would've been the one teaching me the rites of her civilization, the rituals she performed so quietly, like combing her hair or putting certain combinations of salt and spices in our food. I kept saying that we didn't know if he was dead until I succeeded in making my mother stop weeping.

Within a year of his first prize-winning collection, Millind was adopted by a university, advised that he had become a great man. He started wearing velveteen sports coats, smoking cigars, and with the help of a transcriber, an *amanuensis*, the word he learned from the woman he hired to be one, began writing and publishing essays critical of the West as well as of the country he used to think of as his motherland.

In interviews, when he was asked about children, Millind shrugged his shoulders, mimicking cosmic gratitude. "I have known what it is to be loved by a child," he said, with the air of someone who'd tried out this particular experience. As if he'd savored being looked up to by such a creature, "child," before moving on to something else, writing another book.

"And before your gifts as a poet were discovered, the story is that you used to be a chauffeur?" the inerviewer might ask, intrigued and sniffling, a person way too young for allergies who'd maybe been snorting cocaine or heroin hours before. Such drugs were activities, pastimes, that Millind would dabble in during his later sixties, once he had been prosperous long enough so he could become bored. But when interviewed, he answered every single question right.

"Driving a decent family, like my employers were, taught me that there is no shame in a decent work," he said, charming the interviewer with his authentic, accented wisdom.

My father's second wife was from a wealthy family with robber baron lineage. His new marriage sent my mother packing back to India. Dad was "only sixty-two," he said, "with still so long to live." He said all of this only in a letter, not bothering, or perhaps not daring, to tell Ma or me in person. We hadn't been invited to the wedding because, as he said, "it would mean too much suffering." When I first heard what had happened, I dreamed my brother would magically appear at the wedding, which took place at a writer's residency in upstate New York that was named after a famous white woman poet.

I wanted him to come wearing his dinosaur T-shirt and brandishing whatever he'd managed to put into his wallet with the S on it, which must have been faded by then. I dreamed he'd offer money to the guests, show them he'd managed to escape from our father, reveal to them he'd left because our dad had never wanted him. Make them look at our dad with disgust.

Instead there was a special article on Dad's wedding in the nation's most important newspaper, and in this article his new, quite young bride described how much they hoped to have children.

In the year 2001, when people in a certain city where the Bang Bang club was located were on the streets searching, lamenting loved ones, posting ads and Xeroxes about missing beloveds, Millind stood in front of a memorial, not knowing that his son watched him.

By then, his son hadn't been a young man for some years. In fact, he was nearly the same age that Millind had been when he discovered poetry. His son was on a field trip from the group home where he lived, where the police and courts had finally placed him when he refused, no matter how they badgered, to tell them where he'd come from.

If Millind turned to look, he could have seen a face that seized his own, that bowdlerized his calm features, combining his serene looks with the anger of a thwarted child. He could have seen determination, intention, the resolution of a man still young enough to realize: he could be more loved by his sister than his father ever was. Unknown to Millind, this man, his son, would tell the people who took care of him the name of his sister. Then he would let them find her, and he would learn how it felt to be an uncle to her child.

That face, my brother's face. My brother's life worth more than poetry. My brother whose life could have been crushed. My father a stranger until his death, until I found a way to profit from his legacy and smile when his poems were recited, studied by schoolchildren, beloved.

ORANGE POPSICLES

THAT SUMMER, ONCE SHE'D SETTLED INTO a new life and moved into a sublet her college roommate Becca had made available from among the numerous properties owned by her large and prosperous American lawyer family, Jayanti felt she understood the rape.

Jayanti was raped because she dared to cheat on an exam. Her understanding was simple by now, unequivocal. She wasn't interested in penance, though. She was more interested in analyzing, as if with three-dimensional revolving diagrams, the pattern of choices that put her in the position of cheating in the first place. Like so many choices in life, like coming to the U.S. for her studies, the instant of cheating felt both unexpected and inevitable. The same day she received a surreal $20,000 check from a women's foundation, a full scholarship her freshman year she enrolled on an impulse in the big Modernist Poetry lecture her American hallmates were talking about, with that dreamy Irish teacher who knew Yeats by heart. He was as cute as they'd promised. But that class made her late for nearly every single Biology 501 lecture, considering how long it took to walk to Science Hill, and how quickly all the seats were filled up by more savvy and realistic classmates, and that precise set of circumstances, at once preventable and inescapable, was what made Jayanti desperate enough to cheat.

Her mother would have said that her lateness for a critical class had been a kind of opening, a vital crack through which the evil eye could peer at her. But Jayanti wouldn't ever tell her mother she'd been raped. The danger began with that one day of giddy freedom, when, check in hand, she'd felt wholly American. Or had it really started way back, much further back?—when she was still in India, sending back course choices by mail, or when she'd made the wrong decision to take the rigorous-sounding biology class in the first place when everyone knew that the painters, sculptors, and English majors on campus took "Rocks for Jocks" or "Stars for the Bars" to pass the science requirement.

But to Jayanti, sitting on her *Athai's* veranda in Madras and feeling the scholarship pressing down on her, learning real science seemed integral to becoming worthy of such a distinction. Scientific thinking was key to making art. There was the same rigorous lack of compromise, the same remove from what anyone else thought, among real scientists as there was among artists. So Jayanti, a painter who had, before college, already shown some of her work in galleries all over the world, conferred with no one before enrolling in Bio 501, or "The Crucible," as it was called—not even telling the nice pen pal the college's International House had assigned to her—though it was the most intense biology course offered to undergrads, though she had taken none of the prerequisites. Though the class was graded on a curve.

On the first day, slightly late and sitting among strangers who were friendly enough, Jayanti felt good. The first few diagrams filled her with reverence for the human body. Nudes by Michelangelo, anatomy drawings, the fact that all the blood in the body somehow circulated, thirty liters per minute, pumped precisely to and from every cell of every living tissue by a heart no bigger than a fist.

Back in her room, listening to an evening sitar *raag*, she loved reading about cytokines and neurotransmitters, invisible signals between the brain and heart that had the reach of seismic waves. She approached science impressionistically, concentrating on whatever moved her. She even brought a sketchbook to class the first day, not realizing until too late, when there were already over two hundred slides to memorize by the end of the first week, that she was in over her head, and that it mattered not at all that the distinctive cilia of a paramecium looked like a Paul Klee painting, or that the luster of a white, skeletal bone brought to mind one of Dali's surreal paintings. Walking back from the last review session, watching her classmates huddle over fiercely-guarded notes, Jayanti finally saw a truth as firm as Koch's postulates. She'd fail.

The night before the final exam—the only test in the course, apart from ungraded quizzes and problem sets, which Jayanti had somehow not registered the literal importance of actually working through—she sat in the expensively appointed Law Library trying not to cry. Her papers were scattered before her, covered with pan-icky, barely decipherable notes. She tried not to think about how, if she failed this exam, she would most likely lose her scholarship and have to go back to India. It didn't do any good now, she knew that, but here she sat thinking and thinking of it, how she'd suddenly failed. She hadn't imagined, until the review session the week before, that everything she'd studied so far would be completely irrelevant. All she had to know was what keywords to write in the exam pa-per, nothing more and nothing less, but her notes from the semester were irrelevant. All she needed were the foundations, precisely un-derstood, like the humble and often-overlooked foundations of the convent school building Jayanti had attended in Madras, but what she had on the desk in front of her, was nothing but clouds.

A boy she knew a little from biology, Dave Sheffield, walked by Jayanti's carrel, stopped at a shelf across from hers. Walked near where she was sitting, loitered. At first, she scarcely noticed. He wasn't the type she imagined would have given her a second glance. He looked from a distance like he'd grown up playing polo. She looked up at last, when it appeared that he wasn't going away. He came closer.

The few minutes they spent talking about the exam made her feel even worse. How could she sit here, flirting with this Abercrombie

& Fitch guy, just hours before she would most likely lose her scholarship? Lose her whole life? She couldn't fathom it. And yet she let
Dave run a finger down the silk of her embroidered sleeve, down to
her wrist, encircle it and observe, with a satisfied smile, how small
her hand was in his grasp. Let him massage her back and even kiss
her on the cheek.

The next morning in the exam hall, Dave came over and sat right
next to her. Jayanti hadn't confided in him, but his sympathetic smile
and whispered "Don't worry" suggested he knew all too well how
desperate she felt. She had been up all night studying, going through
the textbook word by word and testing herself on key concepts, writing out practice answers, reviewing old exams. But the process had
begun far too late. She'd phoned her mother that morning, when it
was still evening in Madras, and confessed to her terrible mistake.
Her mother said she would make a special trip by train to the Meen-
akshi temple in Madurai that weekend and offer prayers. The exam
results would be back on Tuesday, time enough for Jayanti to be rescued by prayer no matter what she had written on the test paper.
That was what her mother promised, speaking on God's behalf.

Dave had reddish-blond hair and a lanky, confident body. He
veered between arrogance and authentic goofy charm. Rumor was
he'd been a real nerd in high school, run some sort of essay-writing
service, worn glasses. But here he was in contacts, sharp-eyed, yet as
always, indolent, even in this tense examination hall. He rested his
hands at the back of his neck as he looked over the exam, stretched
his legs close to Jayanti's, jiggled his foot until his Birkenstock nearly
fell off. Jayanti was too afraid of failing to allow herself to look directly at any of his body parts. She went through the exam once
quickly, then again, filling in everything she remembered in a few
bursts of rote recall, then fading as she reread the answers and began
doubting herself.

Jayanti tapped her pencil on the desk, making a noise before she
realized she was doing it. Dave nudged her leg with his, once, then

for a second and third time. She looked up finally. They were in the middle but near the back, away from the proctors' gaze, and Dave had a typed sheet with what looked like notes from the review session. Quickly, she glanced at it: there was something about nematode locomotion she could use for the last problem on the test, asking for an invertebrate evolution example. She looked toward the front of the room before she wrote: the proctor was staring at her, but Dave was busily writing, no sign of the typed sheet on his desk, and Jayanti herself was looking down at their feet, so close together, barely allowable. "No touching your neighbor," the proctor called out, and Dave looked up at the sound before smiling at her and exaggeratedly edging his foot away.

When the proctor circled back to the front, Dave's typed sheet was out again. This time she saw phrases—"antigenic shift and drift," "founder effect"—before looking away. It was enough to jog her memory; if nothing else, seeing the words restored some of her confidence. Along one edge of the paper was a long column of letters that Jayanti stared at blankly, confused until she realized it held the answers to the multiple-choice section that made up one-quarter of the test. The column raised all kinds of questions about how Dave had gotten the typed paper, which up until that moment she had assumed was just a crib sheet. There were rumors that one of the TA's habitually sold parts of the exam to the highest bidders, although this had never been proven and no one had ever been caught.

Library. After the exam. At first, Jayanti had thought to avoid Dave at all costs, but he'd come up to her, bashful and almost sweet, saying, "You seemed like you needed help." Compassionate. She'd blinked at him, surprised, stunned that he would speak of their cheating out loud. How sure Dave was. How much he'd been given. Finally, she nodded at him and even smiled but kept on walking.

He must have thought she was only playing hard to get. He followed her into a cubbyhole, a claustrophobic cabinet with a desk and a sliding door that only the most studious inhabited. She imagined he'd probably never been in one before, but before she could turn on the light his hands moved over her back, pushing aside her *chunni* to find her nipple under the cotton tunic and then seizing her throat to kiss her. She pushed his hands aside, freeing her breast and her head, but his taste was intoxicating, and they tangled. He was the one who pulled away, looking down at her.

"Test wasn't so bad after all, was it, Jayanti," he said, pronouncing her name so that it sounded like the name of a cheap perfume, "Jean Nate." She could have sworn Dave was sneering as he left her there, but she was too ashamed to look at him.

The letter came to her regular mailbox, in the post office next to the building where the Modernist Poetry class, now a painful reminder of her looming failure, was held. It was on the Dean's letterhead, and at first she assumed it was junk mail, the Dean's Newsletter or something equally useless, until she read it again and saw that it was addressed to her and cc'd to Dave Sheffield. She had to sit down because she could hardly think for the blood rushing to her head. They'd been found out. The proctor at her exam had named her and Dave as two "candidates for investigation" in a large cheating scandal that had contaminated the exam process for over five hundred freshmen class students in pre-med biology and chemistry. The letter encouraged the two of them to come forward together, rather than try to lay the blame on each other. While they weren't promised amnesty for coming forward of their own accord, they were "assured a reasonable process" that "would not necessarily result in their expulsion, though a brief suspension and automatic failure of Biology 501 was likely at this point."

Jayanti couldn't imagine what to do. She wondered if it was too late to stop them from sending a copy of the letter to her mother. On the walk back to her dorm, a boy with broad shoulders and short hair like Dave's swooped by on his bike and she turned to look, nauseous with fear.

In her room, she sat down on the bed. Her hands were numb and the weight of the suitcases in her closet was too much to lift, though she would have to start packing. To lose her scholarship! Her maternal uncle had taken her to a posh restaurant in Nungambakkam High Road the night before she left for the U.S., told her she would be able to earn the money to treat them all someday.

When Dave called later that night, she'd been doing nothing more than lying in bed silently. Her roommate wanted to know what was wrong; when Jayanti didn't answer, she assumed it was "some stupid boy."

"And don't tell me it's Alok," Becca said, "because if I hear his name again after what he did to you, I swear I'm disconnecting the phone so you can't call him." As Becca got ready for one of her many evening meetings, this one for an on-campus lesbian feminist group though Becca was not a lesbian, Jayanti wondered if her no-nonsense, even self-righteous roommate would still want to be her friend when the whole cheating scandal came out.

Becca knowing about her ex-boyfriend Alok was different. Every girl, even if gay now, had been with some man, at some point, who was a snake. Jayanti's very-much-ex-boyfriend Alok had cheated on her with a Pakistani girl he met at one of the SASA conferences, tall and thin with green dishonest eyes in the photos Jayanti had seen of the two of them, but then he regretted it, tried to conceal what he had done and even proposed to Jayanti when she'd confronted him. Alok's brand of cheating was allowed, maybe even expected. He was handsome and single, turning twenty-one in a few months. His false promises to Jayanti and the other girl would never get him expelled.

Dave Sheffield too gave the impression that he would be exempt from any consequence. When he called later that evening, after Becca had gone out, he was edgy and belligerent, describing how he'd already spoken to one of his father's lawyers, how the letter was nothing more than an intimidation tactic, how all they had to do was stand their ground. The main thing, he told her, was not to say anything directly to the Dean or anyone else. Refuse to cooperate. Above all, don't act like you're about to leave the campus anytime soon.

When Jayanti brought up the issue of her scholarship, Dave was silent. "Well, maybe you could find an immigration lawyer and fight that too," he said off-handedly. She didn't reply. "So, friend, you can be counted on?" he pressed.

"What?" she asked, hardly absorbing what he'd said.

"I mean, like if they come to you and say there's a way to save your scholarship by putting it all on me, you won't do it, will you? Because you know my lawyer would take you down, you're completely in this mess, and if you don't keep your mouth shut I'll start talking about how you begged me to help you, that you offered me a free fuck. You can't imagine you're the first to make the trade. And I've gotten A's in every other science class this year. I'm a star in the biology major. My Dean says that I'm headed for a top-ten US medical school. You can't exactly say the same."

Alert at last, wholly repulsed the way she wished she'd been from the beginning, before the test, before she failed the moment she didn't raise her hand and ask to change seats, Jayanti hung up the phone. She wanted someone to confide in, not Dave, that she had wanted to be an artist, not a doctor, that it had all been a mistake. But there was no one to talk to.

The phone rang and rang, until she took it off the hook. Calls came to her cell phone too—easy enough to block. For a few days, Jayanti succeeded in avoiding him, but then one day they both received a second letter, instructing them to come to the Dean's office in a fortnight and advising them of their right to contact the student council (and a lawyer, although the college "didn't recommend that at this time"). The night they got the second letter, Dave was waiting for her inside the stairwell when she came back from dinner. It was too early for anyone else on her floor to be back. Becca was out again.

Seeing Dave in the hallway, Jayanti resolved to get inside her dorm room and shut the door quickly. It wasn't as if he'd force his way in. Tonight, he was wearing glasses, nerdy and timid again the way he must been in high school chemistry. His clothes were shabby, plain. He was thinner than she remembered. Only his watch looked expensive. He leaned against the wall and seemed to be trying to look sincere. "I was scared, and I took it out on you. It wasn't cool. Will you accept my apology?" Without warning, he reached out with long arms and pulled her close. She held her body rigid, not wanting to make a scene. "You smell good," he said, rubbing her back, and at that moment, she did step away, saying, "It's okay. You can go now. Go, please."

She spoke softly, not wanting strangers to look at them, and he didn't go. Instead he slid past her and pushed open her door, which Becca, had left unlocked. Dave pulled Jayanti inside and kicked the door shut behind him. "Becca," she called out as loudly as she could, trying to put a note of warning in her voice. The lights were off in the living room.

"She's at one of her dyke meetings tonight. Don't worry, we won't be disturbed," he said, taking off his glasses, the seducer again. So much taller than her. Jayanti nodded, looked at where the phone was. It was in its usual place, on the serviceable wooden table outside her bedroom, the same table as in everyone's dorm. It couldn't have been more than twenty feet away.

Her cell phone battery was dead; she'd been intending to rush home and take care of it. The charger was there too, on the table. She stood rigid, hoping for a chance to grab at help. But Dave was watching too closely. Jauntily, he walked to the phone, pulled the cord out of the wall. Pocketed the charger after winding it up.

When he smiled at her, his features reminded her of Rob Lowe's, Brad Pitt's. Glinty blue eyes, cleft chin, dimples. Rumpled, shining hair. Taut arms. Every white cocky American actor, whose cockiness secured their sex appeal.

"So tense. Has Becca got her lesbian hooks into you?" he asked. "You two do a lot of licky-licky?" he whispered. "I'd love to see that."

He grabbed and held her too tightly. His arms were muscular, nearly bare in the cheap white T-shirt, the kind that ordinary businessmen, including some south Indians, wore as underwear. Jayanti struggled to lift his heavy arms off her before he pushed her down into a sitting position on the wood straight-backed chair in the living room and someone else, someone who must have been waiting inside the room, stood behind her and pulled a dank cloth, possibly an unwashed pillowcase, tight around her head, making seeing and breathing both finite and infinitely meaningful. Jayanti stilled, praying that she wouldn't suffocate. By then, Dave had released his grip from her shoulders and throat, and she tried to stand up.

But someone, not Dave, perhaps the person who had put the cloth over her eyes, sat down on her then, sudden and hard, astride her hips, right on her lap, and pressed his crotch into her. There was cloth jammed into her mouth. She couldn't utter a sound. The cloth, tight between her lips, looser over her nose and face, blacked out the room.

Two big hands pushed down on her upper arm—the humeral head, she remembered, right out of the glenoid fossa of the scapula, the Netter drawing she'd seen in the Biology 501 anatomy textbook. Those hands shoved hard enough to make her nauseous from pain, lifting the round ball out of the shoulder joint, detaching it from its moorings and pushing it back so she was completely immobile. She was dizzy; she tried to kick with her feet but couldn't lift them. She retched but couldn't vomit for the gag in her mouth. She tasted bile, dimly aware that her right arm was now a strange thing, hanging loosely at her side. She was a right-handed painter, she thought, trying to say the words. They had to stop. She'd do what they said. They had to understand. She needed that arm.

The word "aspiration," came into her mind. Not just the hope of doing something, of being an artist, keeping both her arms, but also what happened if bile from your mouth came down into the trachea. She saw the diagram of an aspirating lung, so vivid now, the clear image from a textbook. Aspiration. Pale pink alveoli smeared with detritus. The way Dave had smeared her. She willed herself to let the wetness pool inside her mouth, to not swallow. To hold steady, breathe as she could.

In the few minutes' respite created by Dave, or someone, turning on Becca's full-throated stereo system, Jayanti forced herself to think instead of giving up. Soon the hallway would be busy with traffic, her neighbors coming back from dinner, going out to meetings or movies. She tried to think of something she could kick or move with her left hand, something heavy enough to make a loud crash, to get someone outside to come knock on the door.

There were at least three strangers in her room, one man who had been sitting on her and was now standing up, rubbing what felt like his smooth, naked penis against her good arm, another whose steps she could hear moving across the room to turn up the stereo knob even louder, and possibly a third still lurking by the damaged arm. The pain was nothing like she'd ever felt. The gag had loosened by now, she was able to spit out and clear her mouth. "My arm," she shouted. "Arm!" Their laughter. She must have passed out.

When she came to her first thought was of Karen, the blond with pursed lips and conservative clothes who lived down the hall, a girl who circulated home-baked cookies every weekend but had actually taken Jayanti aside once and told her that she was the laughingstock of their dorm for how loudly she moaned and cried out during Alok's energetic lovemaking. "Everyone can hear how much you like to have sex," Karen said. "But in this country, we try to honor people's privacy. It's not like the black hole of Calcutta or someplace like that where everyone lives practically on top of each other, you know? This ain't no slum-dog millionaire," Karen said, giggling. "We're all just cool. You want to try to have more dignity. I'm just trying to help you."

The gag, the cloth slipped free at last and Jayanti screamed and screamed, to no response. When the cloth was taken off her completely and she could see the room again, only Dave stood naked over her. No other men. Her right arm was useless, and her pants and underwear had been pulled down. Crying, she used her good arm to try to put them back on. Dave stopped her with a vicious squeeze, turned her around, and quickly raped her from behind.

He finished with a grunt. Technically, she'd been a virgin. Alok had made her come without breaking her hymen. It was irrelevant now. The minute she'd cheated on the test, that was when she'd lost virginity, she thought. She'd closed her eyes when Dave ripped into her, opened them again when he stepped away, gathering her strength. She wanted to scream but couldn't. The stereo bedlam silenced her. Metallica. *Master of Puppets.* Dave stood back, singing and playing air guitar; she didn't look at him but sensed that he was cleaning himself, perhaps getting dressed.

She used the energy of not screaming to compose herself, to dare to look around. She confirmed the phone was still disconnected. Two cups were undisturbed on the table, as if she'd invited Dave for tea the same way she invited nearly everyone she met. Suddenly he was on her again, rubbing her breast and laughing when she kicked at him. He held her down for another quick, revolting kiss on top of her head, right on the exposed scalp of her part, before finally letting her go. "Good girl," he told her. "I'll feed you a lot more of my horse cock unless you shut your mouth"—a line, Jayanti surmised, from porn Dave might have watched when he was in high school. The minute he left, Jayanti got up and staggered to the door, careful not to move her right arm. Using her good hand, she locked it. Then she lay down on the floor for what felt like hours, wishing it were dark. Later that night the door opened again and Jayanti felt her heart jump, but it was Becca, immediately upset and outraged, swearing more than asking Jayanti any questions.

"Hospital," Jayanti whispered urgently. She said it more than once but Becca wouldn't stop saying "Who did this? What the fuck is this?" as she turned on lights and bustled around their living room, turning off the stereo, picking up traces—strewn pillows, a bloody chair, the empty pillowcase—of what she quickly understood was rape. She turned back to Jayanti, face pallid, lips drawn and angry, throwing a clean blanket over her and saying, "Don't move, the police have to document, just stay where you are, sweetie, they have to do the kit." But Jayanti managed to pull herself up, walk, reconnect the phone with her good hand, feeling less dead, somehow, having done this. Then she sank down on the sofa, depleted. Becca, weeping, called 911.

In the emergency room, all around Jayanti there were people with open, bleeding gashes on their arms and legs, and as Jayanti looked around she was struck by a peculiar belief in her own luck. "At least I'm alive," she said to Becca, remembering many news stories in India where rape victim's bodies had been found in a condition that didn't even allow the women to be identified.

"We're going to get those bastards, count on it," Becca said. They'd come back from the X-ray and sat in a tiny room with a curtain, waiting for a doctor to "reduce" Jayanti's shoulder. A different, motherly nurse was seeing to them now, and Jayanti was glad. Reminded of her own mother, she resolved never to tell her what Dave had done. The new nurse brought her a long, narrow, pinkish-orange Popsicle. Jayanti chewed at the end silently while Becca talked, liking how it numbed her tongue and mouth but hating it, at the same time, for how much it looked like a man's penis.

"The arm is broken, I think," Jayanti said. "Not just a dislocation. My fingers feel numb. I'm scared, Becca. My grip—I can move them, but my grip isn't right." The series of etchings she'd been working on, fine, detailed work of animals inspired by some of the earliest cave paintings in the world, the ones drawn with a single line starting in the animal's mouth and winding out in convoluted, brain-like sworls, out to the tail—how would she do those etchings now, how would she hold the scalpel, incise the copper plates? How would she have the confidence to make permanent marks?

While Becca ran to get the nurse, Jayanti sat looking at herself like a stranger in a tall mirror across from where she sat. Her face was drawn and pale, her lips orange, hair thick and wild. Like an actress in some Hindi movie about rape, but unlike that actress, Jayanti had no one to avenge her. Jayanti was an only child, no brothers, father passed, mother in India.

Jayanti was supposed to bring her mother to the U.S., to prosper here. She'd wasted time. Wasted her chance.

She began sobbing quietly, shutting her eyes, just as Becca returned, without the nurse, shouting imperiously for a doctor, pain medicine, X-rays, a lawyer, the fucking police.

"There are only two guys who would do just about anything Dave Sheffield wanted, and believe me, they're going to pay too," Becca muttered.

She could hear Becca continuing to promise her justice after the nurses and doctors came to hover over her, injecting her with morphine while they made her arm feel almost right. But Becca wasn't there when Jayanti woke up and was ready to go home. Her roommate was already knocking on doors. Organizing.

That night, once she was safe in bed, with women she didn't know sitting on the floor of her living room, talking, Jayanti listened, passive, until she finally fell asleep. Over only a few days, she watched Becca evolve a full, effective campaign. The two boys Becca suspected of helping Dave were on the basketball team with him. A fury of calls to Becca's sisters in her various informal sisterhoods—"Take Back the Night" committee, queer womyn's painting collectives, Asian American and Latina Women's International Rights Association, the Rotary Club—led to the suspected boys being followed day and night by volunteers. Vague sexual bragging by the boys was overheard, reported to the police immediately. The police had inventoried the dorm room, but surfaces had all been wiped. The only fluids were Jayanti's own. The perpetrators had worn gloves, exercised care. Dave hadn't ejaculated when he raped her.

Two weeks later, the police knocked on her door. When Jayanti opened it, she noticed, almost as if it were a dream, that the small picture of the god Ganesh which she had taped onto the dry-erase board was covered in shaving cream. "A prank," the police officer said. She looked away from it, saying a short efficient prayer very softly, under her breath, part of her wondering if the police had finally come to arrest her. She had cheated on an exam, after all. But Jayanti learned that one of her neighbors, a quiet black girl, had called the police about a fourth boy coming out of Jayanti and Becca's room that night, a boy she recognized from the college's Daily News front page. He had just joined the basketball team that year. Like Jayanti, he was on a scholarship. He didn't want any trouble. He not only confessed, but also named Dave and two of his fraternity brothers. He'd told them to stop, but they wouldn't, he claimed. "Gang rape, a fucking lawsuit," Becca insisted, excited, puzzled but eventually accepting of the curious, exotic fact that nothing could make Jayanti press the case. Nothing could make her talk to reporters.

"Thank God you got justice without having to testify in court," Becca would say afterward, sometimes during the rare moments when Jayanti had momentarily forgotten. Months later, when Jayanti learned that the college administration was going to take action against the men, despite the campus movement and the rallies led by sorority sisters who supported the men, she refused to talk to Becca at all, unless Becca promised never to mention the rape again.

None of it really mattered. Jayanti was sure that she would still lose her scholarship, and spent every day thereafter head down, wondering if she would have to kill herself when the decision came. Wondering if there were an easy way to make a suicide look accidental. Thinking about a plastic bag over her head. Drawing it closed the way the rapists could've done.

It took nearly another year for final decisions, during which a special committee involved in Dave's and the other boys' hearings thoroughly reviewed Jayanti's entire case, determining that her half-done problem sets showed effort that was clearly her own, and that she hadn't cheated in any other course.

It took another year for Jayanti to stop waking up each day convinced that it would be her last as she knew it. She didn't lose the scholarship. She was pardoned for the cheating, in large part due to the rape, she thought, sickened by how Dave had saved her. The fissure that had opened in her life had closed before destroying her whole life, but the evil eye had claimed its mark on her. She would never be unmarked again. Never be free of its disapproving glare.

Faced with imminent college discipline, Dave chose to leave for good, rather than risk getting expelled. The rumor was that he had transferred to a small, upscale liberal arts college, changed his name, changed his interests from pre-med to politics. Becca kept tabs on him, insisting that Dave and his rapist fraternity brothers remain on the agenda of the campus women United Against Rape.

"Imagine, someone like Dave in politics," Becca repeated, her pudgy, kewpie-doll face screwed up with disgust. "He'll never get far in the public eye, don't worry. You don't have to talk about what happened to you. We'll be your voice. Me and my sisters in the struggle, my cousin who's a civil rights lawyer. We'll make sure the fucker won't forget."

Jayanti didn't know how anyone could make Dave truly regret what he had done. But Becca made good on her other promises. She'd stuck with Jayanti through her physical recovery, her rehab for the injured arm, her make-up work for Biology, the extra credits Jayanti agreed to take. And here Jayanti was now, long after finishing school triumphantly, living in a clean and well-lit studio sublet thanks to Becca, hurrying forward in a new life she wasn't convinced she ought to have.

As benefactors went, Becca was sterling. But there was still the acid in her mouth, though college was behind her and no one was trying to hurt her now. Jayanti couldn't imagine trying to make Becca really understand.

Her mother had come from India to see her walk in the black gown, taken a thousand pictures, and beamed as proudly as other kids' parents, never suspecting a thing. Well into her second year of graduate school in art, Jayanti was doing nothing but working, producing a few canvases that sold, and she had even made a handful of work friends.

The women assumed that Jayanti's distant quality came from her being foreign, and they seemed to like her more because she never asked for anything from them. Jayanti was their sounding board for "bad relationships," "casual sex," "affairs with teachers," and all the other topics that felt to Jayanti as distant as the headings of glossy illustrated flashcards. Young, single, city woman. Cards Jayanti was glad she'd never be required to memorize.

The men in her art school classes, both gay and not gay, often held barbecues on the roofs of their building, and this evening, in the middle of August, Jayanti had been to just such a barbecue. B: It was so stupid, she thought, hating herself the way she often did. She was raped four years ago. Four years the length of time Jayanti had been in the US. At the barbecue, a container of orange popsicles, exactly the color and shape as the one she'd had in the emergency room, had been sitting on the foldout metal table. The sight of them had made her nauseous enough to flee, to stand nearly an hour waiting for her train.

At home in her tiny, peaceful studio—a few blocks from where Becca lived with boisterous, womanist friends, all of whom left messages on Jayanti's answering machine that she admitted were comforting to get, though she deleted them without listening all the way—Jayanti lost no time in setting up her work.

Soon after, the buzzer of the apartment must have gone off three, four times, before she heard it—just one long buzzer that went on into nowhere. Jayanti, shaking, forced herself to press the button in response. What if there were a fire, or delivery of art supplies? First there was nothing, then a cursing, angry male voice that sounded familiar.

Dave. Her mouth went dry. She held her cell phone in her hand for 911. A knock at her front door. Before she looked through the peephole, she texted Becca. "Might need help. Please come." But the knock was single, courteous. The voice saying hello unlike the man she'd heard downstairs. Opening her door with the chain on, she saw that this stranger was tall, around her age, with blondish-reddish hair. The glasses, similar. The smile. Not Dave. But, still, her heart pounded harder. She couldn't speak.

"Hey, there. Thanks for opening up. It's Becca's cousin, Jake," the man said, his voice still kind. "Jake from Portland. I always crash here." He stepped closer. "I thought Becca lived here. Do you know her? Are you—" He laughed, staring at Jayanti. "Hey, who are you? She owns this apartment. Do you belong to—?"

She shut the door before he finished his sentence. He knocked again but only once. She kept the chain on, double bolting it, then set her back against it, looking at her phone. Becca had texted back: "I'm on my way. Call the police if it can't wait. I'm in Brooklyn, it'll take me at least another hour to get to you. CALL 911."

There were footsteps fading away from her door, the stranger calling out, "Hey, so sorry, I didn't see she'd emailed me. No worries, I'll be at Becca's if you want to meet up, you must be that friend, I—I'll—well, maybe I'll get to meet you." Once she'd confirmed the man was gone, Jayanti sent Becca an "all clear" text.

Jayanti returned to her work. The etchings of animals and cells she'd started to work on two years ago, back when she was in Biology, were nearly complete now. A firebird. A beautiful woman. Goddess in a cave, the one Jayanti prayed to every day. Fractals assembling around her, diaphanous cells like paramecia on slides, the viscous gel of them like sclera of the eyes. Everything Jayanti had paid so much to know about. To see. To engrave into memory. But as she worked on for hours, through the night, forgetting how all day she had barely talked to anyone, Jayanti believed that whatever she created would endure. That her artwork would earn her a place of belonging. And it was this belief that drove the strong force of desire into her arm that was broken and healed, that held her safe till morning light. Till next morning.

NEELA: BHOPAL, 1984

YOU ALWAYS TRUSTED THE FOREST. Here, danger can be seen and is known. The floor is layered with cool leaves that can be used to cover up faces. You're lying here, laughing and out of breath; your brothers are lying beside you. The first one to move will be tickled by all the rest, who pretend to be monsters and fake-growl with the hunger of thin ghosts. All of you will watch out for the glint of teeth and dazzling, predatory coils.

The dense brush hides tigers, snakes, and a tiny creek that tastes fresh after the rain. Your youngest brother knows the best places

The edge of the pretend forest, a neglected city garden, is where you and your brothers purchase time by tickling each other or run and scramble over rocks as if the four of you never had to work. As if your father never accepted a packet of rupees and four quintals of wheat, one for each of you. As if he never told you, *Neela, go.* As if he didn't stop you, when you were nine, from holding onto your mother's sari. As if he didn't hold you and your brothers back, including the youngest one, age five, from nearly tearing the sari off her body when they wouldn't let go.

Your hands could be washed of the clay, of the hard coal, and every day your fingers moved more quickly than the legs of men who carried finished pyramids, fresh bricks for the furnace. In summer, you and your brothers first broke coal, then walked without bending into the brick kiln, cloth protecting your mouths from the smoke.

December was joy and cold, the fumes of the kiln more bearable when you could rinse your mouths with water, which was not so scarce then. And after working, you and your brothers knew that you could leap over everything jagged you saw. In seconds, you could place many yards between the intimation of a threat, its small or large rustle, and yourself. You could easily outrun strangers' hands, and rejoice at the chill. Walking outside, into the kiln and back, and then sleeping on the ground of the shanty was still better than working in the factory.

Then early one morning, coming back with a vessel of water, you spy a pile of bright folded cotton cloths on the ground and, because of the weight you carried, you carefully make your way toward it, even though you want to run.

December. Your birthday.

Maybe a *pavaday* from home—a dream. But all three half-naked little boys, the brothers who'd once thrown stones at palaces with you, or come at you with sticks for swords, are sleeping on the ground near the shanty, tensed and at odd angles, as if they'd tried escaping even in their sleep.

Still hoping they're playing a game, you set down the water and tickle them. You listen for breath, but hear nothing. You've understood the danger too late. Eyes burning now, you run. To the forest. You arrive stumbling and unsteady, but are forced to stop because you can't see anymore. You are afraid.

Once, when you and your brothers were caught trying to run away from the brick kiln, the debt master who'd bargained with your father punished all of you with no water for a day. How light your body felt then, how small, how free, as if you had traveled in some unseen way to your mother.

December is cool and morning fresh, but your lungs are scorched now. Not for another thirty or maybe a hundred years will the water and land be safe again, as pure and unpolluted as they were hours before. Before the air burned and became a hateful thing.

Eight thousand years ago, children huddled with their mothers in cool caves. Those caves are hidden deep in a forest, miles from here, and would have been so much safer than shantytowns around the factory in Bhopal City, the easily penetrated houses of corrugated metal and scavenged plywood. The walls of those shacks are sheets of plastic with small holes to breathe, set at the height of small children unable to refrain from peeking out.

All three of your brothers, limber and clever boys, were gifted at nosing out delectable refuse, edibles in the garbage. They were like scavenging dogs, little ponies. Long ago they nicknamed you *Neel-agai*—antelope, for your thin quick legs, your skill at finding enough unspoiled food for all of them—and when they pretended to hunt you, none of them could find you here.

Other hunters have found you at the edge of your forest: methyl isocyanate, fleet-footed mercury, and Sevin, the most experienced killer, creeping like ground brush.

You remember rope. Remember being pulled up into the kiln, then told to walk on bricks since. Like the other children, unlike the adults, you were light enough to walk on bricks and leave them whole. Ropes hauled by strong men brought you release. Now instead of rope it feels like snakes coiling around you. Or dense vines, tight around your throat. Water. You need water now, for the burning thirst, the invisible thief of your air. Your chest hurts. You push out poison air but breathe in more.

The death toll among Bhopal's shantytown families is estimated by the number of shrouds that were ordered. Twenty-thousand, excluding families who didn't have money for shrouds, fathers who didn't have money for children. Eyes watering, fathers and older brothers were coughing too much to talk, to bargain. After the burning, many eyes turned sightless. Corneas clouded; ulcers branched like thin cacti.

Cacti are plants you'll never travel to deserts to see. You and your brothers saw some once in a comic book you found in the garbage.

A small man with a red beard and a large hat, a cactus with cockeyed spikes. Your youngest brother laughed and laughed, when you tried to imitate that frowning man.

You die seeing your brothers' faces, but not the other faces of the dead.

In death, you match the image of one young girl, asleep after a bath, who hundreds of years ago was engraved in the emperor's miniatures by artisans so skilled that, when they finished crafting monuments, Emperor Jahangir ordered them to be blinded. This forest, where you played, can be trusted to absorb you.

All this was caused by someone important, an American, used to ordering some work to be finished somewhere else, the back of his head under a beam of light from a window that has been opened on a summer day, allowing the Houston air into the office for a few seconds, before his air conditioning starts going full blast.

CHRONICLE OF A MARRIAGE, FORETOLD

MIKKI WAKES WITH HER HEAD TILTED to the side, her young face, neck, and whole body reaching for a person—somebody with a vague but extremely attractive description, who has been lying with great patience and anticipation next to her and must be tall—though she has been alone in bed for all the hours of the night, as she has been every night here. And yet this unknown person takes up space. During the moment of waking, she realizes that her lips have formed a kiss. She wakes kissing her hand as if it belonged to someone else, but also to her.

This isn't the first morning Mikki has found herself curling up to an invisible, impossibly generous, unfailingly exciting lover. Kissing her hand, conjuring him in bed with her eyes tightly shut and almost feeling that he's making love to her—it's no wonder that her husband, passing by their bedroom once and catching a glimpse of what she was up to, shouted in Arabic from outside their room, "*Wlih*, what are you doing now?"

Though Javed hadn't come in, to see if it was something he could join.

The great difference here, at Ridgebrook, is that Mikki is unseen, alone for now, at this women writers' retreat her husband gave her his indifferent permission to go to. Here each indigenous and Third World woman writer, her artistic ambitions as ancient as cave art, is given a literal small cave, a cabin carved out of the rock. To come here, she had to take a boat. This boat, little more than a small, fragile raft, wouldn't have been safe for children, but in any case, children aren't permitted on this island full of caves.

The feeling of living in a cave is balanced by running hot water and lunch delivered every day. There are strict rules about giving each other ample space to work. Naturally, the caves here have no Internet or phone connections. The decision to prohibit men came out of the cave retreat's history, when, in the early years, some men were caught lurking at the entrances of certain women's caves, or following especially lovely women home under the pretext of "only wanted to make sure you're all right," or any number of other behaviors and actions that, added up, imposed a constant pressure. Still, there are women here who want to make love to her; Mikki knows this as clearly, from their close hugs during the occasional communal dinners, as the fact that at thirty-three, she may be the youngest woman here. Those women talk about missing their kids, giving Mikki indulgent, affectionate looks as if, because she has no children yet, she might be one of theirs.

That Mikki and Javed haven't had kids yet is a source of great apprehension to his semi-agrarian Egyptian family, but not to either Mikki, short for Malliki, or to Javed himself, since both have acknowledged, cordially and with a kind of love, that there is distance between them, and that this space, this distance, rather than being negative, will lengthen the course of their marriage indefinitely. She likes that she can't speak Arabic, that he doesn't know one word of Tamil. His world is one of hookahs and soccer games; hers of rice and lentils, temples resembling ships. The architecture of crushing love, which would wash over them without their trying for it, that defining love that makes every choice different—such love for their children would surely have bound them, she thinks now, the way she did a year ago, when she was actively trying to get pregnant. She still feels reverberations of this intense, imagined baby-love whenever she sees a child with its mother or a cluster of unknown children laughing and playing on the street.

Love, love. Love, love. She stirs herself to get ready, drink a cup of coffee, settle down to work, so that when the old women who bring her lunch in a basket, leaving it at the entrance of the cave, look in on her without realizing that she can see them—when these women watchers come to do their daily task, Mikki will appear in control and studious. A woman dedicated to her art.

Instead of one who, given the smallest excuse, would get back into bed to rendezvous with an imaginary man, a man who, if she were to admit it, strongly resembles a male character she's been attempting, here in this cave, a place of fecundity, to fossilize inside her mind. Then lay his bones out on the page, see what the pieces of him can add up to.

HOW COULD YOU FUCKING TRAP ME IN A BOOK LIKE THIS?

By this time in the morning, he is talking. He's been talking all the days that she's been on "retreat." But there is really no retreat from him. He's a weathered forty to her juicy thirty-three. Unlike her husband, the man is white.

JUST COME HERE AND TALK TO ME. YOU WON'T AN-SWER. I'VE WRITTEN TO YOU A HUNDRED TIMES.

She's counted. He's spoken to her like this, in this presumptuous tone, a hundred times—plaintive, demanding, yet self-assured, as if there is this *thing* between them that he can appeal to, even though she hasn't even named him yet.

HARRY. YOU KNOW I HAVE A NAME. HARRY. CALL ME TO YOU. CALL ME BY NAME.

She can't tell if the stranger is actually someone she knows. If the man she feels she might have spent last night with has the name "Harry" because it is the name of the beautiful boy in first grade whom she has never forgotten. The boy had milk-pale skin and un-real, painted-black lashes over blue eyes, which seemed to illustrate "violet," the color of eyes in the story about the rich little princess from England who found a garden behind the house next door, or the color of eyes that could go coy and spill over with tears, any mo-

ment, like the baby-doll eyes of spoiled, rich, flaxen-haired Amy in
Little Women.

Thinking of *Little Women*, Mikki imagines being warmed before
small fires, making do with scarcity, writing novels by hand, only
to burn them when told they're immoral. In most legends and stories, hearth fires are endemic to caves, but there is no firewood here,
despite the trees that look like they have been cut down by wind,
stumps darkening the snow and and ice outside that cover the island
in a bleak, impossible white. The walls of the cave are freezing to
the touch, and yet thanks to the ambient heat from tall lamps and the
garments she and the other women have been given, insulated robes
and electrically heated pants and shirts, Mikki has started to break a
modest sweat. Even though she's been doing nothing more physical
than writing in a notebook, the best quality, Swiss-bound moles-
kine pages with a story about Harry. Marking the pages indelibly,
with a Mont LeBlanc pen.

Pretending to herself that she's alone, she takes off some of her
clothing.

YES. YES. YES M, YOU ARE SO BEAUTIFUL. I ALWAYS
WANTED TO SAY THAT, OPENLY. EVEN THOUGH I PRE-
TENDED TO BE DISGUSTED BY YOU.

This man, this eccentric character, whom she admits she's been
kissing every night in bed for two weeks now, despite this Harry
person remaining invisible, though with a distant outline reassuring in its elegance—yes, Mikki remembers somehow (though how
on earth, if this particular Harry isn't real, unlike other Harrys she
knows, whose voices she's heard as normal voices, in real life, could
such a memory have been encoded?), she remembers the moment
that Harry, sitting in a room with Mikki and their first-grade teacher,
accused of having bullied her and forced to defend himself, shrank
back from her when she passed by, as if she reeked of shit.

COWSHIT, WAS WHAT I WANTED TO IMPLY. FRESH
COW DUNG, OF A THIRD WORLD PROVENANCE. DUNG

YOU'D SOMEHOW BROUGHT FROM INDIA IN YOUR LIT-
TLE KNAPSACK. DAMN WAS A I PRECOCIOUS SIX-YEAR-
OLD.

If Harry was a real man, as Mikki has recently begun to suspect—
maybe someone she'd had a real-life, passing tussle with, then blocked
out like a terrible hair day—if this fellow, Harry, had harassed her, it
had been by Chinese water torture, by psychological drip by drip. That
was how it struck her, the process, day by day and moment by moment, by which he sought to insinuate himself into her consciousness.

It was days ago. At first, he, from wherever he was, spoke in a
conversational, pleasant tone.

HOW ARE YOU? HOPE THINGS ARE GOING WELL.

Nothing different. Nothing awry. But then his words became in-
trusive, personal, she had thought she ought to tell someone, especially
since she was alone here. That he was pressing on her, like the men who
had once followed women to private caves. That talking back to him
at all—a mistake! An error! The sight of her lips moving, the sound of
her voice, the mere act of her responding to him—had stimulated him
to press her more.

I KNOW IT'S HARD FOR YOU, GETTING ALONG WITH
PEOPLE IN AUTHORITY, WITH COLLEAGUES, HELL, REAL-
LY WITH EVERYONE. I KNOW IT'S ALWAYS JUST SO HARD
FOR YOU. LET ME BE YOUR ALLY, MIKKI. LET ME HELP.

Even in what he was shouting, he kept misspelling her name.
And she wasn't sure, either, whom he meant she ought to be getting
along with. Her husband? A man who never criticized her. Coworkers? Her coworkers had brought cake for her birthday, celebrating at
the daycare where she taught two and three-year-old children as her
day job. Authority? She'd had a big fight once with a white woman at
a bank, who insisted that, since there was a discrepancy in how she
spelled her name on her gas bill versus how the government spelled
that foreign name on her license, she couldn't be who she said she was
and didn't qualify for a promotional account.

O MIKKI YOU'RE SO FINE, YOU'RE SO FINE, YOU BLOW MY MIND. YOU ARE A PASSIONATE PERSON. AN ARTIST. NOT TOO MANY MEN HAVE ANY HOPE OF UNDERSTANDING YOU. YOU HAVE TO LEAVE YOUR HUSBAND AND COME BE WITH ME. IF YOU AREN'T GOING TO LET ME OUT OF HERE, IF YOU INSIST ON KEEPING ME IN HERE, THEN WHY DON'T YOU COME INSIDE THIS PAGE, COME HERE TO ME.

If only this character weren't so awkward, so sincere. Two qualities Mikki has learned not to associate with men. Now she leans back from the desk that faces the entrance of the cave, gets up, assumes a Warrior pose for just a few. Now she walks over to a sculpture she has built. A kind of *installation* is the term for it now, though in her head she refers to these works of art as dioramas.

When she was five, just on the verge of finishing preschool, she made her first diorama, a crayon-colored representation of life with her parents. They had died when Mikki was two. She didn't remember them, strictly speaking, yet she had memorized what memories of them she'd constructed. The photo of her mother graduating from college—surely that must have been the source of Mikki's memory, real and sure, of running toward her mother after getting off a bus, running across a field where the usual warnings about traffic and cars didn't apply and she could just run, be a child, and not have to watch out for anyone.

Her father and mother together, in a bed the size and color of the rafts that carried Mikki and other women artists to their respective caves.

Back to the sculpture Mikki has built on this retreat. This more recent diorama Mikki has built in secret, during this retreat, is of a place she's never been. A house on the edge of a tall cliff, white and cream, the awnings bright with red flags on which she's painted intricate designs. A small cave opens out. Inside of it, there are rooms, like an artist's studio, with a daybed upon which there is a woman and a man, the architecture rendered sharp, the human features indistinct. And the diorama is tiny, scaled small so that it makes the viewer live inside her mind.

There is that story she is writing too, now nearly two hundred pages long, a whole novel, from which this Harry character seems to have sprung, fully formed, uninvited, and won't go back into whatever place he's from, whatever sphere where he exists. As if her imagination cannot contain him.

The diorama, now that she stands back and looks at it, owes a debt to Salvador Dalí. There are no obvious melting clocks, but the sense of wide spaces and unaccounted time, reflecting Mikki's own sense, here, dwelling in caves, that all manner of things could have already happened in the world outside. Nuclear war, the overthrow of a demented president. Her husband, cheating with the neighbor's wife. Not like she hasn't noticed that last thing.

HE'S WHAT? THAT FUCKING DOUCHE. THAT WOM-AN HAS SUCH A BIG ASS. COME ON, MIKKI, COME ON. WHAT ARE YOU WAITING FOR? JUST STEP INSIDE. COME IN. GIVE ME A KISS.

It is ridiculous—she is ridiculous, she knows—but Mikki finds herself pressing her own lips against her wrist, deeply enough to leave a mark in saliva. Isn't this what some famous writer told her students to do, when they felt low? And doesn't it make sense, to inject each rumination with compassion?

But this kissing isn't born of karuna or upekkha, or any of the Hindu/Buddhist words ascribing compassionate motivations that Mikki has nearly forgotten how to say, ever since she married a handsome but agnostic, cruel, perfidious Muslim. The neighbor's wife really is no one of note. Just an exceedingly plump, rosy white woman whose major attributes are near-perfect cleanliness, including housekeeping; robust cooking, including Egyptian treats she re-searched after first meeting Javed at a barbecue; and above all, silence in bed. Mikki knows this because one time, when she'd come home from work without warning, she'd crept up the stairs and even slid open the bedroom door, only to find neighbor's wife, fat and naked, splayed and moaning silently, apparently satisfied beneath Javed.

Neither of them had seen Mikki. But maybe he'd guessed that she knew, when only two weeks later she'd contrived a way to be separated, in this cave.

It wouldn't be the first time an Egyptian man—the descendant of kings, Javed jokingly or not so jokingly likes to remind her—has chosen to consort with pale, fat women. In all the emperors' and even in minor sultans' harems were such women, hair shining, wet lips succulent. Mikki has seen them in period paintings, the nineteenth-century European imagination of a slovenly despot's concubines.

Javed has never personally been slovenly, though. Even in the midst of Javed's taboo lovemaking, the covers of the Tempur-Pedic bed were neatly folded, just as usual.

In his well-paid job as a bond trader, Javed is courteous, pleasant—one might even say *gallant*—with women who literally weigh half what this white neighbor does. Women with sheer stockings over worked-out, slender legs, women who put on their silk blouses and perfume every morning, expecting strange men to admire and covet but not harass them. Javed is stranger than most. Instead of *Playboy* or *Penthouse*, he has a stash of BBB porno magazines—big bold and beautiful, plus sizes, pre-gastric bypass surgery sizes. Folds of flesh gleaming, rendered inhuman and therefore more erotic, huge flattened breasts like those of seals or bloated dogs.

In the state of uncertainty immediately after her discovery, Mikki decided she had to go back to work. Not at the odd jobs she cobbled together. Like, not walking the neighbor's dogs (she'd just as soon avoid seeing the lush garden on the other, hateful side of the fence); not painting old houses for cheap; not standing at the register in the hospital gift shop downtown; not tutoring the Korean children whose parents paid Mikki well for every session, though the kids spoke not a word of English and she not a word of Korean.

Before she'd taken all the odd jobs, she'd lived on what was left of her mother's inheritance. Before she'd married Javed, Mikki was unashamedly writing and making art, living off love, the love her mother's mother had for her, leaving Mikki's mother—baapre! That much money to a girl!—enough so she could be an opera singer. Mikki still loves to play her mother's records.

YOU'VE NEVER COME OVER TO WHERE I AM, PUT YOUR FEET ON MY LAP BEFORE A FIRE, AND LISTENED TO OPERA WHILE DRINKING WINE WITH ME. YOU'VE NEVER LIVED, MY LITTLE MALLIKI.

Malliki. She considers her name. "Now is that sort of like Malachy, the Irish bloke?" one of Javed's old-slash-distinguished British banker friends once asked. Malachy McCourt, the brother of Frank, who'd had the chance to write his memoirs too. Saint Malachy, who'd restored the sanctity of marriage in Ireland. Whose prophecies, for centuries, had been poo-pooed. All of his doomsday prophecies.

YOU HAVEN'T PUT MY MEMOIRS IN THIS BOOK. I'M READING IT. IT'S GOOD, IT REALLY IS. ESPECIALLY THE SCENE WHEN SHE REFUSES TO TAKE HIM BACK AFTER WHAT HE DID. BUT WHAT ABOUT ME? WHAT ABOUT OUR TIMES TOGETHER, THOSE AFTERNOONS YOU SAT PREOCCUPIED WITH ME?

Who will write her memoirs, Mikki wonders. What has she ever done that is really worth writing about? Not children, since she and Javed had never succeeded in creating any. Not Javed, whose ideal woman she fell short of by at least fifty pounds. No one will write about her life, she surmises. And who knows what this Harry guy will do to the pages she'd written. Nothing will stop him from mucking around inside there, distorting the truth.

YOU KNOW I'M NOT GOING TO GIVE UP. I'M TELL-ING YOU, I'M NEVER GIVING UP. COME IN, COME IN, WHEREVER YOU ARE. I'M WAITING.

Since Mikki has never talked out loud to him, she wonders if the man, this character, whoever he is, might be so shocked by her addressing him that he'd stop heckling.

"Hello," she says, out to the dark beyond the cave. "Hello? Hello?" Silence.

Emboldened, she begins to sing an Indian religious song, a bhajan about lotus-eyed gods, while putting the finishing touches on the diorama and thinking, for once not of Dalí, but about De Chirico. Old churches, echoing emptiness. The feel of thrilling desolation similar to how she felt, Mikki remembers, when she first read 'The Crying of Lot 49." That nauseating, sickening feeling that forces of darkness too elusive for her to even name could be responsible, somehow, for all manner of losses and false turns. Thurn und Taxis. Something going bad. A handsome man who, upon closer inspection, might turn out to be no better than a seedily aging movie star, a man no one would fantasize about anymore.

I'LL FANTASIZE ABOUT YOU, MY MIKKI, EVEN IF YOU DON'T COME ANY CLOSER THAN THIS EDGE. SO GRATEFUL THAT YOU'RE NOW TALKING TO ME.

Mikki falls silent. It is nearly time for the old women to make their promenades around each cave, officially clearing excess snow and making sure the pipes were functioning smoothly, unofficially snooping on the indigenous women artists, among whom Mikki alone has no children.

She has a choice to make; she can see that now. She can say yes to this old Harry—

FORTY'S NOT OLD!

—especially since Javed's infidelity frees her from guilt. How she would say yes, she isn't sure. The diorama has grown bigger in the last few hours, though. Of that, she is certain.

There is a haunting, eerie smell—of jasmine hair oil, from when she visited India when she was very young, though she hasn't rubbed her scalp with even one drop in years. That such a long-ago smell should be here now, here in this cave-studio where characters from novels are speaking out loud, is only logical, Mikki supposes.

"What about that whole cowshit thing? Are you that Harry, too?" Her own voice out loud, in the cave.

I WAS WAITING FOR YOU TO FIGURE THAT OUT. THAT WAS THE HARRY FROM ELEMENTARY SCHOOL. DO YOU REMEMBER? HOW HE SAID THAT YOU SMELLED LIKE COWSHIT, AND HOW YOU COULDN'T WASH THE BROWN DIRT FROM YOUR HANDS?

"I guess I remember now," Mikki murmurs.

I'M NOT THAT HARRY. LOOK CLOSER NOW. COME HERE. COME TALK TO ME.

In the diorama, installation, cave within a cave, really, this house built on a cliff, its male and female figures on a bed, one old woman cooking dinner, other old woman sweeping floors, and still another one, witch-like, peering from outside—in the small place she's built, inside this place, Mikki has never imagined Harry, but now she does, giving his heckling, needy voice a human form. Suppose she believes he's not that bully from elementary school. But suppose he isn't innocent either. Suppose he's that white guy about whom she'd gone to Human Resources.

Mikki remembers why, in her book, she might have picked the name Harry.

She has been working a holiday retail shift at the hospital gift shop. Evening shifts. There was a Harry something who was a doctor, psychiatrist, relatively early on in his career, only forty. He'd come every evening, buying chocolates "for my two kids," he said, his wedding ring glinting, even laughing a few times and asking if Mikki had kids.

One day—she remembers this—he came forward, trying to offer her advice. The day after she found Javed cheating. He'd seen the tear marks on her face. That was the moment this adult Harry dared to touch her. She'd been wearing a silk blouse, ruby-colored, with a gold chain and gold earrings. "You look like a Gypsy," he said, completely free of irony. Since of course he didn't know.

I KNOW IT NOW.

Harry (she'd looked him up online, using her phone)—the well-heeled psychiatrist Bostonian, both father and grandfather trained as famous analysts—had no idea of Mikki's ancestry, from real Gypsies who'd once traced their ancestry to western India. How the Romani bone structure, hair, gold jewelry reflected in Mikki's own weren't accidentally similar, but reflective of Mikki's own Tamil forebears. An ancestry that Harry, unlike Javed, wanted to know more about, though he claimed he couldn't be sated by a few minutes' conversation, she was that interesting to him.

WE'LL TALK IN BETWEEN YOU KNOW WHAT. PILLOW TALK. HEH HEH.

She'd made him remember, he said, the history he'd learned as the former leader of a clinic in Somerville for Nepali immigrants. His friendly, progressive views were nonetheless a bit rigid, she thought. Staunchly anti-Palestinian, for one. Not that comfortable with queer identities. Judgmental about sex workers forming a union. Almost Puritanical in his tastes.

WE HARDLY GOT TO TALK! I TOUCHED YOU THAT ONE TIME. WE EVEN KISSED IN THAT GIFT SHOP. I CHEATED ON MY WIFE AND KIDS. BUT THEN YOUR BOSS SAW YOU, AND YOU REPORTED ME TO HUMAN RESOURCES.

"I didn't report you, actually," Mikki says, still softly, looking at the entrance of the cave but not seeing anyone, wondering if the old women are coming today.

WAIT, COME AGAIN.

"I didn't report you. I only went to Human Resources to see if it was allowed, any kind of dating between someone like me, a part-time employee in the gift shop, and a tall person, a fine person, like you. Doctor and all. Because I liked the way you kissed. Just that one time."

KEEP TALKING.

"I only wanted to make sure it was allowed, what we would do. I mean, if we did anything."

WHAT DO YOU WANT TO DO?

The old woman assigned to clean Mikki's cave comes then. She sweeps out the dust that, even in snow, remains all over the island, a testament to its hot, twisted birth out of volcanoes with grand gusto, like millions of champagne bottles popping.

BELIEVE ME, I WANT YOU TO MAKE AS MUCH NOISE AS YOU WANT.

They all say those things in the beginning, Mikki thinks with irritation. She nods to the old woman, pretends to work.

"What else?" she finally speaks the words softly, thinking that perhaps he won't hear. Her hands are in the diorama now, now that the old woman has finished and gone, sparing only a quick glance of curiosity to Mikki with her taut self-dialogue. Now she is alone, Mikki reminds herself, feeling strange and desolate, like she is being given a fake thing, a false clue, a hopeless and demoralizing view from a window, like Pynchon's crazy psychiatrist in "The Crying of Lot 49," calling the heroine Oedipa Maas in the middle of the night. Mikki could swear that not only her fingers, but her whole *arms* are in this diorama now, her whole face and neck and hair and, within minutes, her whole body.

And now she can see the features of the man and woman on the bed. In this newly warm, cave-like space, so much warmer than the one she's been in for the women's retreat, Mikki can make out the dim outline of a bed covered in a down blanket. And in this large raft-sized bed lies someone, not the Harry she'd seen in the hospital, the real man, albeit white, who'd seen her sad, and alone. This Harry *isn't* that psychiatrist who, until that afternoon, when he'd first touched her ruby-silken-covered shoulders, then her face, and then kissed her, had never done more than smile at her warmly. It was a moment like a moment from the inexpensive paperbacks the hospital gift shop was selling. The moment of a handsome, distinguished stranger kissing a much younger woman whom he's seen in distress.

This isn't him, Malliki thinks, excited. It actually isn't that random guy from the gift shop, whom she had feared would get her in trouble if anyone saw the video footage. She'd gone to Human Resources to assure her job as being safe. At that point, Mikki couldn't know, even, if Javed would leave her for some BBB. If Javed would keep essentially bankrolling her art in exchange for Mikki pretending not to have seen what she had seen. The odalisque with her slick, decadent rolls of flesh and Javed, uncharacteristically subdued and content.

YOU MEAN YOU DIDN'T KNOW WHO I WAS? I'M CRUSHED.

This isn't a "Harry" she has known before. This is an unknown person. He turns and could almost frighten her with eyes like a sorcerers'.

I WANT TO FIND OUT WHO YOU ARE.

That's her voice, not his. Mikki finds herself speaking the same language he does.

I'M GOING TO MAKE YOU WISH YOU HAD COME TO ME SOONER.

HARRY, THAT SOUNDS LIKE A PROMISE.

DO YOU EVER HAVE TO GO BACK?

THIS CAVE IS MINE AS LONG AS I WANT IT.

THEN MY JOB IS TO MAKE YOU WANT TO STAY.

YOU'RE DOING FINE.

And so it goes, this back and forth—so loud inside each other's minds—

EACH OTHER'S HEARTS, they say in unison.

Until, instead of being able to talk spontaneously at all, and instead of moving wherever she likes, Mikki finds herself pinned to the diorama's bed, displayed, not nude but even more exposed, making a kissing motion toward her own outstretched right hand. But this time Harry, the *right* Harry, is kissing her hand too, and holding her there with his whole body, which feels heavy and immovable, as if it has been carefully glued into place.

HEITOR

ONE OCTOBER EVENING IN THE Year of Our Blessed Lord, fifteen hundred and forty-five, a male Indian slave once advertised as being in the most robust health, his young skin shining like sturdy striped mahogany from all the healing scars of past whippings, stood chained in the cool courtyard of the convent in Evora, in Imperial Portugal. He was awaiting punishment.

As a mercy, one of the sisters had allowed him to continue wearing a loincloth, though, at the moment of his death, he knew that even this insignificant black rag would be forced off. The covering was for the benefit of the fifty or so women, some of them girls, who lived in the convent for lifetimes, and who, like Mariana, a sixteen-year-old novitiate, were never supposed to see any man's genitals, yet who had contrived once to see Heitor sleeping on the ground outside the stables, had found his body beguiling, had ordered him to stand guard outside her bedroom door on several nights, though he had resisted doing more.

When death came, it would be a gunshot. Heitor would not be blindfolded. But no one would prevent him from closing his eyes when pistols were raised, and seeing vivid memories.

As a child, Heitor was taken at the age of seven by slave traders from Lisbon, remote but proud descendants of da Gama, who'd entered the Indian Ocean a century before. Heitor's tiny mother was struck to the ground in a village in Bengal after the elders, without informing her, captured her son and then sold him. Small for his age, easily bound, Heitor was brought by ship and force, by sons of spice traders, by members of large prosperous companies, brothers of men who had settled in Goa, the place in India where the first human remains of the Old World were found. Those traders had married the most beautiful Indian women they could find. With jewels stolen from their own ancestors, the women were converted to Christianity.

Heitor was sold for an elite price to work for the nuns of Evora, and their novitiates. Indian, Chinese, Japanese slaves were bought and sold in Portuguese cities, believed to be more intelligent, and less potent as males, than African slaves, and thus allowed to work in the convents.

As a child, he was striking for his quietude, his gentleness, which formed a graceful harmony with the aggressive energy of his hard and strong limbs.

Beginning at the quick, observant, diligent age of eight, Heitor was saved from harder labor, given to the convent's Indian gardener and its cook. They were nowhere to be found on his last night. The men, lovers, were hiding for fear of being chained. They were both drunk and in despair that they had not foreseen his fate. His two passionate, adoptive fathers, who knew how to grow the choicest sprigs of lavender to place on dinner plates, also knew the art of capoeira, a fighting form evolved to fend off slave traders, one of many methods of survival that Indians would learn from Brazilian men, the black crewmembers who frequented taverns and inns in the city where the cook and gardener were sent to do errands. These crewmembers, in their turn, bought young Japanese women as slaves and bragged of how much they had enjoyed them.

The cook and gardener also were devoted to pleasure. Believing Heitor should have the same, they taught him capoeira, cooking, and all the other arts. The men had intended Heitor to inherit their small trove of possessions. Those two men, slaves of the convent, suggested which girls in the village Heitor could make love with in secret.

Mariana, the rich virgin who desired Heitor, didn't know about those girls.

If the oldest and most powerful of the nuns of Montemor had known about the welcoming village girls, each of whom were after all some respectable tradesman's daughter, by now the police would have torn off Heitor's balls and forced him to go oneliving and working.

Less than an hour remained until Heitor would be killed for different crimes.

Every week, at least two policemen searched the convent's surrounding gardens for criminals, all seeking sanctuary on holy lands, all trying to evade having their hands and feet cut off for stealing. No one dared covet the king's gold, won back as it had been only a few centuries before from the Moors, from those stealthy, marauding dark ones—and before that, seized by the Portuguese explorers and traders, those daring wise ones, those Europeans unafraid to travel to the far end of the world.

Mariana was from one of Lisbon's wealthiest slave trading families. A year away from permanent vows, she talked of leaving the convent. She teased Heitor, allowed him to see her nude body, left him gifts at the slave quarters, even compelled him to stand near while she took her bath. She pled sick so she missed prayers; through cook and gardener, she had sent word asking for him, only him. Her merchant father could have bought Heitor from the nuns, at Mariana's pleasure. Terrified of being sold again, Heitor pretended to run away.

Caught, again enslaved, Heitor could die knowing no one would ever learn the truth. That he, Heitor, had stolen back the conqueror's gold, the stolen Christian gold, stolen before that from Indian temples and palaces, from statues melted down so that the features of gods and goddesses were long ago forfeit. That gold, accumulated, stacked, a pestilence to the native people, a providence to the Portuguese, and which they seized, triumphant and knowing, at their first opportunity.

The bags of gold he'd filled up with pilfered coins, only a few at a time, would pay for Sita to escape to America. She would be a stowaway, a crewmember's concubine. To gain her freedom, Sita would smother this man, once he was drunk and asleep. Once Sita freed herself from him, whoever would be her last master, as soon as the ship reached Manhattan Island, she would tell her descendants that it was Heitor, a man possessed of his full powers though forced to pretend otherwise, whose gold had carried them across the waves. A man who'd been a slave, yet staked the mother of his beloved child, so she and the baby she carried could hide in the New World.

NEWBERRY

VINITA TOOK HER LAST DRAG from the stolen cigarette. From under a tree outside the salon, she watched the morning ladies as they passed. She felt proud of how much smoother her own skin was, and how much flatter her stomach than theirs, even though she couldn't tell if any of them had given birth, and she wouldn't have judged their bellies if they had. But none of them walked holding the hands of their children. These women paid others to do the morning school run.

"You really shouldn't smoke here," one of the women muttered, making brief eye contact with Vinita before walking on.

Being this close to so much money made Vinita want to smoke. She'd made sure that the purse she lifted the cig from was not only designer, but well stocked with packets of nicotine gum bursting from one of the pockets, so she could tell herself that by stealing she was helping the owner. Vinita wasn't one to lie to herself, though. What she and Marco were planning had nothing to do with helping anyone. Maybe they wouldn't even help themselves. But they were in it now; she'd taken the money. They had no choice but to finish it.

Later it would be tempting to offer up reasons like: "My father had a stroke and we needed to pay for a home nurse," or "Marco was frightened that he'd be deported because his visa was expiring in a month." These were facts but weren't exactly excuses. The real fact, the one she allowed herself to enjoy as much as the cigarette, was that if they pulled it off, Vinita would never have to stand on this street corner again.

In this city, what counted as a city, a single street that substituted for city streets that were riotous, out of control, lavish with loud inequalities, on this staid Newbury Street, Vinita had spent the past year hating herself but saying, in her mind, how much she hated everyone. It gave her flickers of amusement, sometimes, to think the words "I hate you all" as she was smiling the smile her boss Leo swore "guaranteed gratuity." To think those words while all along saying a comforting *mm-hmm* or *really?*, while Vinita settled a stressed-out customer in the deluxe manicure chair.

The regulars paid for manicures daily. Then they went on their way to the Commons, stopped at the N'espresso store for coffee, nothing more, probably liking the absence of pastries, distractions. Then to the Taj Hotel, just near the park, for champagne brunch or a meeting. Maybe dressed down in new-looking jeans, high heels, sleeveless blouse under a blazer, if the woman was on the executive team of a biotech or pharma company, or even one of the younger hedge funds or venture capital setups that had their unpretentious offices upstairs in some shop building on Newbury. Nothing too fancy.

But Leo. Leo's name a jinx even to think.

Leo said Vinita looked a lot like Rachel Roy. The designer? The pert Indian girl born in the US? The one linked to famed black sportswear entrepreneurs, though her own parents were Keralite Christians, just like Vinita's. Rachel with her "good" straightened hair, which Vinita copied. The rumored "Becky with the good hair" from the Beyoncé video about Jay-Z's cheating. More than once, Vinita imagined herself photographed like Rachel in a recent glossy *W Magazine* spread, draped in white silk, pushed down onto a couch with her young husband's muscled and naked back showing. Like Leo's back.

Vinita's smoke break was well timed. A customer she loathed was just leaving. Soon three more women came to take her place on a backbench. It wasn't the woman's obesity Vinita detested. It was that the fat cow had once accused Leo of stealing. That was a few years ago, under the previous owner, who'd thankfully let go of the whole thing when Vinita saw the supposedly missing gold chain dripping from the customer's pocket. The thoughtless woman, who'd fallen asleep during her pedicure, had forgotten that she put it there to keep it safe. The woman grudgingly apologized without looking at Leo, went on about the necklace having "sentimental value," but Vinita took it as proof. That people like that woman deserved to have things taken from them.

That perhaps it could be justified, how, using the hacking skills she'd picked up in college, last night Vinita stole forty thousand dollars from this nail salon franchise's overseas bank account.

Vinita's boss—*Don't call him Leo,* she told herself—was still away, still on a planned two-week vacation to a spa in San Francisco where he would be without Internet or cell phone access until next week. His absence meant Vinita was unofficially in charge, overseeing the receptionists and the front desk, making sure there were fresh flowers and water jugs containing lemon and lime slices within customers' reach. Her boss had recently become the franchise owner of this nail shop, one in a chain. The others were in malls in Chicago, Detroit and Oakland. Places Vinita knew she and Marco would have to avoid going to, once everything played out.

Today would be her last day at work, if all went as planned. Only eight hours remained. The normal routine meant taking her lunch break at around one, to bring her boyfriend Marco a sandwich like she often did. Then she would come back with a bag from the dubious Indian "street food" restaurant. That would make it credible for her to call in sick tomorrow with "stomach problems," giving her and Marco about six extra hours to disappear. And in that time, she could make sure that the metadata changes she'd made, to make it look like hackers in India had stolen the money, didn't contain any mistakes.

Like checking over work before turning in a school exam. Like catching glimpses of others' papers, whenever she could.

The owners of the nail salon franchise were rumored to be related to the heirs of a Malaysian syndicate. But far from being brutal overlords, these living remnants of the pre-Mao Triad system didn't interfere with the salons. The night Leo, drunk, told Vinita about the syndicate, she'd promptly looked up "Asian gangs" on Wikipedia. The salons, like other shell businesses, were where the syndicate supposedly laundered money. There was nothing visibly different about the franchise's "miscellaneous expenses" bank account. Their passwords were appallingly easy to crack. The previous owner of the franchise, a chubby, comfy Mrs. Jairaman, was now retired to India. She'd frequently browsed bargain Indian websites, ordered cheap decorations from New Delhi cottage industries, and even used Indian Independence Day and her own birthday for the account login passwords. Every so often, a good-looking, slick-haired Indian male "relative" would come to visit Mrs. Jairaman, chatting about the weather with Vinita when she brought him tea. Then he'd leave with heavy-looking leather briefcases.

Vinita discovered the old laptop in a closet, left behind by Mrs. Jairaman. The screen still opened into the record of the bank account number and location when "Jairaman" was typed in, which Vinita tried doing once, long before the thing with Marco, simply out of curiosity.

"All I was hoping was to confirm the old biddy looked at porn," Vinita said, showing Marco the printouts of the account's past balances. Its maximum was in the tens of millions, she noted; its fluctuations, by week, varied by as much as four hundred grand. "No one would ever notice, like, forty thousand," Vinita said.

But Marco didn't bother going there with her. He never even brought up having money, or more accurately not having it. All he said, looking at the papers with their tiny, narrow columns, was, "Damn, am I lucky my girl's a math person. Our children will be geniuses." Now Vinita had to hold onto the scheme for both of them.

Back inside after her smoke break, pouring fresh water into the pitcher at each of the stations, Vinita mentally rehearsed the steps again.

At 1 p.m., two and a half hours from now, she'd walk the four blocks down Newbury, in the direction where suburban commuters got on the Mass Pike. Newbury Comics was very close to that Mass Ave end of the street. That was where she'd first met Marco almost a year ago. He'd surprised her by not looking at the usual vaporizing villains and big-breasted women comics, but actually reading Gene Yang's *American Born Chinese* graphic novel. Very different than the *zap 'em* and *shazzam!* stuff Vinita herself happened to be buying.

While Vinita waited her turn in line, Marco—barrel-chested, black-eyed, shaggy-haired with his soft beard—was staring at her from over the top of the novel. When she saw the title and smiled, he hadn't seemed to realize he'd already earned a thousand points toward getting her in bed.

"My ex-girlfriend was from Beijing," he'd told Vinita, in a voice of needless and sheepish apology. "I just couldn't deal with all her gambling. She even took her teenage sons out to Foxwoods. And no matter how I tried, I couldn't love her food. I'm Mexican."

Hesitant, he'd tried out Spanish on her, and Vinita answered, near fluent, admittedly a little formal, remembering her AP courses in high school Spanish. The ones she'd done in homage to the actress and lifestyle blogger Gwyneth Paltrow, who'd once lived with a host family in Spain. Marco, chuckling, said he'd stick with English.

"Your parents came from India, didn't they? Doctors or something, right?" he'd guessed, as if he knew this as a fact, though neither of her parents were doctors, and in fact there were no doctors in her family. "Your eyes. Indian eyes," he'd said. Like those two proofs that she was beautiful made it impossible for thirty-year-old bohemian Marco not to fall for Vinita.

Marco was a softie, no question. Vinita wasn't going to think he was a wuss, though, not today. For the twenty-four hours, about two months ago, that the two of them believed she was pregnant, Marco and not Vinita was the one crying his silly and impractical tears of happiness. Naming their daughter and praying out loud that she would have Vinita's eyes. Why he was so sure the baby was female, she had no clue, except Vinita suspected it had to do with Marco being a poet.

How else could one explain his joy in accidentally fathering a child with Vinita, who at that point he'd only been dating for a month?

Despite Marco's deadening day job as attendant for one of the Early Bird Special! parking lots on Newbury, his mind remained both starry and suggestible. He still sent his poems, written in English with crucial Spanish words, the sound of which Vinita admitted she liked, to little magazines that she'd never heard of, nowhere that paid him actual money. He still submitted poems widely, every week.

Marco could have stuck with it, writing poems eternally, for all Vinita cared. Probably, she would've become bored with him. She would have moved in with Leo. Let her cool boss be Damon Dash to Vinita's beauteous Rachel Roy; get her nails done, like Rachel did, so she could scratch up his velvety skin. She would have broken Marco's heart, left that old sentimental screw-up to languish.

All changed, "changed utterly," Marco repeated, on Monday morning, and here it was the Thursday with only days before Leo's— before her boss's—return. Before she'd gone, Leo had somehow earned Mrs. Jairaman's trust. He was the one responsible now for maintaining and securing the syndicate's money, Leo was the one thugs would come after and punish, if those criminals did discover the paltry but still missing forty grand.

The men of the syndicate were criminals, murderers, pimps, Vinita reminded herself. No different, except in sophistication about skirting punishment under the law, from any of the hedge funders and their wives on Newbury. Just people who should be stolen from.

Leo, the name she shouldn't say. Leo, the one who'd smiled so sweetly at her when Vinita, looking through *Paper Magazine*, lingered for a while on an old photo of Madonna visiting Malawi, holding a beautiful black child Vinita hoped the pop star had adopted legally. "Vinnie, let's go and make us one of those," Leo said, squeezing her shoulders.

Damn Leo for always being involved with someone else. For not seeming to care when she started dating Marco, as long as it didn't stop her from going out with Leo too, for drinks, when he wanted. For never answering his phone in front of her, but always checking it for texts, for sexts, chuckling. Diversified.

"Decisions and revisions that a minute will reverse," Marco had muttered, over and over, after the episode Monday, when he had almost killed a child. He hadn't been drinking—he never drank. "Kills the brain cells I need for writing poetry," Marco always said, when Vinita wanted to go out for a few beers. But that morning, Marco was distracted. He had been working on a new poem in his head. That was allowed, but he'd made the error of getting behind the wheel while daydreaming. The three-year-old son of some corporate vice president, a blond boy actually dressed in seersucker, Vinita saw from the newspaper photo, had nearly been hit when Marco backed his black Land Rover out of its space too rapidly. Marco hadn't thought to check below, behind. The child was standing, unseen, watching God knew what. Maybe composing a poem too.

No harm was done, per se, the child quite startled by the mammoth car moving sudden and heavy toward him, not stopping, as if seeking him, the mother having to snatch the boy away, but the boy's mother was nervous, a wreck for how she'd been texting on her cell phone and not holding his hand. ("Probably sexting some tennis pro she's cheating with," Vinita said). The mother said Marco was "dangerous," and now that Back Bay white woman was threatening to have Marco fired. And deported.

The woman's famous portfolio manager husband hadn't even donated to the RNC. Vinita checked his campaign contributions on the Internet.

"It's the Trump age, what can you do," said Anthony, Marco's boss at the parking lot. A tall, mournful-looking man from Ethiopia, Anthony had sympathy for Marco, but just so much. Anthony hadn't said anything when Marco pleaded, somewhat desperate, not to lose his job. "But we could all get deported," Marco's boss reminded him.

"She could Homeland all of us. It takes one call. Thank God your visa is still valid, for now. You have a chance to move out of her way. Take ten days, man. Settle things down. But please, do go. I'll have your last paycheck next Friday."

Marco, like Vinita and her parents twenty-two years before, was all along planning to overstay his visa. He lived in a sublet in East Boston, in nice-weather walking distance from Newbury. His landlord never asked for reference checks, proof of citizenship, or any other paperwork. He drove using a fake license that his cousin Hector, who'd become an American citizen last year, charged him a discount to obtain.

"If you can give me twenty grand, I'll get you and your lady to Canada, easy," Hector promised Monday night, when Marco couldn't get the word "deportation" out of his head. Luckily, Hector didn't know that, by Wednesday, Vinita had stolen twice that amount.

At just past one, Vinita eased on a delicate black cardigan to cover the skimpy camisole she always wore inside the salon. Her shoulders were hurting, as if she'd carried heavy loads, but all she'd done was lift bowls of water, the larger ones for clients having pedicures with special stone washes. One of the treatments even flecked their skin with gold. Vinita, hands still sparkling though she wore no wedding ring, slipped through the door of the salon, only to find her whole body pressed against Leo's. He stood still in the doorway, blocking her from getting out, but looking, to anyone, like a macho boyfriend pressing flush against her. She almost moaned. She had forgotten the lemon and sweaty smell of Leo Jones.

"Too early in the day for dirty dancing, girl," Vinita heard in the background, the receptionist tittering at the sight of her breasts crushed against Leo.

Leo, unsmiling, took Vinita's hand and pulled her outside.

"What," she said weakly, not questioning why Leo was back two days early from vacation, already accepting that he knew what she'd stolen.

But he didn't. Or, rather, what he knew now would soon stop being relevant.

"V, I really, really liked that Ashis Nandy shit," he said. "I read the whole thing on the plane. *The Intimate Enemy?* Shame, and all of it? It would have resonated deep for Malcolm X. Thank you for giving it to me."

Why had she given it to him? She couldn't remember now. Probably there was a day he'd seen the cover peeking from the bag she carried, a tattered canvas tote, only something cheap. Liking that it was so out of place on Newbury, Vinita wore the old bag like a signature, for which Leo teased her. "That's like your new berry," Leo had said. "Your new thing looking so delicious." She was new to the manicure shop then. Long before she'd ever seen Marco. "Sweet like your body," Leo whispered, making Vinita giggle. The bag, so faded now, had once glowed with vivid red cherries and strawberries.

The books in her bag, including the one by the leftist sociologist Nandy, were from her father, who was once a literature professor in Khottayam, but now scarcely ever left their Brockton house, and often lived as if alone. The house had once belonged to crack dealers. It stood opposite a methadone clinic, where addicts reported every morning at seven, oddly cheerful and carrying Starbucks, usually obediently lining up, but sometimes ugly and obstreperous. On a bad day, they'd stand in the street shouting oaths or roaring incoherently. Vinita's father couldn't sleep through their tirades. Most mornings, she woke to him at the window, peering from behind the white lace curtains her mother had begged Vinita to sew. Years before, Vinita's mother had gone blind. But the lace, the touch of lace, like bursts of berries on her tongue, like sunlight still generous on her face and hands, this her mother said she still enjoyed.

Vinita's father had supported the family. Worked night shifts as a janitor at a hospital. Taught adjunct courses in South Asian history until he had his stroke. Her father could still see and notice everything. Vinita propped his chair near the window, and every morning, the most exuberant among the recovered addicts waved to him, calling, "Hey, Gandhi, what up?" and "See something you like?" They didn't know how his expression, regardless of mood, would stare men down. Would stare Vinita down as well, when she arrived home from bar nights with Leo, late nights when Leo told her about the syndicate, "the life." Saying, "I mean, you need to know. Where all the money is. Where it comes from. 'Cause one day, baby, I'll train you to be like my right hand."

That was before Marco. Marco and the peaceful temptation.

Now, back from his California vacation, on this morning when Vinita had already vowed to stop thinking of him, Leo tipped her chin upward, looked serious, asked, "Is your dad okay?" A few months ago, she told him about the stroke; one day she'd had to call in sick. Leo had even come out to Brockton. Actually, because of Leo, Vinita went back to the church. Only for a single service, but after long years.

It was the music she loved. AME Church on Turner Street, Brockton. Vinita had worn a hat, hair tucked inside. Kind of a brown late-night-to-early-morning impeccable sophisticate, with her well-painted red lips and tailored dress but punk nose ring. A sort of Indian Gwen Stefani. With Leo like Tony Kanal, the brown boyfriend Gwen had long ago discarded. During the service, Leo took Vinita's hand. Then during the singing, he was silent, "because I just wanted to listen to you sing. It was so beautiful," he'd said.

Why didn't she and Leo get together at the start, before they'd become "friends"? Or at least move in together months ago, or even go on proper dates? They'd never even kissed full on the lips. Only the cheek tantalizers, as Vinita thought of them. Those moments of air kissing. Leo's lips had come too close to hers, when with a bold lick of her tongue she could have tasted his soft mouth.

"I would've loaned you money. Why didn't you ask?" she could hear Leo saying, in a conversation they would never have.

"Don't waste your life," her father always cautioned her. "None of us knows how long we'll get to be ourselves." Vinita, an only child, had been his hope. But then she'd only gotten into an average college, and in that place, there'd been a small scandal where she had been accused of stealing her roommate's diamond ring and emerald choker, the two together worth thirty grand. Vinita hadn't been able to prove it wasn't her, and in the end, she'd left the college completely, muttering about "racism" and "mediocre assholes," thinking to work awhile and save up, then reapply to somewhere really good. Now it was nearly two years later and Vinita was twenty. According to her father, she was headed "nowhere." Spending her money on things like Japanese hair straightening and a cable TV subscription, wasting her time reading *Us* magazine and watching e-News. Picking up extra shifts at the salon, where she would play receptionist, only to spend the money going out with Leo or, more recently, helping out Marco with his rent.

Vinita resolved her father would never find out how she had paid for the home nurse. The one who would sit patiently and read to her father. The one who'd be paid to remember that her mother loved the sun. The nurse was supposed to start tomorrow morning.

"I'll take a quick lunch," Vinita promised Leo, on his first day back from vacation, as they stood now in the sun on Newbury just a few steps outside the salon.

Before he could answer, the receptionist poked her head out the front door, calling to Leo, "You need to come quick." The girl in all black didn't look at Vinita, didn't say hello or excuse herself for interrupting them, or even make polite eye contact. That bitch had slept with Leo once, Vinita remembered. So had the other two girls at the desk.

With a quick nod to Leo before setting off, Vinita walked at her usual, preening pace down Newbury, carrying her old bag with berries painted on the front, sashaying just a little bit when gangs of European boys who liked the cafés on Newbury slowed to check her out.

The way Vinita sashayed for Leo's enjoyment, sometimes. Watching her walk out of a room. His gaze on her felt like an oil spill. Viscous, too heavy. As if she'd feel too content with him to ask why he sometimes carried a gun. As if, once he pressed himself down on her, she'd never slide away. As if she would stay beneath him forever, her painted talons caressing his back.

When Vinita's mother had first gone blind, she asked Vinita's help to keep doing her nails. "I can't see the color, but I can feel where they're painted," she'd said, smiling, still gentle. Her MS diagnosis was a fact of life by then, like where they lived. Vinita was a freshman in college, before the incident, carefree in the dorm room watching Rihanna videos.

Leo taking off Vinita's camisole, nuzzling her young breasts. Leo in the salon backroom sitting before a laptop, reviewing the whole month's take. No shirt, only his baggy shorts. Proud of his stomach too. As he ought to be, at thirty-nine.

She could hear Leo's voice with hers now, talking in bed. As if they'd had a night like that, even one night, and she had not imagined it. As if they'd started living together. "That's some cool shit," Leo would mutter, settling back against the pillows, back into the Ashis Nandy book once he fucked her. "Check out how he starts up this thing. Camus. 'Through a curious interposition of the times, it is innocence that is called upon to justify itself.'"

🐘

By two forty-five, instead of heading back to the salon, Vinita and Marco were driving down the Pike. She didn't want to take the chance of those extra few hours; at two, from a payphone, she'd called Leo, said she felt sick and had to go home for the day. Over the phone, he said nothing that wasn't professional. Leo would deduct five hours from Vinita's sick days. In the background, she heard one of the front desk girls laughing with him. She heard him quiet on the other end, patient but preparing to go.

Vinita would never see Leo again. Never hold him. That was what she had decided four days ago, the morning Marco called her in a panic about being arrested. When it felt like it was too hard to have faith in any other choice. When suddenly it felt like rescuing Marco could be a way that she rescued herself.

Both her and Marco's cell phones had been dismantled so they couldn't be tracked. This van unmarked, bags and fake papers in the backseat, as Marco's cousin had organized. Vinita's new name would be Kim, as in Kardashian. She and Marco would have to be the bolder migrants, heading farther north. Canada. No Trump. And if the syndicate people pressed Leo, which they might not, and if he figured out she'd taken the money, which he had no reason to do, Vinita was sure Leo would never lead them to her parents. He'd find someone else to pin it on. She could count on him.

In the backseat, guidebooks on the state of Alberta. The money left after paying their fixer was already in a Cayman account, according to the new records Vinita set up and checked on the new laptop, right before she started driving. It was a nest egg, even after Vinita had also left a wad of cash in a drawer, with instructions to her father, whose facial droop and weakness all on his left side had left his major hand intact, right dominant. Two plane tickets for her parents to Cochin via Bombay, Cochin where Vinita's grandparents on her father's side still lived, vendors of the spice trade that had persisted over centuries. They hawked bottles of various cheap spices they labeled as "saffron" from a roadside stall. Just in case the syndicate's men threatened her parents, or ever came to collect what they considered debt.

There were glossy magazines in the backseat, pillows, chocolates. A day trip, two lovers, not a thing that could be objected to. There were hours ahead to drive, but she wouldn't share them. She wouldn't have trusted Marco to drive them anywhere, not now. But he didn't mind. A passenger, he slept, indifferent, the lines of a new poem stretching themselves tight, plucking the music from his sleeping thoughts and closing his kind eyes.

ASHA IN ALLSTON

THE ONE THING YOU PROMISED, you *swore*, was that you'd never allow her inside our house. Remember, when we came here, you believed we'd have four sons. An optimistic belief but not impossible, since I come from a family of ten, you from just five, and the astrologers had said we'd have sons. Their predictions made us get engaged.

You said this was the house where we'd grow old. I say "this was the house" because, though you don't know it yet, there was a kitchen fire last week. Your patio, gutted. Water damage to the tiles, the basement. Cheap melted plastic and disjointed machines, the sound of a soft female voice droning all her broken syllables. Don't bother asking what became of her. I won't answer. You shouldn't care. You have her download stored somewhere permanent. You have what you need to make as many new Malins as you need. I can't say the same for making me.

I know you've got enough to think about, nodding and bowing your way through the summer retreat with VC's, trying to make sure you keep your job. Everyone at Ganesha Inc. is aware now, aren't they, not only engineers, even corporate, that Malin became one with you, somehow? That like an animal researcher who gets too attached to his primates, you seek to protect her still?

I shouldn't say "her." I never forget *what* Malin is. A mannequin with hardware, an old-style robot encased in new-style coverings, turning her tricks. A plastic dream. The sum consciousness of notebooks, graph paper, comic books you used to read and collect long years before I ever met you, where women's breasts were large and conical, leg muscles strong and well-defined so they can leap between buildings. Malin's a fucking joke, the sister of inflatables. She isn't real. She never will be real. It doesn't matter that her legs and arms can move so precisely. Her smile isn't her own. She can't own anything.

But that must be why you love her. Malin has nothing to lose.

That old stupid question: *What does she have that I don't?* I know the answer without having to ask. Her sight. She can see better than most people, nearly as good as an eagle. But that reflects on you, not her. You designed and built her laser gaze. I recall just how intent you were on that detail.

I was just back from the neurologist, a cold morning that left me shivering. The doctor in JP was still too—what? I couldn't say. Empathic? Guarded? Practical? All of the above? to make my diagnosis definitive, even though I'd read enough by then not to be fooled. The best we could hope for was relapsing remitting. There would be good days, even Richard Pryor funny days, days I could walk and even dance a little bit. But the doctor wouldn't confirm the name of my disease, let alone the number of bad days. "How many children do you have?" he'd asked, the absentminded and respectable doctor.

"Zero," I forced myself to say, only because at that moment, I craved his pity.

By ten-thirty I'd taken a cab home because of how pressed-down I felt, held back by the silence in the examining room, the sense of life moving so fluidly all around me. I hadn't exposed myself on public transportation—by "exposed" I mean even sitting on the T among strangers—because of how frightened I felt. What would go first? Speech or hearing? Memory or mind? Where would the plaques surface, white clearings where there should be brain forest? I did not want to know.

You had equipment spread on the table, a naked blond woman open and smiling before you, flat on her back. You had a headlamp on and tiny screwdrivers and tools I did not recognize. But most of all you had the room, and there was no way I could have entered it. It wasn't until three weeks afterward that, spent after your run around Jamaica Pond, you came to me smiling, wanting to make love before you showered, and I had to show you the neurology report, the patient education handout. Wait for you to read it. Blame and even hate myself for turning you so grave. We stayed in bed for hours. I can't remember what we did, except that I had you completely, you had me, yet all the while, I felt empty-handed.

That was six months ago. Nothing has changed since. Everything has changed. There is a taut anticipation in our lives. We wait for the worst. I lose my balance often. You catch me before I fall. You're dutiful, perfect. The best neurologists. Second and third opinions. The articles you clip, saying it might be Lyme's disease, Guillain-Barre, benign tumor, even a mild case of herpes. Anything reversible. Anything but what it is. And yet, the more attentive you are, the less I have of you, the less you're here. You disappear into the closed garage, the place where I once thought of gassing myself while I still could. While I still have enough control to decide. But the garage is your space. The place where Malin was constructed, after a big check was written to your AI program from no less than Paul Allen; after your postdoc at Stanford and you being recruited to a Kendall Square biotech; after you'd earned a big enough bonus to bring me to you from India and bid high for this house.

And now there won't be any sons, or daughters. There won't be birds singing in the trees. Sunrises, sunsets. First my balance, then all my senses, ephemera, sometimes working, other times blocked by muffled synapses, ghosts in the machine of me. My cellular catastrophes.

But you'll have Malin, won't you? Yes. This being, first inert, named after a Swedish actress, your crush from a superhero movie at first. Now quite a bit more. This thing that's come alive. She can think now. You look like you could spend eternity watching her think.

No doubt, when you build her next version, salvaging whatever you must after the fire, she'll tell you how frightened she was. When I approached her, leaning on my cane, dousing her with kerosene, lighting the match. At first not caring if I burned myself too, but in the end running while she stayed still. I'd glued her feet. I'd tried to think of every possibility.

I couldn't kill her. It shouldn't surprise you, given that I couldn't kill myself either. The fire was only for her physical body. Your files, your work in the garage, I left intact. So, you will be able to rebuild, of that I'm confident, and also—that you'd rebuild me if you could. That if you had to choose between Malin and me, there'd be no choice. But, my love, we don't get to choose

THE LIFE YOU SAVE ISN'T YOUR OWN

.

By her forty-third birthday, Seema Venkatramanan had almost stopped minding how much she'd messed up her life. By then her wrong decisions had all bloomed like seeds. They'd flowered into vines that bound her tight, though without the titillation of some fifteenth-century naked satyr-nymph, S&M scenario.

First, in college, making the mistake of thinking that she didn't love him enough, and that they would never be alike enough, Seema had broken up with her tall and handsome white, blue-eyed boyfriend, who promptly found Indian Girlfriend 2.0—smarter and calmer, with prettier tits and less traditional parents. This decision led to seven years of Seema alone, followed by a quasi-arranged marriage with an alcoholic engineer who'd been in love with his ex, too. On top of that, Anand was sterile. Weeks after their third anniversary, Seema learned via a cable that he'd divorced her and moved to the U.K. to start over. By then she was thirty-two, with her own problems. Miscarriage number five from the sperm bank only confirmed what she'd already suspected: there wouldn't be kids.

And then there was her job in insurance. Four years of college, graduating as a nurse and coming to hate the hospital, but instead of quitting to be an art historian like she'd always wanted, Seema had sold out and gone into managed health care nursing mid-level leadership, boring meetings, endlessly pedestrian white binders full of pages no one would ever read, and miniscule numbers on screens.

Her company job paid well, but more than that, it soothed her fear, assured her that she wasn't a loser. She was successful at sustainable unhappiness, stable enough so that she came to work without fail but soaked so thoroughly in misery that each night she couldn't remember what she'd done that day and melted like a rum cake in her whipped-cotton-sheeted, cool white bed.

The sight of numbers, staccato black strokes, soothed and suffocated her. To the dollar, Seema knew what was in her bank account. So much went to an IRA, so much to her parents' expenses, and just a little bit for that one trip, to the Uffizi. She'd been to Florence, to that museum, on a vacation by herself, only weeks before the big fire bombing in 1993.

When Seema had seen the news about the fire, she'd wished for a second that she'd managed to curate a completely different life. As if it existed somewhere, the colors bright, like a painting she had yet to see. As if there'd been a moment where she could have been in it.

The rumors were that disgruntled Mafiosi bombed the street adjacent to the museum. A famous tower was destroyed, never replaced; brutalized too was the room that worshipped Niobe, the mother who'd lost all her children for bragging she was more fertile than the gods. For one moment of exuberant maternal pride, Niobe paid with centuries of weeping, turned by the gods into a rock gushing water.

A two-month old Italian baby, child of the Uffizi caretakers, was also killed in the bombing.

Seema wondered, if she had been working for the museum, whether she could have prevented the whole thing. She imagined herself late at night leading a special guided tour for some fat-fingered gangster in exquisite Armani. Standing close enough to the David to see her reflection in his beautiful torso, the lean abdomen into pubic triangle, that gleaming stretch that left gay men and straight women weak. Being a protective mother to the reddish-blond Venus with breasts of pink champagne on the half-shell, every day noticing the timelessness of that beautiful face, the wide-spaced eyes, the long, almost boyish torso, a counterpoint to the doe-eyed expression, the duplication of the same beauty in numerous other paintings by that master.

Botticelli. Wasn't it the name of a guessing game as well? A word game based on biography and one letter. Know me by my life, my deeds, each famous person said, speaking through each raptly listening player. It was too painful to think, to acknowledge, that Seema would never be known. Seema's life didn't intrigue anyone enough to lead them to guessing. Her name would never rise to the level of symbol.

She was an only child, without children. Pointless to think of playing Botticelli anyway, back then, in 1993, Seema thought, because it was a game played at parties, a social game. She couldn't remember the last time she'd been around other people by choice.

At the end of her twelfth straight year at the insurance company, in May 2000, a week before she turned forty-three, Seema comfortably made her bonus by persuading many doctors not to spend money caring for patients. There was an announcement at a staff meeting that Seema was number one for hitting the target. The day she confirmed that the money was present in her account, Seema bought her first major artwork, just so she would have something to say when people asked her how she planned to celebrate. The work, a few hundred dollars, was a print of a famous Caravaggio made by a promising student. *Boy with a Basket of Fruit.* The student succeeded, probably beyond his own expectations, in making a sketch that fully captured the leaves' irregularities, the boy's fanciful curls. Seema stood looking at the painting in her living room, fighting her pride in this young man, reminding herself that this single decision, because it was one in a set of decisions, would doubtless prove to be as shitty as all of her other ones—she just couldn't recognize how yet.

The Medicis had left entire museums to descendants. She'd seen other shrewd, skilled, yet somehow discontent executives devote their lives to building similarly vast collections. Rare wine, books, and dolls in elaborate costumes. Permanent objects of devotion that never made demands like children would. There was, however, only so much satisfaction to be gained from each acquisition. Seema knew that, going in. To make the pleasure last, she considered cooking the numbers that she entered on the spreadsheet she'd been keeping, rating each purchase alongside the objective data like its sticker price and estimated resale value. When quantifying how much she enjoyed each on a spreadsheet, she might buff the numbers slightly, so that when she looked at the whole thing and saw numbers like "ninety-nine percent", she would experience a flush of happiness, a pinkness of the cheeks like one of Tintoretto's demure girls.

In other areas of life, she'd often try to fool herself this way. Look at a photo of an interracial couple, in some trendy ad, and say out loud, if she were alone, "He's probably going to break her heart." Pass by a flyer for a university lecture starring some historian or art critic and think, "But how much, hourly, could some professor be earning anyway?" She avoided completely any images of children. It sometimes worked, unless the couple looked too much like they were really in love or unless the art historian looked like he had a great sense of humor. Then the pain stayed, and all she could rely on was her art. The Janson textbook she kept in her office, the pair of leopards staring at each other in the section on Titian, top folds of the pink robe thrown back against the wind behind Bacchus's head. Her eyes moved there; she pictured the leopards whispering their growls. She supped the blue of a woman's dress; a visual feast, the eye going from blue to pink, rich texture to texture, wave of the ocean to a rose. Contentment she couldn't measure.

But each image in the textbook was so distant and condensed. She was never close enough to see the texture of the paint. She'd never had a feeling of being inside the picture, of letting it contain and soothe her, even when she bought high-quality prints and hung them on her walls.

Still, the act of collecting, at least for a time, satisfied Seema. She'd scout out gallery shows in small Northeastern seaside towns, drive out, eat clam chowder—which for some reason, out of all dishes, she never minded eating alone. The thick salty whiteness comforted in its sameness and solidity and made her feel more like one of the locals than eating a salad would have. Despite the rich food, Seema remained thin, and always came to galleries wearing her corporate uniform: black blazer and heels, cultured pearls dangling from her ears. Out of sheer habit she still wore makeup every day, and since she was miserly when it came to personal expenses, she drew from her stores of deep red lipstick and purple eye-shadow, the same paint that her college boyfriend had enjoyed seeing on her dark mocha skin. People either mistook her for being a well-organized wife from one of the banking enclaves, like Marblehead, Back Bay, maybe the Vineyard, or wondered if she were some rich man's Oriental mistress. Only the gallery owners who became friendly with her, who sold her meticulous reproductions, learned the truth by asking about her husband, her employer—*Any men? Any at all?*—expected to weigh in on the sale. In a series of awkward moments, the owners learned that Seema had no one.

Soon enough, she tired of answering their friendly, or maybe prurient, questions. She used a whole week of vacation time to go to San Francisco, boarding the ferry to a Sausalito gallery, where no one would know her history.

The gallery was rococo, not austere. Its doorway framed in golden curving arches, the Palace took up much of the Main Street, where previously there had been small sandwich shops and smaller galleries. Its oval windows overlooked the dock where the Sausalito ferry would sit waiting, its captain reliably patient with how slowly rich shoppers walked when laden with their purchases. The captain was always a white and sunburnt man. There were few naturally dark faces to be

seen anywhere on the island, Seema noticed. The captain was less patient with the kids than single adults. The open sun and dream-white
spaces of the boat made a physical prelude to the gallery.

Seema knocked. The mustachioed proprieter looked startled to
see her but let her in after a pause. She must look different to him,
she imagined, from how she sounded on the phone. Perfectly white.
Inside, the walls were also bright eggshell, the gallery somehow containing preserved rubble from reclaimed antique palaces, its floors
gleaming, its hallway inlaid with tapestries like those that once lined
the hallways of the Uffizi.

Seema found it comforting that Uffizi meant "offices." Her office at the company was where Seema forced herself to go, hating the
weight of her heels on carpet, the strained smiles of people forced
to live as closely as families, yet never able to trust as family should.
Seema's parents had become kind enough now that they were im-
paired by dementia, living mostly in comfort on savings and Seema's
contributions. Or maybe it just seemed like they were kind, now that
they could only smile absently. Soon her parents would be out of
money except for what they counted on from her.

Walking in a dark corridor behind the fat mustachioed man,
who turned and smiled periodically, encouragingly, saying, "We keep
originals from Europe in a vault here, just for security," Seema justified her plan to spend fifteen thousand, more than she had spent so
far on any single visit, by assuring herself that she'd be making a sure
investment. Better than buying the work of some modern hotshot.
Life sculptures, meaning the artist sat on a stage pretending to be
inanimate. Mobiles made from toilet paper. Decapitated heads made
from real, presumably donated, frozen blood. None of these qualified
as art. Whereas the work in front of her now, in the room the man
opened with grace, hung by itself on a clean, well-lit wall, security
walking just outside—this was art without pretense. She'd come to
the island to buy this reproduction, again by a talented student from
Tintoretto's studio, of an early sketch of what became the master's

self-portrait, somehow capturing, as if in advance, the bottomless black stare of the artist, simple and pitiless.

Seema appreciated, too, that the gallery owner had the sense to let her stand before the painting, to possess it mentally, even before he took possession of her check. This man, the bearded artist on the wall, particularly satisfied her, she couldn't say why. As if he wouldn't bother trying to fool her. As if he could commiserate with how she'd chosen the wrong life.

When the blast came, Seema felt peaceful and was already on her way out. There was a boom and shattering, the combination loud enough to dull her ears. She and a guard dropped to the ground, holding their knees, eyes shut tightly. After sustained quiet, they made their way to the front room of the gallery, the guard cautioning Seema to stay behind him, though it wasn't as if he carried a gun.

Once in the open air, her full hearing returned. It helped too that the front room was colder than it had been only a few minutes before. One of the big windows had been smashed, that was all. The light coming in danced with fury, varied colors a sudden spectacle on all the shards of broken glass, on walls, even on the lone face of the young and slender woman in black who worked for the gallery owner, and whose face, Seema was glad to see, was free of blood and unwounded. But the fat man in the grey suit and the mustache, had blood on his hands and was standing near the doorway, shouting down. The boy at the entrance was cowering and brown, his faded white T-shirt streaked with blood. Without thinking, Seema ran forward, realizing quickly, with a surprising surge of joy, that he was still alive. She pushed aside the gallery owner and instructed him to call 911.

Seema held the boy, who could have been no more than ten, precisely in the way that she'd been taught. He breathed, he moved. Then one by one she asked him all the questions she still carried in her heart, though she had not been in a hospital for years. Palpated, checked, confirmed, counted. Saw he was fine, though his face, arms, and hands were bloodied by the glass, with most of the cuts at least appearing to be superficial lac's, only one or two needing sutures. The firecracker he and his friend were playing with had gone off suddenly when he'd thrown it, but only broken the window and taken no life, damaged no sculptures or paintings. Severed no fingers. "But it sounded exactly like a bomb," the owner shouted. "Why would you bring fireworks here? Why on earth would anyone," repeating the phrase, over and over, over the phone with the police, until Seema asked him to please lower his voice and bring some gauze and bandages.

"What is your name?" the boy asked. His lashes were fluttering black brushstrokes. His friend had disappeared long before the police and the ambulance came. He refused to answer when they'd asked about parents. By then Seema had a bed sheet around him, the kind used to cover paintings in a state of repair.

There was confusion everywhere, police sirens blaring, people talking loudly into walkie-talkies, the street cordoned off, so all the glass could be cleaned from the road. Seema helped the boy into the ambulance. Settled into the space next to him, nodding to the paramedics that she was riding along. Finally, she whispered her name in the boy's ear. She didn't mind, not even a little, that once he was handed off to others, at the hospital, he would likely forget her.

THE ORPHAN HANDLER

AT DAWN, ANOTHER VAN WITH GIRLS comes in and Sister Agnes takes them onto the back veranda, branding them with a tattoo and warning that they'd better not scream. Then she checks for scabies and lice, wearing non-latex hypoallergenic gloves. Then she leads them, even the ones who are weeping quietly, into a vast gay room with bright-colored streamers and balloons and glittering signs spelling out birthday greetings, even though not one of them has given us their real birthdays or names. Then she initiates the change that is our little spiritual secret: the transformation of orphaned girls with special powers, the powers to change into wild creatures of various kinds, into future housekeepers, grounds cleaners, toilet scrubbers, perhaps a secretary or two, or God-fearing wives. After the birthing rite come songs, a ritual that never fails to irritate Mother Superior Devi. Before erecting this orphanage-cum-vocational school, Devi had been arrested for drug trafficking in Kamathipura, where prostitutes lived and where indeed she was involved in heroin. In jail, she learned to read the Bible and took orders as a nun. Now she gives us orders and sporadically allows us to watch a blue movie or two, just to remind us that God accepted her because of, and not in spite of, where she had been, and how blind we would be to think that anything we ever did would be beyond his Love.

Post-birthing ritual, during the songs, in between clapping after each number, I write fake letters home and to the government.

These are to advise any last living relatives and state welfare agencies that the girl in question has died. Sometimes I throw in their new names, the names I assign to the girls at my pleasure. No one can select names better than mine, not even the girls themselves, who usually claim not to remember who they were. "They're orphans, all orphans," the sisters say, but whispers abound outside our colony that in reality the girls all have parents somewhere, or aunts or other relatives, wondering what's become of them, concluding that they ran off once and for all like the unruly girls they always were. In order to allow themselves the privacy they deeply craved to become eagles or panthers or wild mares, the girls had often disappeared, through-out their whole lives. When the government aid workers call with their concerned voices, wanting more details of how the girls died, I'm reassuring and solemn. I cry only at the conclusion of the tragic ends I narrate, holding my voice steady and calm and factual when I talk of accidental drownings, suicides, auto rickshaw crashes, kitchen fires. Then, as per Mother Superior Devi, I ask if they'd mind sending us the girls' remaining possessions, so these can be buried like relics, just as was done for the Catholic saints the Hindu government work-ers aren't all that certain existed. The possessions may look cheap but sell well. And here and there is a treasure: a bracelet of the finest gold, a piece of ivory carved into sandalwood. Once, in my memory, even a thick packet of coins.

These days the girls' possessions are my main joy. I'm too old to attract male company. I am nearly seventy. Even among permissive nuns, allowed to watch blue movies, masturbate with each other, and bathe the girls alone without being questioned, I'm considered past my prime. I don't like it, considering how long it took me, a nun ordained at age sixteen, to find permission for my wants, but like the girls' fates, the situation is beyond my control.

I am unique, alive, organism, the girls cry out to each other in their regional languages, or, more often, telepathically, and these are only the words I and the other nuns imagine are broadcast on young faces. After the branding they know better than to implore us. They see the fates of girls who fight the Mother, hear whispers of how some are sent to the cages in Kamathipura, remote stations, and truck stops, to service drivers bringing heroin from Thailand. Then the shouting stops and with it the girls' old beliefs about justice. It's not that we teach them right from wrong. It's more like we show them a rainbow spectrum of cobalt blues and subtlest orange hues, whereas in their previous lives they only saw red, indigo, and green.

The colors of their clothes alerts us to how many will need to have told more than one story. Those in bright, fresh, clean-looking clothes shouldn't be here. At ten, eleven, twelve years old, it means they have mothers who will not rely on fathers to find them. They have the kind of mothers who may show up at the gate, and in the years that I and my sisters of mercy have been here, there has been one mother or two dragged into the compound for branding. Mother Superior Devi can smell women who change—and the girls, the special girls, with powers to transform into animals, well, many of them inherit this capacity from their mothers.

Girls in grey are easy fish: calls are cursory, inquiries disinterested. It isn't even grey that they're wearing. It's filth, their clothing washed, if you can call it that, in refuse-tainted water, in puddles that slum dwellers make do with for small ponds. There is a smell on these girls that is distinct, not just a smell but a texture—the unwashed clinging even to the newly-washed, the smell of their hair still rank though it is combed and gilded with flowers.

Only the transformations astound me. At night, manacles aren't enough. Mother Superior Devi has gone into deep pockets, money retrieved from her former lucrative life, to build tunnels and dungeon rooms equipped with chains and cages and even one exhibit with rocks and grass where girls who become panthers can be contained, where the wildness of these girls can be transformed in changes more powerful and still more devastating than their earliest age, around age five or six, when they first must have discovered that, as girls, they had a secret; when they first sounded a different voice, thrilling to them in its forbidden and unexpected grace. *What was it like when you discovered you could roar?* I asked a beautiful fourteen-year-old girl-cub-lioness one time, a girl whose eyes were golden brown and her hair matted from life in the slum. But by then she had already been branded and subdued. Doubtful that she knew anymore what to answer; nor how grateful she'd be, shortly after, for how the Mother made her forget, helped her attain a quieter, more durable power.

IN ALLEGHENY

IN THE PARKING LOT OF THE Pittsburgh temple, the priests were painting the Ganesh Chathurthi float. In late September the festival season would begin, and the float would be carried by worshippers, most of them middle-aged husbands from all over the Northeast. The women who were mothers and wives would watch as the men kept the float aloft on their shoulders, often for fifteen or twenty minutes longer than they were required to. Then the men, usually flabby though always energetic, would admit that they had reached a limit of physical exertion and move as one set of arms to put the float down, with great gentleness, in the parking lot.

The children were brought as reluctant observers. They were often blamed for the occasional clumps of litter in the lot. The young Indian girls wore long tunic dresses over high-waisted pants that were tight and emphasized their calves, always tied with an invisible drawstring that held their backs straight no matter how bored they became. The boys wore T-shirts and even jeans, although when they were inside the temple they often took off their shoes without being told and stuffed them in nooks and crannies, away from the religious statuettes.

This was only the second time Michelle had attended the dance recital of her neighbor's daughter, and while few of the families were friendly, some of them did recognize her from the supermarket, or maybe from the hospital. The husbands seemed to know she was a

surgeon. They talked to her about wars and amputations and bomb-
ings and accidents that might have made women like their wives flinch.

After the recital, when everyone was waiting to receive sweets
and milling around the temple entrance, three of the husbands approached Michelle, wanting to know all about John. They wanted
to know if it was a high school student whom they saw mowing her
lawn every weekend, his arm resting on the leaf blower every now
and then, waiting for her to come out with lemonade. Michelle told
them he was not in high school. Then another man, an older one,
slapped his friend's arm and said, "I told you not to ask."A third man
said that he had read about a schoolteacher getting in trouble with
the law for "taking in" a fourteen-year-old boy. The two of them had
corresponded until the boy turned seventeen, and now they were
going to get married. "But that boy was a Filipino chap," the man
added, as if reassuring her.

Michelle nodded, then left the men and started up the stairs of
the temple. The white building was set against a hill that accounted
for the choice decades ago to build it here, in honor of the Lord of
the Seven Hills. These hills were part of the Allegheny Mountains,
according to a pamphlet she had picked up near the temple entrance,
after she'd taken off her shoes. The rain had stopped.

Midway up the stairs, three women were holding onto the railing. The women looked in the direction that Michelle was heading—
where, on one of the temple's highest peaks, there were tiers of golden
engravings stacked in the shape of a ridged dome denoting the 'head'
of the temple, its 'body' a tall building with two side wings and two
side entrances, like a heavy, still bird.

Michelle looked at the women's necks. All of them wore heavy
golden necklaces. "Mangal sutram," John had called them. In college
he'd studied abroad in India for a year, the lone white man in a South
Indian university. She thought then—with increasing annoyance at
her shame—that she should have just told the men that John was her
lover. That he was a medical student and that she had been his surgery

attending. All they wanted was to confirm she was sleeping with him. That was what all husbands and their wives, looking at an unmarried woman with an unknown man, wanted to know, in all cultures.

For Indians, unmarried sex was especially exciting, she supposed, something they couldn't even see in cinema. The Indians—who seemed able to introduce song and dance into the most dire of situations—could probably make a Bollywood film out of her affair with John, as long as they skipped over certain parts: Michelle first ignoring his letters and small gifts, which had started after he'd worked only one week in the surgery clinic, as a junior student when she was a junior attending; then agreeing to go to dinner with him and standing him up because of work but also out of fear; then having sex in the coat closet of a nightclub where they'd seen each other unexpectedly; then refusing to answer his calls after she'd become a full-fledged faculty member in the Surgery department and he was doing his clinical rotations. Then finally letting him move in once he'd reached his fourth year and determined that he was going to be a psychiatrist, and so would never again be her professional subordinate. He had decided to apply to residencies only in major cities where there would be a job for her. But only a month ago she learned that, during all those hot, sultry days as a foreign student in Madras when he'd mastered vegetarian Indian cooking, he had carelessly slept with one of his South Indian classmates, and unknowingly fathered an Anglo-Indian child with her. He had a ten-year-old son who lived with his graduate student mother in a tiny apartment in Berkeley. John was somehow managing to support the two of them, despite being a medical student at thirty.

🐘

The rain had started again when John pulled her car into the temple parking lot, waiting for other guests to leave so he could drive closer. He had not come to the recital, though Michelle said more than once that she was sure the invitation included him. By the time she got in the car, her hair and face were soaked. "There's a towel in the back," he offered, keeping both hands on the wheel as she shook her hair and lay back on the seat. She flicked on the heater and watched the passenger window steam up.

"This'll do," she said, tracing wiggly lines in the foggy glass the way she'd done since she was a small child. She peered out through the clear holes at the now-distant Indian families holding umbrellas over their children or wiping the rain from their faces with white handkerchiefs.

Was it just a few months ago that, whenever she met him after a day of work, or even after a fifteen-minute trip to the grocery store, John would grab her by the waist and kiss her on the mouth no matter who saw and no matter what she looked like? Odd to recall how it annoyed her if he tried to do it anywhere near the hospital. Back then she hadn't known about Shalini, mother of his child, or Jack, his son. Michelle wondered now if what she'd interpreted as passion was really desperate need—if he'd just been lonely, sending a check every month for a child he'd hardly met.

"Dollar for your thoughts," John said.

His eyes were on the road, but his right hand snaked over to her thigh, which was dry and warm from the car heater.

"Trying to keep up with inflation," he added.

She let him keep his hand where it was, but didn't cover it with her own.

"Better keep your dollars then," she said.

For a moment, he needed both hands to guide her old Honda Accord around a narrow curve. They were still up on the mountains, traveling a scenic road from Penn Hills back to the city of Pittsburgh. The other day, John had been talking about a short story collection that he'd read called *The Mysteries of Pittsburgh*, something he compared to a "bisexual *Midsummer Night's Dream*." After practicing medicine for nearly eleven years, non-medical books had little meaning for Michelle. More than specific books she'd read in college, she remembered the undergraduates who once sat in classrooms with her. Michelle wondered if they now mourned the smooth elasticity of their skin, the reckless vigor of their hearts. She wondered how they might react if they needed emergency surgery, or if someone they loved had died in an OR where the nurses were playing something loud and oblivious on the radio, and a strange woman, Michelle, were to come out into the waiting room in the middle of the night and offer explanations. Michelle was now forty-one, and her own body had remained intact. Never split in two for a miraculous moment and then remade, as a mother's. Never distended, full and precarious.

"Stop here," she said. "Oh shit."

She got out of the car before he'd turned off the engine. Another car, a black station wagon with two young children in the back, had pulled over to the shoulder; a thin, crew-cut teenage boy was holding his chest and grimacing, his heavyset father holding him close and waving a white cloth with his free hand. An Indian woman she took to be the boy's mother was still sitting in the car, fumbling through a purse and shouting through the open window, "Abhijit, Abhijit, saans lena, baccha, saans lena." The boy's eyes were nearly closed, the woman's heavy jewelry gold and garish in the light.

Gently Michelle pulled him from his father, shouted "Call 911" to John, and took him to the grassy lookout point off the shoulder of the road. She laid him down and did mouth to mouth, encouraging him to cough and to stay awake. By then John had parked their car and helped the parents find the asthma inhaler. The Indian father, obese with a kind face, rubbed his bald head while John ran the device over to Michelle, who was busy murmuring reassuring words, "It will be all right. You're going to be all right now," as she helped sit the boy up and operated the small, flimsy but vital device, hardly looking at John when she took it from him.

"Did they call 911?" she asked. The boy was still coughing and pale, but much better.

"I think yes, I'll check," he said. She kept going with the inhaler.

As John made his way back to the parents' car, they both heard the sound of the ambulance, the sirens loud and near. Michelle had been continually checking the boy's pulse and respirations. The father stood near him, holding the boy's hand; the mother stayed in the car with the door open, holding onto to their other son. The asthmatic boy's eyes were wide open now and his pulse had come down to the low 70s, from the 110s. His color was good, and he could speak; no need for her to make a hole in his windpipe. That was a relief, because all she had was Swiss Army knife, the same one she and John had used on a last-minute picnic that June, when life together was new and untroubled and they found it amusing to pull off the side of the road, having been driving through Brandy-wine Valley after a day of kayaking, and make love under the trees, to lie down and feed each other grapes, expensive cheeses, honey and bread.

"Like college kids," he'd said at the time. "You could pass for a freshman."

The paramedics looked like freshmen themselves, no more than nineteen or twenty. When they learned Michelle was a surgeon at University Medical Center, they weren't just deferential, but flirta-tious. One of them asked, "You wanna grab a drink after this?" not seeming to care that she said no. He lingered with Michelle once the kid had been taken into the ambulance, hooked up to oxygen, and had two sets of bland vitals with a normal cardiogram, once his mother had settled in the back of the ambulance, press-ing her hands together in gratitude and bowing her head slightly to Michelle. The father had gotten back in his car with the other children by then and was watching the scene, ready to follow when the ambulance got going.

"He never arrested or lost consciousness," she told the young man with his clipboard, smoothing down her hair, which was still a mess from being caught in the rain. John had come to stand beside her.

"This your medical student?" the same paramedic asked, not bothering to listen to the answer as he kept writing. "Your students are lucky, I bet."

The other man stepped up into the rear and took a seat next to the boy and his mother, closing the back door with a thud. The boy's father honked; both John and the paramedic near Michelle shot him a wave.

"Later then, ma'am," the man said, brushing shoulders with John as he strode past, taking the ambulance driver's seat and winking at her from inside the cab.

"And what the hell was that?" John asked, when they were alone, Michelle started back to their car, not looking at him. "Hey, answer me when I'm talking to you," he said. She kept walking. Muttering "Goddamn," he followed her and slammed the door behind him, starting the car before she'd had a chance to put her seatbelt on.

Was there something new and harder in his voice? A lean tension in his hands? He didn't try to touch her now. She looked at him with renewed interest, with hot but temporary lust. In Allegheny, that's where it had changed, she thought she would say, years afterward, when she and John were no longer in touch.

In Allegheny, she had begun to prepare herself for the thick envelope that came in the mail about six months later, in March, announcing that John had matched at Stanford for psychiatry.

He would be living and working just an hour from where his son was being brought up. No way to deny the opportunity. And so Michelle worked up the conviction to say carefully, folding a towel as meticulously as an OR tech and standing a little apart from him in their bedroom:

"John, I think you should go alone."

In the Allegheny Mountains, where the air wouldn't stop being bluer or thinner even when you'd come to pray to God. Where your child could lose the power to breathe in a heartbeat, in an instant, unless the right person decided to go out of her way to do the right thing. In Allegheny was where Michelle's decision had begun, she told herself, now patting the towel on the top of a pile, its perfect neatness proof that she'd made up her mind.

"You should ask for family housing and help Shalini with your son. You should be—"

"What? A family?" John spoke the word too bitterly. She'd been right, Michelle thought, with the odd sag of relief. Yes of course, she knew what he meant. His parents had divorced; his father remarried a woman who didn't love John and his sister; his mother had a string of boyfriends who already had children of their own. He had already told her everything. He had a son with no father.

Three weeks passed. After their most recent fight, followed by several days when she didn't allow him to touch her, Michelle told John it would be better if he moved out of the house.

"I can't tell you what to do," Michelle said, thinking again, with a glassy remoteness, that he really ought to go be with his child. When she was alone, she admitted she was taken aback by her decision's clarity—so different from the more instinctive, tense and doubting decisions she'd grown used to making all the time in the OR, the ones she made quickly but would constantly revise, the decisions that, when they affected or cost a human life, haunted and tormented her until she was convinced she'd learned enough to be better next time.

"I just don't want you to feel like I'm holding you back," Michelle told John again. "Like I kept you from being with the mother of your child. Like I broke up you and Shalini."

"There is no me and Shalini," John said again. "There's me and you."

He was obstinate, repeating his position even after he started staying at a friend's run-down apartment, in a building across town, and he and Michelle were talking on the phone late every night. She'd thought it would be easier to give him up, to have no contact. She'd thought she could easily revert to the life she'd had that was contented if boring: solitary hikes along the Ohio River, days spent running, reading magazines, sleeping or eating takeout while proofreading academic articles while old movies played in the background.

When John had lived with her, she'd often missed that life. Now there was the absence of John's quirks. His reading in bed with the lights off, never minding how hard he strained his eyes. His gentle insistence on seeing grainy, obscure black-and-white Japanese movies Michelle had never heard of—about solitary women swallowed by sand, about rice. The bite marks he left on her shoulders. The non-alcoholic drinks he mixed her before a big case—iced tea with fresh-squeezed lime and orange peels, strawberry virgin daiquiris. The way he carefully packed lunch for the both of them, every day, putting aside the money he saved to send to his son, to Shalini.

"Listen, Shalini has never, not a single time, asked me to move in with her," John said. It was the middle of the afternoon, the kind of Sunday they would have spent having sex if he'd still been living in Michelle's house. "She just wanted money for our son, and she was right to want it. She wanted to make sure he didn't lack for anything. But her life is a mystery to me. I don't even know if she's dating somebody. I don't know where all this duty and sacrifice for my kid, who's doing perfectly fine by the way, and whom you've never even met, are coming from. Or is it something else, Michelle? Have you just fallen out of love with me?"

Michelle hung up. Wanting to get out of the house so she wouldn't be tempted to call him again, driving alone on a mountain road, she found herself near the Hindu temple again after she'd passed signs for a local Hooters bar and Chick-Fil-A. She wondered if the proximity of those places to sacred ground bothered the vegetarian, sexually conservative Indians. Then again, the Indians showed plenty of breasts in their movies, even if covered by tight, often wet clothes. Maybe she'd been looking in a far-off and exotic direction thinking about Bollywood as a reflection of her life. Maybe the movie of her relationship with John could be written as a Deborah Kerr and Cary Grant movie instead, or better yet, a Bette Davis vehicle about a stubborn, smart woman, proud until the end, slurring her final, regretful monologue.

"I haven't fallen out of love with you," she said out loud, though she was the only one there to hear it.

She stopped the car and got out. The temple looked smaller and quieter than she remembered. Michelle walked around the whole structure once, making a wide circle, like she remembered her neighbor saying she would do because her daughter had gotten into college. Making the circle was how the family would set their minds at peace about such a major decision, such a large outlay of money. While the neighbor was talking, too busy with her own family to ask where John had gone, Michelle felt glad she didn't need things like superstitions, rituals, because she was at peace already, letting John go, knowing she was doing right.

But here she was, walking the same path as the other worshippers, adrift and confused and waiting for mercy. She stopped short of actually going inside, thinking it would be too strange, not wanting to make the effort of talking to the people she'd see there, whose questions were inevitable.

She stood still, next to her car. For the next two days, she wasn't on call and would probably be at home. There would be too many hours to fill. Then she saw two boys spilling out of the temple, laughing and trying to hit each other as their parents followed slowly and heavily behind. The mother and father looked around gloomily and bent with effort to put their shoes back on as the boys raced in circles, picking up their shoes only to aim them at each other. They couldn't have been more than nine or ten, the same age as John's son.

The sight hurt her. How happy and how utterly careless the two boys were in their happiness, knowing that the mother who mumbled angrily at them to stop fighting, the father who slapped their shoulders to get them to stand still, would always be there watching, knowing what was wrong with them and able to fix it, the parents solid as a house. What every child deserved.

Before Michelle could move, in front of her, a lone man appeared, his hips and legs wrapped curiously in excess layers of white cloth edged in festive, almost garish gold. The costume gave an unexpected grandeur to his sad, brown chest. His old-man skin was speckled with white and grey hairs, and despite having the look of someone with an important job to do—he shushed the two boys, beckoned them to move aside, and started scattering spoonfuls of water from a sort of gold scoop he dipped into an equally burnished pitcher, muttering and dropping the water on the ground in a pattern known only to himself—he also had the look of someone resigned to staying late at work, to going home alone. Later Michelle would learn, from John, that the faded orange thread around the priest's shoulder and neck meant he too was the head of a household, a married man, a dad. But at that moment, John wasn't there to point out or explain anything; he was packing his things and thinking about California and the future, she supposed.

She stared at the priest's bare, mottled shoulders, seeing how alone he was and probably always would be. One of the boys, the younger one, looked over at the man and made a face, sticking out his tongue and trying to cross his eyes. "Ho," his father said, pulling him away from the priest's view, sheltering him in a corner with his body.

The father's face was familiar. His bald head, the way he scratched with one hand, held on so tightly to the little boy with the other. And the mother. The Indian mother stood thin, worried, wrinkled, the smooth, elaborate chains of gold around her neck as gleaming as the temple's roof. Their other little boy butted his head against her waist.

Without intending to, Michelle found herself back inside her car, revving it up and turning sharply, the steering wheel a wild thing in her hands as she sped off. She wasn't heedless but did not take extra care. The Indians noticed her and took a step back.

She drove away, intent on following each curve of the road, no longer curious or compassionate toward that family or the boy, the one she'd helped to save that day in the mountains. No longer interested in seeing how these strangers lived, what they believed. Only when she reached the building where John was staying, slammed her car door and ran to the door that he'd opened, only when she was stripped down next to him and safe in bed did she realize: nothing could sustain her loyalty, nothing in medicine or religion, nothing more than the rhythm of their breaths and pounding hearts, the mystery of them.

THE GODDESS OF BEAUTY
GOES BOWLING

Mr. Neelakanta Vaikuntashyamala Gopisundaram Iyer, Gopi to his friends, stood on the staircase of his house, leaning on his cane.

The cane could have belonged to a wandering Buddhist ascetic with nothing but outstretched palms and a cheerful disposition to see him through old age. In contrast, Gopi was seething, tired, resentful. His cane was made of young bamboo, from shoots that grew past the inquisitive, cruel snouts of wild pigs outside his sister's garden of jute and banyan trees ten minutes from the Kapaleshwar temple at Mylapore. Walks in that garden were truly serene; how he missed it.

Somewhere in the US was a serenity, probably for rich people, he didn't doubt—a few moments that some tycoon spent in a gold-plated bath, on *Lifestyles of the Rich and Famous,* or sunning his pink, fleshy face in the pages of a magazine. Somewhere in the US, it was quiet—but not in Elmhurst, one block from the subway and right under the Number Seven train, where Gopi lived.

His wife was still young, stubborn enough to run up the train steps and then come down looking worried, roaming the street. She would be looking for Shree, always for her. Shree, of course, would be safe and comfortable. Oblivious—but not in a serene way, not like the god Vishnu asleep on a serpent in the cold deep. To Gopi, rather, his daughter was the serpent, rapaciously devouring them.

At fifty-eight, Gopi shouldn't have felt like an old man. His wife Lakshmi's face was as young-looking and round as it had been on their wedding day. Though she looked more like a younger sister, people knew her to be his wife. His hold was too possessive anything else. From the beginning he had worried not only that she would outlive him, but that she would have to care for him as an invalid.

There was nearly a twenty-year age difference between Gopi and his wife. To some it seemed like a scandal, a thirty-eight-year-old bachelor finally marrying a nubile, intelligent nineteen-year-old girl from a good family. It was Gopi's reward for his father's years of company service and longstanding friendship with Lakshmi's father. But her father knew, after all, that he would love her to his death, care for her, shelter her with the last scrap of clothing he possessed, like Nala in the Mahabharata, who took off his one remaining garment and used it to cover his beautiful, half-naked wife once they were exiled into poverty.

Gopi made his way down the steps slowly, listening to the sounds that filled the house. In all these twenty years, he'd never expected to be where they were now, like this, in thrall to a child he could hardly recognize as his. His daughter, Shree, the Goddess of Beauty, was brushing her teeth and gargling theatrically as usual. It was as if, knowing how irritated he became, she did it more. Next would be prayers, to which he couldn't object. Reverberating through the whole house like the noise from a passing subway train—relentless, low-pitched, rattling his teeth as it lurched on overhead.

Praying was the way Shree could talk as loudly as she liked and for as long as she wanted, without ever having to ask permission. There was a story she had started reciting in a monotone, making it something else, not quite an incantation but dangerous-sounding. He had no idea how she'd learned this myth, how there could be myths and legends in a mind the doctors had said would never develop beyond that of the average five-year-old. But there she was at twelve, able to tell the story of Narasimha—half man, half lion, the form of Vishnu that had come down to earth to protect a faithful boy from his father's threats and curses.

The father in the story was wicked and vigilant. Constantly aware that his power as a king could be taken away, he prayed for unlimited power using the severest penances. He forbade his son from praying to the god Narayana because it reminded the king that he wasn't a god. But the boy continued to pray. Had the father listened in the night, he might have heard doom in the silence, the lack of a reply from God until it was too late for him to repent. "No man, no beast, no god. I cannot be killed in the daytime or in the night, inside of a building or outside. Go on and pray, my boy."

To Gopi, the ambitious king's voice, in its certainty, in its roaring, grandiose monotone, was not like Gopi's own voice at all, but like his daughter's. Shree prayed every morning and every evening for their health, without asking him how many more years he wanted to live. But prayers for others were just formalities; her real intention was to make special requests to gratify herself. Let my mom live forever, she said. Let her keep working with me every afternoon. Let Dad not yell and scream, yell and scream. Let Dad love me. Please let him, let him.

Gopi and his wife Lakshmi lay in their beds every night listening to her. Lakshmi could fall asleep right after, first calling out, "Goodnight, sweetheart," and feeling satisfied by Shree's answering chortle. When Shree was two or three, and Gopi sat looking at her from a few yards away on the bare, perfectly clean floor, imagining her being the same way at forty years of age, at fifty and sixty, he'd offered his own prayers silently—that she wouldn't outlive either of them, that she would die when it was time to get her married, so no humiliation would come to the family, especially to his son. He hadn't wanted to send Romesh to boarding school, but Lakshmi insisted, saying that the distraction she always felt, the preoccupation with Shree's safety and routine, would prevent her son from getting all the attention he deserved. They had no family here to cherish him, unlike in India.

She didn't want him to feel the day-to-day cares of worrying about Shree; Romesh was already too compassionate, getting into fights with the neighbor's child who had thrown dirt at her. Scolding Shree, when he was only eight and she was ten—once imitating Gopi with his hand raised and his face drawn in a scowl, making her pick up a bowl of cereal she'd spilled and saying he would beat her otherwise. Not knowing, as Lakshmi told Gopi afterward, that Shree's clumsiness was part of her disability, the same thing that made her use up shoes so quickly and need special inserts from the podiatrist, some unknown but ill-fated process by which her movements would never have Romesh's exuberance.

When their beloved son Romesh was three years old, Gopi remembered him playing with his sister. Going into the room where she had her toys and stealing them, leading her out into the other room on his fat toddler legs, laughing with delight. Laughing even more when she fell backwards and hurt herself. That was the natural state of things, Gopi believed. Not something to be banished.

"But I want Romesh to stay a child," Lakshmi had said. "And she needs my care."

He'd answered, "Why send him? Why not send Shree away." The children were at the playground together; he didn't worry they would hear. "God has already punished me. Why do you punish me too, khannu?" His tenderness hadn't made any difference, in the end.

Romesh was only eight but had quickly been settled in the excellent school at Coimbatore, where generations of Lakshmi's male relatives had studied and done well. So Gopi had accepted things. The boy's grandparents were taking great pleasure in bringing him up.

Now it seemed Gopi had little to do but wonder if he had sinned in a past life. Like the hero Rama's father had sinned, accidentally killing the son of a powerful sage, for which the sage cursed him to also feel the grief of losing a son. God was listening; God was keeping score. So Gopi would say nothing whenever Lakshmi went on. "I think she should have singing lessons, at least a few.

I found a lady who'll do it for only five dollars a lesson. She used to sing for the dancers at Baby Kamala's school in New Jersey; now she sings on and off in the temple and so on. It's worth it, isn't it? She said she wants to sing like the radio, and she has a good voice. You know she sings along to the bhajans every single Saturday on *Voice of Asia*. She's very good."

Lakshmi was content with his usual answer, a grunt. By the time Shree was eleven, he had learned not to mistake his conversations with his wife for the picture of marriage he'd cherished for years, a man and his wife reminiscing, taking pleasure in each other's company, proud of each other. Also, his Lakshmi was the bread-earner of the family. He was "retired," he told people, and had been so since eleven years before, when Shree was born and Lakshmi came ahead of him to America.

At that time, he had been forty-six and jobless, an unexpected bruise on the golden body of Lakshmi's illustrious family of lawyers and judges and engineers, though he had never hit his wife. Lakshmi was fair-skinned, his parents had insisted on that—so where did Shree's stubbornly dark color come from? "She favors your side of the family," Lakshmi said.

Soon after Shree was born and the doctors had handed down her diagnosis, Lakshmi had fled to the US, first telling him she wanted to consult with specialists, then finding early childhood programs for Shree and deciding not to go back. She'd even gotten a job in one of the programs looking for a part-time aide. When Lakshmi, not once consulting anyone, least of all him, had sold her marriage jewelry to put down a security deposit for the apartment in Elmhurst, he'd said to her on the telephone, "What if I refuse to come?" Gopi could never remember how she replied, just the sound of her crying on the phone, then the surprise of his own tears, not shed since his father's funeral, at the thought of never seeing her again.

He'd taken the first plane he could on a student visa, done a short business course at City College. Then failed, fired from a few jobs, refusing to look for anymore. There was a small inheritance he contributed at first, then promises to go to interviews, then staying at home. His communications degree from Mylapore College was useless here. He could communicate, but no one would listen. In India he'd worked for a small advertising firm, writing in Tamil and English and making phone calls, but mainly talking and sharing tiffin with the college friend whose father had helped Gopi get hired.

Leaning on the side of the armchair in their small living room, before lowering himself into it, he tried again to remember precisely what Lakshmi said to bring him to the US, where he was now marooned. As if there were words he could change, different inflections he could add, that would have made their lives different.

He knew he wasn't the only one who felt the way he did—look at the movie made just that year, *Geethanjali,* where a perfectly reasonable and decent chap, a father interested in providing for his other children, tells his wife that a child born with problems died at birth. When she discovers the falsehood and finds the child, wrenching the daughter away from the institution and only home she's ever known, the whole colony where they live descends on the mother, trying to make her see reason.

But that was a mother's love. Reason didn't enter it. At any rate, these days, when he and Shree were home alone together with Lakshmi at work and his son studying at boarding school, Gopi had the freedom to tell Shree exactly what he thought of her, *Those glasses are awful and ugly. Stop eating so much or I'm going to get the belt. Why do you take so long to bathe? Oh Shanyanay, deerdramay, pishashu.* Fitting names for demons, all of them. As she would for years to come, perhaps for all her life, Shree lacked any comprehension of these names. She didn't respond with tears, only the same benign, determined stare that Lakshmi said was partly a result of her visual defects.

Another morning. There was silence in the house, meaning he had avoided Shree's prayers so far. The sound of the Queens public bus screeching to a halt just outside was like a school bell—he eagerly pushed himself up and went to the door before Shree could come down to fling it open. Somehow depriving her of this joy satisfied him. There was too little she hadn't stolen. Lakshmi had just come back from the market. It was eight o'clock and she had twenty minutes before going to her job as a special education teacher, for which she'd gone back to school when he was forty-six and she was twenty-seven, full of energy and hope that learning techniques for strangers' children would help her with Shree.

Her life was a blur of things to do for Shree and for her work. She no longer had the time to go to the market in the morning and buy him fresh food, as his sister and his mother always had every morning, since he was a child.

But today was a special day, a holy day—the achingly proud day of his son's Avanay Avatam, the thread ceremony, with an uncle taking Gopi's place in India, because they couldn't afford a ticket home. Lakshmi had shopped for special foods, to make the prasadam she would offer to the gods so that next year they might save enough to bring Romesh to the U.S. for a visit. This morning, no matter how uneasy their togetherness, Gopi and his daughter both inhaled the smells of coffee, fresh papaya and coconut milk, steaming idlis from the cooker, mint chutney. As he ate, he flipped through the newspaper she had brought, fingering each page as he read, since each proved that Lakshmi had been thinking of him only, and not about Shree, when she bought the paper.

"Heartshare has a bowling trip for school-aged children," Lakshmi said, sitting next to him. "Normally, I wouldn't let her go, but she really wanted it this once, and she's told me she can do it even with her legs like that, so…it costs only twenty bucks. Can you please take her to return the bottles? She can get some pocket money that way, for the trip."

"She's not a school-aged child," Gopi said firmly. "She's a retard, in a program. It's not a school. School is where you sent our son. School means there's a future that you're learning for."

Lakshmi looked down. She hadn't bought a second newspaper, which she sometimes did, at fifty cents; it was something she could read on the bus to work. Too much else to do, he thought. Or she was saving the money. "So will you go?" she said. "Today I just cannot, and she needs it."

"Seri," he agreed. "I need to buy some iced tea anyway. At least let her help me."

Lakshmi agreed. She got up to clear the table, their breakfast finished after less than twenty precious minutes. She was busy thinking about her lesson plan for the day, he supposed, how she would teach children who couldn't do more than play with their own fingers. They liked to trace the letters of the alphabet in sandpaper cutouts she had carefully pasted.

The night before, after dinner, Gopi watched her making them. He'd looked away from her then; now he wondered how she'd thought of the project. How could she stand to be creative for those kinds of children? The mistakes?

His walk to the store passed without incident. On the corner, Shree took his hand as they waited for a stoplight. He was certain she felt the power she had being alone with him; he felt sure that she was goading him.

No matter, he wouldn't be irritated today. For once, he let his daughter hold him. His son was ten years old. The boy had been away at school, away from them, two long years now. Today was his Avanay Avatam. One of Lakshmi's brothers would stand in for Gopi and, when saying the prayer, Romesh would call out "father" to that man. That man, who wasn't his father, would hold the boy's hand. They would laugh while waves of the ocean rose and broke over the two of them.

He tried hard not to feel the knife pain of imagining this. The grocery store doors swung open and closed of their own accord. Shree was entranced by them, stepping back and forth across the dirty linoleum and laughing when Gopi reached for her in outrage and embarrassment. "Ula po!" he commanded, shouting at her to go in, as if saying the words in Tamil could hide his fury.

He tried not to care about the curious stare of the redheaded boy who overheard him, a boy only a few years older than his son, whose job it was to collect the shopping carts that people left outside. Back home, he told himself, someone in that position wouldn't even dare to make eye contact with a Gopisundaram like himself. They were all the same, all paravans, as far as he was concerned. Untouchables.

"Do you need help?" he thought he heard Shree say. He turned around. The look in her eyes was the same as usual, the sturdy body his to either take with him into the store or push out of view, onto one of the benches near the registers, where elderly ladies waited to be helped with their groceries and where Shree might even sit quietly for once, with dignity.

He told her to wait for him, left her sitting on one of the bench-es, and took his time buying a few things. She would wait, he knew. No one would approach her, but if they did? Imagining Lakshmi's reaction if he told her something had happened to Shree while they were at the store, he hurried and banged one of his arthritic knees against the metal display case holding gum and magazines. She was still there on the bench, waiting for him.

Now she stood up and waved her hands, calling, "Dad, look out!" In hastening toward her, he had almost bumped into one of those el-derly ladies, this one using a motorized walker and hardly aware of people in her path. It was the same thing Shree would do when they took the bus, calling out, "Dad, this is our stop" in such a loud voice that he feared one of the vicious-looking, leather-jacketed teenagers sitting next to them would decide to follow them and throw stones at Shree, as one of the neighbor's children had done recently.

As they left the store with his bag containing iced tea, a half gallon of ice cream that she'd insisted on, and a packet of naan for the night's dinner, it was Shree who remembered their errand. "I want to do the bottles. Can I? Can I?" She had been carrying a bag without complaint, all this time, with at least a dozen heavy glass bottles and forty crushed cans. The whole bag might give her at most four or five dollars. She gave a deep chuckle, feeding the cans to the machine first. "Grrrr," she said, imitating the grinding sounds.

Shree looked at him. The smile was there, as expected. Smiling at him as if she were a tame and trusting animal. If she had been normal, seeing the rage that must show on his face, she would have run out onto the street, calling desperately for help, running without shame to strangers.

At that moment, Gopi was holding a glass lemonade bottle in his hand. He could feel the heft of it. The machines for recycling, he noticed, were in an alcove off the main exit from the store. No one could see the two of them. People moved inside and out of the main store, including a security guard, without even knowing he and Shree were there.

As if propelled by a curse, he raised the bottle to strike her. The ritual of Avanay Avatam took place in the ocean, as Brahmins washed their bare bodies and chanted before sunrise. Brahmin boys, Brahmin men. The glass that he held up, how brightly it gleamed, like water.

ADRISTAKAMA

Two years ago, when I went back to Agra, India, at the age of twenty-two, to visit my grandparents and let two of my uncles set up my marriage, my ex-girlfriend Lauren, whom I work with now on a daily basis, came after me, hoping to stop me from giving in.

We both work for a domestic violence services agency. She's arranged her hours with care, it's obvious, so that we won't see each other except at big staff meetings, over a hundred strong, where Lauren melts into a crowd of pale faces. Whereas I stand out, my ego stroked, my seat at the front table assured, my smiling brown face never omitted from the shiny cover of the organization's annual report. My face again, inside, under the section called "Diversity."

The summer I saw my grandparents, my family was searching far and wide, preferably for a traditional man from a religious family who could get me "under control," as my father said to all the sympathetic relatives. In my grandparents' house, I didn't even feel like I had the right to touch Lauren's hand. Her visit was brief. It was the summer of 1985. We should've been in a bar in the East Village, doing shots and strategizing about how to fight Reagan's budget cuts, flirting and swaggering. Instead we were in a hot, quiet place where even talking, just the two of us, would've been too intimate.

Lauren tried. Right in front of my grandmother, she said she was going back to Delhi after her visit to volunteer at Sangini. "Sangini" meant "soulmate," but it was a codeword too—a helpline for gay, lesbian, bisexual, and transgendered Indian women set up a few years ago by students, social workers, and lawyers. Set up for Indian women like me. My grandmother smiled politely and offered her some more tea, a little curious about this "Sangini" fellow. But I refused to follow Lauren's lead.

I was the one resisting her attempt to combine worlds. I was the one who wasn't swayed by her grand gesture of following me to India. I was the one who told her *It's over, forget it.* Now two years later, I'm the one here in New Haven, starving for a glimpse of her.

Fast forward to that fall and my failed, arranged marriage to a frightened gay man who insisted his "best friend" could come to live with us, even though my family was the one who put the down payment on our condo: we were expensive, but history in months. I think of my marriage as a brief penance, for hurting a woman who loved me, but I couldn't expect Lauren to sit around waiting.

A whole two years have passed, but I remember everything. I imagine everything.

On the way to see me in Agra, to save me from locking myself up in an arranged marriage, Lauren rests her lean body against a dark grey concrete pillar, reading a Hindu comic book. An old woman squats a few feet away, spreading a large black cloth on the ground and setting out her bronze statuettes for sale. In the story Lauren is reading, the god appears suddenly as a coy enchantress, Mohini—smiling at the demons as she steals their nectar out from under them. Lauren looks up from her book only when she hears a sudden whistle blast, but there's just some delay—men in white shouting abrupt commands, a family being helped out of a black Rolls Royce. The daughter emerges, dressed in jeans and a red silk blouse, stands long-legged on high heels, waits for a coolie to follow with the luggage. The line of people eager to get into the train sighs, stands aside as the golden girl and her parents steal ahead of them on line, wondering if she's a celebrity.

Finally settled in her seat, Lauren pushes the hair out of her eyes, thinks she should have gotten it cut before blowing her entire graduation allowance on this trip. Her parents loved the idea, told her it was a romantic adventure, that she should enjoy her freedom while it lasts.

Lauren talking to her mother on the phone from the airport:

"It doesn't feel like freedom, Mom. With me and Nisha, it's a lot more like compulsion."

"My love, you haven't yet seen how marriages and partnerships can fail. It takes two. You want Nisha, but if she doesn't want to be with you, you'll move on. You've got your whole life ahead of you. Call me when you're there, India has national phpone service now, the paper said."

Lauren as I imagine her on a train, in India. She checks whether her cell phone is still hooked into the belt of her jeans and sits back as the train begins to move. She thinks about the first time she and I met and the first time we made love, two events that were barely hours apart.

We happened to sit next to each other at a production of Kalidasa's *Shakuntala* put on by the Queens College Indian Cultural Association. The little boys who run such organizations are always enamored of Princess Shakuntala. This character is basically a hooker with a heart of gold—a sort of ancient Indian *Pretty Woman*. Anyway, this girl that everyone liked, Uma Narayan, was in the title role. God, she was a fox. She walked around in a skimpy forest-dweller costume made of leaves and string. We'd had a one-night stand in our freshman year; she said she'd never been with a woman before but always fantasized about doing it with her sister-in-law. But much more available was this blasé, single chick Lauren sitting next to me. She had very stylishly cut, reddish-blond hair, a buzz cut in the back and long soft bangs in the front. No lipstick, not that she needed any; a leather jacket like mine, incredible green eyes. So I leaned close and said to her, "Look at her boobs, they're going to come out of that top."

Lauren, winking at me: "That'll improve things." And there was the dirtiest expression on her pretty face. Right there I thought—it's on.

We talked first, we did. I was a little embarrassed to tell her my major. I was studying to be a dietician back then, a degree my parents thought would go well with an early marriage. It felt so plebe. Lauren was in lit theory, interested in Marxist critiques of Harold Bloom. She'd read *The Book of J*, Bible studies from a feminist viewpoint, comfortable in the English department at Queens College where her father was a scholar of Renaissance studies and her mother had gotten a PhD under him, literally, before becoming a writer of freelance articles and romance novels, and going around the house in her Birkenstocks saying things like, "The Western canon is dead, I'm serious, totally dead."

Our first night we talked on and on, confirming happily that yes, we both existed. Soon we were standing in front of Lauren's car, about to get in. It was that moment before intimate knowledge, before the other person becomes familiar enough that on a day-to-day basis, you forget what she looks like. Then we kissed for ages, forever.

"O! That you would only kiss me with the kisses of your mouth," Lauren whispered.

I like to think Lauren remembers that night, a singular night in our lives, when she was on her way to Agra to stop me from throwing away my life, both of our lives. The train journey from Delhi to Agra isn't more than a few hours, especially if you take the Rajdani express and like the idea of resurrecting the British Raj in small, more or less innocuous ways, which Lauren kind of does. As long as it doesn't involve anybody suffering. Sitting on the train, she opens her eyes, surprised to see a young man in a white turban and tunic standing near her seat and holding out a warm, damp, dazzlingly white towel in preparation for a complete lunch service. Given how much dust there is here, a lot of labor was involved in that whiteness, Lauren observes, deciding to tip him extra. She asks if they have lassis, a sweet milky drink, deciding to ignore what her mother and most people have said about avoiding ice in India. The boy is solemn and polite, not more than fourteen at the most. He has an even younger cousin who dances in the tourist park they recently put up outside of Jaipur, complete with elephant rides and puppet shows. The boy writes down her order carefully, asks her more than once if that will be all. "I ate a big lunch," she says, smiling at him. He waits, unsure. She presses a fifty-rupee note into his hand, which crumples in his fist from how hard he's holding it. "You're doing a good job," she says. Despite strict orders from the cook, about turning over all baksheesh, the boy vanishes with it and Lauren doesn't see him or her order again.

The end of our year together, a day I've gone over in my mind many times. Lauren and I went to an Indian restaurant in Jackson Heights, where boys like the one on the train were the waiters.

"You look like a mermaid in that thing," she'd said. She fingered the soft edge of my new sari as we waited outside the restaurant on a Monday afternoon. Lauren looked good too. As we made our way to a table in the back, she turned to me with an exuberant smile.

"Listen, I'm going back to India," I said, before Lauren could ask me anything.

"What do you mean, 'back'?"

"I mean to get my marriage arranged."

"Honey, you'd be miserable! You know it as well as I do. Even if you don't want to be with me anymore, don't do that to yourself. Stay here."

"You can't know what makes me miserable."

We were loud. Lauren seemed more angry than surprised.

"I thought you might drop a bomb like this one day. I knew you weren't going to come out to your family anytime soon, and I accepted it. But you don't have to go back to India, Nisha. Don't put yourself into the ground. You have a choice."

"No one has a choice. The whole idea of choice, it's just a Western myth designed to make people uncertain, prevent anyone from taking responsibility. It makes people not know who they are. But *I know* who I am."

"This is bullshit. You're not leaving and we're not breaking up. You just want to please your family. It's understandable, but you have to move past it if you ever want to have a life."

"Whatever it is, it's who I am. It's mine. My heritage."

"No, baby, you're mine. You're mine and I'm yours," Lauren said. "You belong here."

"We'd like to believe that, but it isn't true," I said.

Lauren shook her head. She reached for my glass, drinking deep. People in hell just want a drink of water, but I didn't pause to take a single sip.

We always drank from each other's cups, ate from each other's plates, but after a whole year of being together, Lauren had never been to my parents' apartment.

Lauren rubbed my sari-covered thigh. But I couldn't touch her. The chubby young couple trying to persuade their two little twin boys to stay put in their chairs; the old woman wearing a white sari and looking around suspiciously, picking at her teeth and eating yogurt with her fingers; the two skinny, short waiters who would have been staring anyway, but were all the more riveted by the prospect of a vanilla-chocolate live girl show—everyone in the restaurant was staring at us, I was convinced of it.

"So when are you going on this big trip to India?" Lauren asked. "Because I was thinking of asking you to go with me somewhere for summer break. Maybe the two of us could go together or something. Stop in Thailand."

"I'm leaving next week," I said. "I'm sorry I didn't tell you earlier."

"You crazy, stupid girl."

Lauren put her hands on my shoulders and kissed me for a long time, right in front of everyone, amid exclamations in English mixed with laughter and languages she wouldn't have been able to name.

That night we fucked in an empty classroom that we found after walking hard and fast through the deserted Queens campus, not looking each other in the face. We rarely did anything physical at school. Usually I was afraid of getting caught, but Lauren persisted. It was like she wanted to show me what being "out" meant. She opened an empty classroom with her father's keys, unwinding the soft sari while I trembled, then pressing me against the wall, pinning my hands above my head. Lauren didn't give me a chance to move, to call my parents so they wouldn't get suspicious of the late hour. She wouldn't let me hold myself back for even a minute so I could listen in the darkness like I always did, for the sound of someone coming close enough to hear us. For the first time, she made me scream, and I didn't care who heard.

But Lauren must be dating someone else by now, I'm sure of it. Because she's stayed away from me all this time, as if I'm a temptation. Because she looks, at least from a distance, calm and well cared for. Because she hasn't come by to hurt me. I want her to care enough to hurt me. Thus far, there's no proof she cares that I exist, or any sign she knows I'm not married.

What I imagine: a week after our breakup at the restaurant, Lauren, getting on the train bound for Agra, detours to make a flower offering at the temple listed in *The Lonely Planet* guidebook. The temple is white like a flash of lightning through a raincloud—the epithet for Hindu princesses in the religious comic book Lauren bought in Chandni Chowk. The marble floor is cold under her bare feet, but she doesn't mind. TThe smell of the jasmine in the garlands around each black stone statue; the sweet, intoxicating smell of sugar candies sticky in worshippers' hands; the heavy smell of overripe bananas being offered; of raisins being thrown by a young priest unconcerned with flies—all of these distract Lauren from the cold marble floor.

She moves to where there seems to be a show, two lines of people looking at one particular, half-hidden statue. Prompted by a short blast from a conch shell nearly as large as a child's head, a middle-aged priest draws back a black velvet curtain to reveal a large stone depiction, over six feet, of the elephant-headed god I had told her stories about.

At this small roadside temple in Agra, the priest bathes the statue in milk from silver pots. Bells clang to empty the worshippers' minds of everything but the thought of God. People close their eyes and chant. Not knowing what this is, Lauren wishes the noise would stop and feels a headache coming on. She leaves her flowers on top of the large pile in front of the alcove, and turns to go. On her way back out to the street, she looks closely at the two stone birds that guard the temple. They have strong, outspread wings. Garuda, she remembers, from one of the books I'd read to her some night. The bird that one of the gods uses to fly across oceans, across worlds.

The street is teeming with weary, subdued worshippers. Someone has thrown a soft drink bottle on the steps below the birds, letting the dark liquid coat the feet of one of the sculptures. White tourists carry Pepsi bottles like this one, as they walk down the street and attempt to revive from the heat.

Lauren picks up the empty bottle, hoping no one thinks she dropped it there, and makes a point of throwing it away.

The Hindu comic book is a collection of epic stories told in color comic strips. In the story Lauren reads last, two people fall in love before they meet in person, influenced by talking swans. The swans have gilded wings, artistic beaks that draw lilypad pictures of the lovers and reveal them to each other. They can see each other well enough to be captured, spellbound. The prince and the princess, for of course that is who the two people are, fall in "adristakama." Love for the unseen.

When they meet in person, it's bound to be awkward. How do they think of what to say? Your eyes are black butterflies, black marigolds. Your neck is warm topaz. O, that you would only kiss me with the kisses of your mouth.

The train at last pulls into the Agra station. Full of excitement, Lauren flips through the guidebook one last time, looking for a five-star restaurant where she thinks she will take me.

A small boy waits behind her in the line to exit the train. People are as eager now to leave as they were to get on. The boy alternates between trying to make eye contact with Lauren and hiding his face against his mother's legs. Lauren smiles at the boy's mother, whose smile in return is polite but rather small. Lauren looks at the boy instead, with his long lashes that remind her of mine. The boy is shy but looks into Lauren's green eyes intensely, no doubt liking them. People are yawning and talking, moving forward, and Lauren moves too. She pictures dazed butterflies and the sheen of frightened wings beating above her head, pictures the two of us having a son, as she searches among the people waiting on the platform for me, the woman she still thinks of as her girlfriend, the unseen one. And in the sequence that I imagine, a woman comes to the station to meet her: that lucky woman—me—Nisha—who has not lost Lauren yet, who knows enough to have said *Yes* to her love. *Yes.*

ACKNOWLEDGMENTS

No BOOK BECOMES REAL without the love of some reader. Thanks go to Michelle Dotter, first reader to decide these stories should be published in the Dzanc Books Short Story Prize collection series. Thanks also for kind, incisive ,and really dedicated editing that made publishing with Dzanc live up to everything other writers said about why they love indie presses. Thanks also to Lane Zachary, agent extraordinaire and a wonderful editor in her own right, for kindness as well, but also fearless honesty and loyalty.

Thanks to the renowned authors who pulled me up into what I have come to recognize as not only a "community" but an aerie, a place of soothing, cool, regard and care for each word that we write. Diana Abu-Jaber, first one to say the book had "magic" in it (I'm now a believer but wasn't at first). Jamie Ford, big-hearted optimist/ realist. Peter Rock, from a slightly amused perspective of integrity. Skip Horack, teacher to so many wonderful writers as well as a thrilling and warm writer of acclaim. New comrades like Emma Eisenberg, childhood friends like Dohra Ahmad, social media comrades like Amber Noelle Sparks, Courtney Maum, and Allegra Hyde, and mentors like Victoria Chang (whose poetry I learn from constantly). Amelia Gray, whose writing is so multidimensional and textured and gripping, it actually gave me confidence in the editing process to learn she'd liked the book. Jeff VanderMeer, both a generous and an incredibly imaginative writer citizen. Anthony Marra, whose stories about Chechnya I remember reading during med school and enjoying so much. And Lauren Groff, whose grace and encouragement of emerging writers is well-known but still delighted and surprised me.

Thanks too to everyone at MacDowell, where one of the stories was written from start to finish inside of a two-and-a-half-week residency, and where I first really acknowledged to myself that I "am a writer," whatever else I might be. Also warm thanks to Sewanee Writers Conference, where I got up the nerve to read and discovered how much I love performing my own work (Randall Kenan: thinking of you). Thanks too to the other teachers and friends at Sewanee who helped me "believe"—Steve Yarborough, Shanti Sekaran, Marilyn Nelson, Michael Knight, Venita Blackburn. The posse. Various amazing and generous editors made these stories better on every level—Tom Jenks at *Narrative Magazine*; Anna Schachter at *Chattahoochee Review*; Mary Akers at *r.k.v.r.y.*; Bill Berry at *aaduna*; Kelly Luce and Jenn Baker and Michael Seidlinger, *Electric Lit* editors who never fail to inspire; and Lydia Kiesling and Julie Buntin and Jimin Han, my comrades at *The Millions*.

Thanks to my writing partners who kept me going before I believed—Anna Depalo, Jennifer Hudson, Christian Mohler—and super smart teachers like Adam Sexton. Thanks too to writers who took out time to encourage me, like Meg Wolitzer and Min Jin Lee; I learn both from your example and also from the kind words you said to me. To my parents, who paid for my undergrad and came to my first "story telling contest" performances. To my brother Ganesh, whom I think of every single day.

And the ones who are the center of the world: Nazli, Orhan, Muhamet. Always. You three.